PIECES OF HONEY

Alan Nelson

A Novel

Doggerel Bones
Multiplex

Published by Andrew Benzie Books
www.andrewbenziebooks.com

Printed in the United States of America

Second Edition: February 2015

10 9 8 7 6 5 4 3 2 1

ISBN 978-1-941713-15-0

There was the sound of voices—faint, lingering voices. Little bells ringing deep in my brain.

I listened for a few moments, pretending to myself that I was still asleep, but when they got louder I pulled off my blanket and stood up. Still clothed from the night before, I stepped into my sandals.

The crescent of desert beach to the north was blue-gray and perfectly still. Rubbing my arms for warmth, I peered out at the lake then up to the top of the Pyramid rock rising up some two hundred feet at water's edge.

Silence all around.

Then there were voices again: from the bluff above the beach.

It's impossible, I thought to myself, who could be after me here? Maybe someone had discovered Biggs' operation and raided the spring site at King Lear.

I scrambled across the beach, climbing into a cluster of tufa formations on the edge of the bluff. I carefully peeked out across the expanse of sage then ducked down in panic—a Reservation Security truck was on the gravel road.

I twisted the oily strands of my beard, all traces of sleep instantly fleeing my body. Son of a bitch, I whispered, quietly terrified at being found out before getting to Nixon for the delivery of the artifacts. I untied the red bandanna from the strap on my overalls, stuffing it in my pocket where it wouldn't be seen. I checked the field again. Two Paiute policemen were going about their business. One talked with a family in front of a Winnebago, the other confronted a couple traveling by motorcycle. Money was changing hands and I felt momentarily relieved, realizing the people were being charged for camping at lakeside the previous night.

Then, from over the crest of the hillside to the east, two blue Nevada State Police cars unexpectedly came into view. My luck's the shits, I concluded angrily, fleeing back to my things on the beach.

I didn't know what to do and was furious with myself for thinking the lake would be a safe place to spend the night. I clasped my canteen belt around my waist then hurriedly rolled my wool Army blanket around a loop of rope, tied it with two short pieces of cord, and draped it across my chest. I felt totally exposed picking up the cumbersome canvas bag—the dry terrain stretching out flat and treeless all around me.

Where to go? My eyes fixed on the Pyramid rock. The previous year, when I visited the lake with Winona, I'd climbed up the side of the craggy edifice on a dare. It was my best bet; at least there it would be a difficult climb to catch me.

I wanted to run, but the artifacts were too heavy. Instead, I shuffled across the hard sand to a narrow peninsula covered with boulders then passed over to the base of the Pyramid. Expecting—almost wanting—to hear a commanding voice at any moment, I lifted the bag up into the rocks; finding a foothold, I pulled myself up, then, step by careful step, I clawed like a crab across the waist of the rock. In five minutes I made it to the southern face, hiding from view in a large crevice, exhausted, my breath on fire.

It was a steep descent down the rock face to the water, so I pushed the artifacts securely behind me then squatted down. I was hungrier than a newborn pup and couldn't remember the last time I'd eaten.

I closed my eyes for a few minutes, ignoring things down on the beach. I could feel the touch of the new morning sun on my face. Strangely, an image from one of Mother's travel books settled in my mind: a naked man falling in a swan dive from the edge of a cliff. What should I do if they come after me? The answer was perfectly clear: I'd respond like any frightened animal and jump into the water. It all seemed so absurd.

A sweet draft of air wafted up from the lake. I opened my eyes, feeling oddly calm and resigned to some ugly fate. Below, in the water at the base of the Pyramid, whitish limestone pools steamed mysteriously, the volcanic rock above the mineral pools connected by long cobwebs, dotted here and there by large gray spiders.

A half-mile out into the lake was a small island. Rays of sunlight hit the rock promontories in the center of the barren isle, casting two immense triangular shadows. I knew the white spots along the shoreline of the island were Great White Pelicans; Winona had pointed them out to me that day we'd made a fire of sagebrush on the lake shore, then canoed over to the island at sunset. A few of the pelicans set off from their nesting areas and took to the open skies above the lake. They were beautiful creatures, floating effortlessly in circles on the high winds, but the memories they sparked in me were dim, half-forgotten, like the actions of someone in a different life.

Restless, I stood up and peeked at the beach below. The police had turned around and were heading back towards the highway on the gravel road. I watched as the vehicles disappeared into a wash, their whereabouts signaled only by a rising wall of dust. I felt sad and confused watching them leave, because I almost *wanted* someone, some circumstance, to stop me from making the delivery.

There was nothing to do but go, so I climbed down from my

hiding place. I decided to stay by the water and avoid Highway 237, wanting to arrive by a safer route through the marsh and grazing land north of town. I trudged along, the green polished lake at my side, changing the weighty bag from hand to hand and keeping my head down to avoid the sun. The pelicans hovered in the sky for a while, eventually disappearing behind me as I made my way south. After an hour of steady walking the shoreline flattened out and bent sharply westward.

I stopped and set down the artifacts. I took a long drink of water from my canteen, then put on my bandanna.

The blunt profile of the Pyramid and the barren island were now small monuments on the northern horizon. Pouring the remaining water from the canteen into my hands, I scrubbed my sweaty face, trying to shake my lethargy, then I turned into the breeze blowing off the lake, wringing my beard dry. Small waves rushed up onto the shore, playing quiet music, leaving traces of foam. Three ravens hung in the wind and scores of white terns skittered about the mirror-like sand, poking holes in the ooze. Even though there was still a touch of coolness in the morning air, the August sun already nibbled at my deeply tanned arms and shoulders.

I gazed into a small valley where the lake merged by way of a thousand rivulets into a brackish marsh that stretched to the ranches and alfalfa fields near Nixon. I guessed I had another two, maybe three, miles to go.

I felt uneasy heading south. It seemed like I hadn't once gone in that direction since leaving my hometown, Cherry Creek, two years before. I had gone in a circle, following the strange geometry of my own blind flight from home, Winona, and the university. It had been pinball geometry: first, Battle Mountain; then changing truck tires in Beowawe; a stint in a mental health facility in Elko; camping in a cave around Deeth and Pequop; up north to Jackpot, near the Salmon river and the Idaho border, to wash dishes for the Henderson Mining Company; a few weeks on the Duck Valley Indian Reservation; then undercover the past six weeks with Biggs, on King Lear peak in the Jackson Mountains. The circle was almost complete now, and I had succeeded in losing everything: the station wagon, the clothes off my back, my savings from working at home, my pride. It seemed that every cell in my body had been transformed from Merle into . . . into I didn't know what.

I hitched my canteen back on a loop on my overalls, focusing my mind on present circumstances—getting to Nixon. The delivery of the artifacts would mean money, and because I was dead broke, money would change everything. I spied the vague outline of a firm trail through the far side of the marsh and started walking again.

When I finally arrived in downtown Nixon, emerging out of the trees near Black Rock Feed, I knew something was going on that had nothing to do with my transgressions. Normally a desolate, sun-baked reservation town, population five hundred, Nixon was now teeming with all sorts of cars and people. At first I thought there might be a festival drawing tourists from Reno, but I could immediately sense differently.

A vocal crowd of Paiutes, law enforcement agents, and miscellaneous officials had converged on the small market and post office across the street. Two television vans were parked in a nearby field; Nevada State Police cars, probably twenty in all, were parked randomly up and down the street.

Beside myself for just being visible to the crowd, I ducked into the store.

A buzzer went off as I entered. No one greeted me, so I peeked back outside through the parted curtains. Two Paiutes were addressing a group of reporters, gesturing with loudspeakers; the police were gathered off to one side, most of the uniformed men wearing sun glasses, drinking coffee, smoking. Then a man dressed in a formal, dark-blue suit stepped between the Paiutes, grabbed a loudspeaker, and began talking grimly, scowling in the sun.

"The store is closed. Did you see the sign?"

I turned back and faced a fat, middle-aged Paiute woman who was wearing a baggy white cotton dress. I set the artifacts down next to the door.

"I didn't, ma'am, my apologies. Lots of Blue and Silver in town today. What's going on out there?"

"Trouble. We've had trouble," she said, walking behind the cash register set in the middle of the store.

"What kind of trouble?" I asked.

"Indian trouble."

"Indian trouble," I repeated. "That's too bad, I'm sorry to hear it. Is Ed Morgan around?"

"He's not working right now."

"He's not, huh?" I asked, skeptical.

"No."

"But he's a famous rock collector, isn't he? I'm a bit of a hound myself, so it's important that I talk with him."

"But I already said, he's not here right now. He's off today."

I figured I was being screened.

"If Morgan's not here then I've come a long way for nothing. A long way after being told he would be here to see me." I stared into the woman's brown eyes, which were hard to find in her stoic, wooden face. "Give him a message, wherever he is. Tell him Biggs sent me here. Biggs, O.K.? He'll know what I'm talking about. And let him know that with all this going on outside, I'm not going to be in town long."

She looked at me coldly then walked to the rear of the store,

6

disappearing behind a red and black blanket hanging in the doorway.

I bided my time walking around the place. Seeing what little dry goods and tack they had for sale, I could tell they didn't do much business.

Morgan had to be around—I couldn't go on without completing the deal and getting some money. Biggs said the man practically lived at the store and would be expecting me, and he was never wrong about such things.

I walked over to a shiny, chestnut-brown saddle displayed on a sawhorse. I grabbed the horn and ran my hands along the smooth leather. Big, fat sacks of grain—chicken and rabbit feed—leaned against the back wall, and I kicked at the kernels spilled about the floor.

When I came to a rack of bandannas on a small table, I stopped and rifled through the colors, finding a red one that matched the one I was wearing. I stuffed it quickly inside my overalls with a quick jerk of my hand, something which pleased and excited me. I waited for a sound that never came then walked over to a row of ten-gallon hats hanging on the wall, feigning interest.

A few moments later, the woman returned.

"You come back in an hour," she said, peeking from around the blanket, "then you can talk with Ed."

"I need to see him now."

"No, that's it. We're closed. You have to go."

She kept watching me and I knew I wasn't going to get my way, so I picked up the artifacts and walked out of the store.

I quickly disappeared around the corner of the building, stopping when I saw a small bungalow behind the store. It had a security door, the windows blacked out. So that's where Morgan does business, I thought, tempted to force the issue, but then I was startled by the rattle of gunfire (from the hills, not the street) and dogs barking, so I fled. I dropped down the hillside into a grove of cottonwoods, dodging between the gray-cracked tree trunks, stopping when I felt I was a good ways away from the main street. I felt physically unable to carry the artifacts any farther, so I hid the canvas bag under a piece of sheet metal, which I camouflaged with some tree limbs and leaves.

Squatting down, I looked out at the small ranches, the cattle and sheep, listening for signs of danger. The cottonwoods swayed above me, and white fluffy seedlings landed on my arms like snowflakes.

What should I do now, Roe? I asked my invisible sister. The question seemed to come from an old, old reflex. I gazed back towards Pyramid Lake, which glowed like a drop of mercury melded to the low horizon. I thought of Roe and what she would say if we were to sit in a quiet place and talk. But the more I let my imagination loose, the more I became furious with myself, understanding, in my gut, the ghost I had become since last seeing her. The wind hit the cottonwoods again, making a haunting chorus of sound, the leaves awash in silver. The hot, dry wind seemed to point its finger at me, touching my arm. The bottom line was simple: I had to keep moving, and, although I dreaded the idea, I knew there was only one place to go.

Fleeing my own train of thought, I left the shelter of the cottonwoods and continued down the hillside, crossing over a sandy wash to a dirt road, feeling stronger without the artifacts.

A short ways down the road was the Waterstone's house. The place was like most reservation housing: a boxy, orange two-bedroom on a graded lot, a satellite dish angled off the roof, a lonely stand of sage taking up the surrounding acreage. No vehicles were parked anywhere around. Thinking I could maybe hide on the premises and kill some time, I walked across the road and stood awkwardly by a cord of wood stacked by the front door. Above the woodpile was a bedroom window, so I peeked in, expecting to see Nanna, Winona's deaf grandmother, who used to sit for hours at a time in her rocking chair, still as a snake. Straining my eyes to see between the curtains, all I could make out were indistinct shadows.

Then there was a clatter to my right, and a dog charged at me from a small opening underneath the house. I was taken aback for a moment, then shouted, "Shut up, Budweiser, or I'll kick your teeth in."

The old German shepherd stopped in his tracks, his growls turning to whimpers. I leaned over and patted my leg and he shuffled towards me, head down, wagging his tail. I knelt down and rubbed the dog's boney neck and patted his dusty head, feeling the coolness of his hiding place all over his thick gray fur. It was satisfying, somehow, knowing that the animal recognized me.

It seemed my presence was a known fact after Budweiser's barking, but I was still too shy and hesitant to knock on the front door. I moved slowly around the corner of the house, trying to act calm and natural, as if I was an everyday visitor who the Waterstone's were expecting. Against the house there was a ramshackle workbench and a metal frame with a car engine hanging from it; the stuff reminded me of Cracker Joe, and the thought that he was living at the house boosted my spirits some.

I finally banged on the sliding door at the back of the house.

"Hello. Anyone home? It's Merle." There was only the whispering wind and Budweiser noisily drinking water from a dish at my feet.

My eyes fixed on the refrigerator in the kitchen. Impulsively, I tried the sliding door, found it unlocked, and slipped inside. "Hey! What kind of welcoming party is this? Anybody here?" No response. I quickly opened the refrigerator. Seeing a six-pack of Miller High Life, I knew for certain Cracker Joe was around. I grabbed a bottle and downed it in large ravenous gulps, the swirling effervescence cutting through my pasty saliva. I hadn't been in a house for months, and all I could do was look around, dumbly examining things. I grabbed another beer, drank half of it down, and stepped outside.

I took off my bedroll and set it on the ground, then filled my canteen from a faucet. Pulling up a milk crate, I sat down and finished off the beer.

I looked out at the tall sunflowers bordering the overgrown garden of tomatoes and squash. A reddish-brown rooster stepped carefully about, pecking the ground here and there. In the corral, two horses stood head to tail, enduring the afternoon heat, tails swatting mechanically at flies.

I took off my bandanna and scratched my crusty scalp. Budweiser came up and I scratched his nose. I'd been happy those two months with Winona, I thought regretfully. Wanting to distract myself, I decided to take a walk to the earth-house that Marcos Waterstone—the youngest son in the family—had built on the rise above the corral. I had always secretly admired Marcos. He was more intelligent than Cracker Joe, always spouting off ideas that I'd never understood or taken seriously. As part of his plan to return to the Old Ways of the Paiute, Marcos had built a low adobe structure with a hard earth floor for the family to use. Winona and I had slept there many times when I was living at the house.

I passed by the corral and whistled at the two pintos—each horse raised its head, half-interested—then followed a winding path through the sage. At a clearing I saw the mounded front of the earth-house, which was just as I remembered it. I stepped towards the entrance.

"Hold it right there," a voice said from inside. I stopped. I saw the barrel of a rifle pointing at me from behind a blanket hanging over the entrance.

I raised my arms. "Hold it, just hold it. Don't be stupid. It's Merle Honeycutt. You know me."

I waited a few long moments, frightened at first, then, strangely, almost wanting to be shot.

"Merle, I'm sorry, is that really you?"

The blanket parted and Marcos ducked out of the narrow doorway. He squinted in the bright sunlight then smiled broadly, his long black hair parted down the middle of his head, tied into two ponytails.

"Shit, I haven't seen you in ages." He walked over and hugged me. "What brings you around?"

"Just passing through. Thought I would come by and say hello to my old family."

"Well, you know we're glad to see you, but you picked a bad . . . man, you look tired, where you been keeping yourself?"

I didn't know what to say. He sensed my awkwardness and continued: "Have you heard what's going on?"

"Just a little. I been up north 'til today."

Marcos dusted off his t-shirt and blue jeans. "Some locals—they're all my friends actually—took some state representatives from Carson City hostage. They've got them in the school on the hill above town. This happened three days ago. It's a long story, but there's been all this political shit happening since you left. My friends are pretty radical, so they took matters into their own hands. But a cop got shot when they made a rescue attempt and now everything has turned nasty.

How'd you get into town?"

"Hitchhiked."

"Nowhere's safe now. They might want to question me, so I've been hiding here."

The warm wind, which had been blowing steadily, died down.

"I guess you want to know where Winona is?"

"Sure," I answered tentatively.

"She went to Reno with Joe and Nanna. There was a big rally at the university about this whole thing. She should be back any time. How long can you stay? We've missed you."

"Not long. I've got some work lined up," I lied.

"Well, you're not going to see me much, unless you come visit me here. I have to hide out until this thing blows over—when that's going to be is anybody's guess."

Just then, Budweiser could be heard barking back at the house. The thought of seeing Winona sent a chill down my spine.

"Sounds like they're home. Why don't you go and see. I'll stay here in case it's someone else, but if it's the family, I'd be interested in knowing what happened in Reno. Good to see you, Merle."

"Yea, likewise," I answered. "You want a beer or something?"

"No. Need to keep my wits about me. I've been reading."

We shook hands then Marcos disappeared underground. I went back and picked up my gear and walked around to the front of the house. When I saw that Budweiser was only barking madly at the sky, I breathed a sigh of relief. Looking back across the wash to Nixon, dirty business came to mind, so I retraced my steps through the cottonwoods to Black Rock Feed.

After I entered the store, the woman emerged again then disappeared without a word. When she returned, a slightly built man with a waxed handlebar mustache followed her. The guy was dressed neatly in a matching powder-blue shirt and slacks, a large piece of turquoise inset in his belt buckle. He was more formal in appearance than I would have imagined, knowing what slobs Biggs and his friends were.

He walked directly up to me, smiling like a poker player, glancing quickly at the bag at my feet.

"Ed Morgan, top of the mornin' to you," the man said, shaking my hand, then putting his hands on his hips.

"Glad to meet you," I said, purposely not stating my name.

"Did you have any trouble outside?" he asked.

"None at all," I answered. I suddenly felt nervous; I was in over my head, a greenhorn. Get it over with quick, I repeated to myself.

Mr. Morgan smiled confidently, perhaps sensing my nervousness, and turned to the back of the store.

"Did you meet my wife? This is Bonnie. She was born and raised in Nixon."

"We met before. It's a pleasure, ma'am."

She looked at me, nodding her head.

"Bonnie, why don't you bring me some coffee out back. Would you like some, young man?"

I declined, still tasting beer in my mouth.

Morgan led me out the back of the store. Two pit bulls immediately came to life in the presence of their master. Each was up on its strong hind legs, pulling on ten-foot chains attached to posts in the ground. He stopped, smiling paternally, pleased by the attention in some obscure way. I stepped back as Bonnie opened the screen door and handed her husband his coffee.

She went inside. He paused a moment, taking a sip from the mug. "She's a good lady—does whatever I say." Yea, that was Nanna as a younger woman, I figured, staring at the dogs.

"The gray one is Crazy Legs; Betty Lou has the spot on her forehead." The dogs leapt about, whining.

"You must've had a dog or two over the years."

The question seemed oddly personal, but I answered anyway.

"My father used to show dogs when I was growing up."

"Is that so? What kind?"

"Russian wolfhounds mostly."

"Yes, well, you know then that men like dogs. They belong together. Nature meant it that way. And you need protection out here, believe me, especially with the shenanigans that have been going on lately."

We went inside the back building. Mr. Morgan turned on a set of fluorescent lights over a large table in the middle of the room, locking the door behind us. The hideaway seemed well-used: a gun rack and the head of a black bear were mounted on the opposite wall; a crowd of baskets took up one corner, a large drafting table with a map draped over it, another; next to a small sink, a bobcat skin was pinned to a wooden frame like a giant butterfly.

"You want to put down your bedroll?"

"No, I keep it on."

"Suit yourself. Well, let's see what you brought," Mr. Morgan said avidly, rolling up his shirt sleeves, looking like a hungry camper about to explore a picnic basket. He took a long sip of coffee and cleared his throat.

I lifted the bag up onto the table and unzipped the top.

I was as curious as Mr. Morgan about the contents of the bag because I'd never seen Biggs pack it in the mountains. With a delicate hand, he spread the pieces across the tabletop, then pulled a knife out of his pocket and started cutting off the thick red cloth and tape that each was wrapped in.

"These are just perfect. Tell Biggs, I've got to give him credit. I don't know where he finds these beauties," he said, holding up two long stone blades. "Rose Spring Period. See how each base is convex and the corners are notched."

He continued on, as if touching each piece somehow bestowed ownership upon himself. There were three clay figurines, a hooded cradle, a bag of carved pieces of bone, some beaded textiles decorated with gray feathers, a small coiled basket with red geometric designs, and, most impressive of all, two pieces of black ceramic pottery, polished to a shine, and engraved with animal figures.

"These are very rare," Mr. Morgan remarked with satisfaction, setting the pots side by side. He pulled a pack of cigarettes out of his shirt pocket.

"You from Nevada, young man?" he asked. "You from the Great Basin?"

"I'm from down south—around Mercury and Cherry Creek."

"That qualifies." He lit a cigarette, quickly placing it in an ashtray. The curling smoke was sucked up by the overhead air conditioning.

"Want a cigarette?" He grabbed the pack and offered it to me.

"No. You go ahead."

"I know your neck of the woods; I know the test sites," he said, spinning the tip of the cigarette impatiently against the side of the ashtray. "So you probably understand the way I feel. All these things on the table—well, the whole damned country really—it belongs to us. It belongs to you and me, not some hair-brained bureaucrat in Washington."

I'd heard the same story from Biggs during my stay in the Jackson Mountains. I didn't believe a word either man said; they were just hypocrites making money off what didn't belong to them. And from the looks of things, I was the same cut of man.

Mr. Morgan reached over and lifted up one of the pots, which was shaped like a bulb of garlic. "This should belong to everybody. Not put in a museum."

"Lots of people go to museums—" I remarked, stopping myself.

He stared at me.

"Well, they do, don't they?" I said defensively.

"My, my, you sure are cultured. That's obvious."

"Mister, I just want my money."

He broke into a laugh.

"I don't know where Biggs finds you guys, but you're all the same—so rough around the edges that you can't even hold a civilized conversation." He spit a piece of tobacco out of his mouth. "Young fella, don't get nervous. I'm a businessman. If you want your money, you can have it."

He shook his head and stepped back and reached into a drawer and pulled out an envelope. "The agreement with Biggs was eighteen hundred dollars. He said to give an additional two hundred to you for your good efforts, and that you'd be returning to King Lear tomorrow with another package I've prepared. There are some pieces, similar to the one's here, that I need to return to Biggs." He knelt down, reached under the table, and lifted up a bag smaller than the one I'd been carrying.

"You need to be very careful . . ."

"But that's not what Biggs said to me," I said in a low voice, trying to mask my uneasiness. "Biggs told me to bring back three thousand dollars in cash. He didn't mention anything about my pay—that was going to be talked about later—and he didn't say anything about another delivery."

Mr. Morgan nodded, crushing out his cigarette. "Biggs is always getting these things screwed up," he complained, smoke pouring out his nose and mouth. "Have you ever noticed that about the man? He's disorganized. He's made four deliveries and this same thing has happened on two of them. I won't pay an increase, and I've told him that." He tossed the envelope on the table.

I needed the money, whatever it took. It was risky, but I

reached across the table and pulled the two pots towards me, cringing for fear of breaking them.

He stood still, watching my hands.

"What's this all about—you starting your collection to donate . . . now just be careful with that." He looked down and lit another cigarette, biding his time, waiting for me to respond.

I remained silent, but took the opportunity to pull both vessels close against my waist, embracing them like children.

"Mr. Morgan, the way I see it, everyone involved in this project needs to work . . . as a team. Understand?" I picked up one pot (it had a light, ancient feel) and set it back in the same position. "One piece of the puzzle doesn't fit and the whole game is ruined."

I asked for a cigarette. He seemed a bit surprised at the request, but quickly gave me one. I crushed it in my hand, then let the tobacco fall into the pottery. I had learned to do things like that—crazy, unexpected things—when I was desperate; it helped get my point across.

He looked right through me, his face now expressionless.

"You son-of-a-bitch," Mr. Morgan said jokingly. "I don't know who you are, but I like you more every minute. I'm going to have to talk with Biggs and tell him about you. Believe me, I'm going to do that."

He stepped back from the table, knowing that I could do nothing until he gave me the money. He put the cigarette in the corner of his thin-lips then stepped back to the gun rack on the wall.

He lifted a rifle down. The long steel barrel seemed to take up the entire room. He brought the butt up to his shoulder, pointing it at the wall behind me.

"This is a great 7mm Remington; used to hunt bighorn sheep with it." He stepped over to a box of cartridges on a nearby table and methodically loaded up.

I shuddered. Even though I knew he was bullshitting, I couldn't be sure. I picked up both pieces and raised them up to my chest, steady and careful—my magical protection.

"Give me the right money, Mr. Morgan, if you want your goods. I'm sure you don't want any trouble with the riot squads outside."

"You shut up," he growled, bringing the shotgun down to waist level and aiming it at me. "Do you think I really care about those pots and pans you're holding? You jackass, you don't think you can come in here and screw with me like this, do you?"

He moved around the corner of the table, trying to get closer to me, but I stepped back. Kill me, I thought, go ahead and blow me to bits. I *wanted* the blast into nothingness; this was easy.

But nothing happened. Morgan stared at me; my eyes moved between his pensive face, the silly mustache, and the silent barrel of the shotgun. After a minute, he turned away and walked to the drafting table on the far side of the room, leaning the shotgun against the wall. For a moment he disappeared. I quickly moved back to the table and saw that he was kneeling before a small safe. In no time, he stood up, took his previous spot at the table, and began counting money into a stack.

"I wish my customers in Arizona could see me now, they'd understand why I charge what I do," he said, adding the cash to the envelope. "Here's your damn money. You tell Biggs that I'm going to be talking to him about this. He owes me—you let him know that loud and clear."

He slid the money halfway across the table. Pinching the lip of both vessels with one hand, I reached over and took the stack and put it in the square chest pocket of my overalls.

Now I had to leave. I knew that by just walking out of the place I'd risk his turning on me with the shotgun again, but I felt I would leave my fate in Mr. Morgan's hands. If he wanted to come after me again, that would be the end of things; I didn't care.

I asked him to unlock the door for me, without the shotgun. And as he took the keys out of his pocket and moved towards the door, I followed right behind him, leaving the artifacts on the table.

"You gonna deliver my package to Biggs?"

"No."

"Well, in that case, don't ever show your face around here again, museum boy," he threatened, opening the door and stepping back. "I knew it was three grand the whole time," he whispered.

"Fuck you," I said, bolting outside. The dogs growled as I passed into the store. Walking quickly through a makeshift kitchen, I passed Mrs. Morgan at the cash register then stepped out to the main street.

The crowd that had been assembled across the street had disappeared. Without a moments hesitation, I walked out of town, hoping to make it out to Highway 47—which wound down the western side of Pyramid Lake—then flag a ride south to Fallon.

Sorry Biggs, I told myself without regret, trying not to walk too fast and make a spectacle of myself. What he would do when he found I'd stolen the money was anyone's guess, but I had no intention of being around to deal with it. The money bulged in my chest pocket like a roll of toilet paper. I'd been broke so long that I was filled with a childish excitement about the gold mine in my possession.

But no sooner was I out of Nixon proper than two white police vans drove towards me from the opposite direction. I avoided the eyes of the drivers as they passed and just kept walking—on pins and needles. My skin crawled at the thought of the authorities confronting me, searching me—after all, I had no identification and was carrying three thousand dollars—and I slowed my pace. After a minute, I looked back and saw that the vans had disappeared into town.

A quarter of a mile down the road, I came to a short concrete bridge which passed over the same wash I'd crossed visiting the Waterstone's earlier in the day. I stared down the dirt road that paralleled the wash, leading north to their house. Marcos had said that Cracker Joe was coming home soon and I was tempted to meet up with him, but there was Winona to worry about. I looked west: the view was nothing but a strip of asphalt lined with yellow scotchbroom, and low, gray hills in the distance. Nixon was thirty miles from anywhere I could find a hotel room, and if I couldn't flag a ride before dark, I was facing the desert again, which was intolerable. Besides, the Blue and Silver were snooping around. I decided to take my chances and visit the Waterstone's again.

This time an old mud-splattered station wagon and a new red pickup truck were parked in front of the house. Seeing the vehicles, I was tempted to turn around and split, but Budweiser was already barking at my arrival.

I knocked on the door and Winona answered. She was wearing blue jeans and a white t-shirt, the words *"Remember Pelletier"* across the front. She looked at me, confusion in her warm brown eyes (I think she was having trouble recognizing me), then stepped outside.

"Hi, Merle," she said, finally, in a calm voice. "Everyone has been wondering where you went."

I pulled off my bedroll and started grappling with my canteen.

"I walked over to town to kill some time."

"Did you? Where were you? I went over there and looked around and didn't see you."

I avoided the question, her eyes.

"Here, let me take that stuff. I'll put it out back." As I handed my things to her, Budweiser yelped and yelped.

"Buddie, you stop that," she said affectionately, his growl subsiding. "He's getting old. He barks at anything." I watched her as she bent down and patted his head. Her long black hair, dark skin, and cheerful round face were all perfectly familiar, despite the passage of time.

"Aw! He just doesn't recognize me," I said.

"Yea, it's been a while." Winona stood up and looked directly into my face, and at that moment, all that I had been and done in the past two years instantaneously rushed through me like a chilly wind.

"When did you grow this thing on your face?" she asked, showing the tiny gap between her front teeth. "I can hardly recognize you." Her laugh turned into a low, controlled giggle.

"In the spring," I answered, blushing. "It's getting kind of long now." I had grown the beard for no other reason than the convenience of not having to shave.

"So what's up? What brings you here?" she asked politely.

"I'm going to work in Fallon. I thought I would come by and say hello."

"Well, I guess I'm glad you did. But I'm not sure," she said, casting her eyes down. "Come on inside. I'll get you a towel so you can take a shower. You need to freshen up a bit."

I sat down on the couch in the sparsely decorated living room, and Winona disappeared into the bathroom. The television was on: five o'clock news. A public official was making a statement about the crisis in Nixon, flanked by Pauite officials. I yawned deeply as I watched the broadcast, the comfort of the couch bringing a bone-gripping weariness into my body.

When Winona returned, she immediately went to the television and turned up the volume, shaking her head.

"Senator Davis is a bare-faced liar," she announced to the room. "He wants everyone returned, but doesn't want to address any of the issues that led to the action. They let the utilities into the sacred grounds near Tohakum; they cut the jobs program; he never visits; and here he is speaking into the mike."

"Yea, Marcos told me about it," I said.

"Poor Marcos, he's been a wreck since this started. He's been worried about all his friends—guys he grew up with and organized with."

Just then, a bedroom door opened and Cracker Joe walked out.

"Hey, you rattlesnake!" he roared. Before I could stand up, he was in front of me, shaking my hand, slapping me affectionately on the side of the head.

We looked at each other in a state of disbelief; being old friends, years of experience passed between us in the blink of an eye.

Overweight, with sad, narrow eyes, and a complexion ruined by acne, he looked even more dissipated than I remembered. I wondered whether he felt the same shock in seeing me.

"Well, God damn, where you been?" he asked, sticking his thumbs in his jean pockets, his thick lips set in a happy, mischievous smile.

"Been up north mostly."

"What you doing up north? I thought you went back home."

"Would you be quiet," Winona said impatiently. "I'm trying to hear the end of this."

Cracker Joe grimaced and glanced at the television. "Little Big Horn," he said, laughing.

Winona turned to Cracker Joe, and when she did, I thought, how different my sister and I treated each other.

"You're a horse's ass, you know that?"

Cracker Joe looked over at me and rolled his eyes as he defiantly pulled up his ill-fitting jeans.

"Merle, I left a towel in the bathroom if you want to clean

up," Winona said, stepping around her brother. "I have to bring Nanna some lunch." She walked into the kitchen.

The thought of food dazzled me, and I considered not taking a shower and just following Winona into the kitchen, but Cracker Joe began talking.

"You want a beer?" he asked.

"Sure, but let me clean up first." I stood up from the chair. "We should talk," I said in a knowing voice that I assumed he would acknowledge. "You gonna be around?"

"I'm always around, Merle, where else am I going to go? Shit." He slapped me on the back. I smiled and went into the bathroom.

After I cleaned up and ate something, Winona suggested a walk up to the lake.

"Where did you go in December?" she asked, as we left the house, the breeze playing with the bangs that fell straight across her forehead.

"Up towards Elko," I answered warily, picking up a handful of small rocks as we strolled along.

"Elko. That's a funny place to go. What took you there?"

"Oh! you know me, Winnie," I said, sarcastically, "you can't get me out of those little Nevada towns."

"Right, you wanted out of here more than anyone I know—except maybe Joe. You just never admitted it to yourself."

We arrived at the lake. With the sun losing strength in the western sky, the surface of the water had turned a dark, syrupy blue. It had been too long since I'd talked intimately with anyone, and I felt awkward, like I was speaking a foreign language.

"I've been doing pretty well since you left," Winona said. She leaned against a large boulder covered with patches of orange lichen, folding her hands over one knee. "I surprised myself really, because I was heartbroken for awhile. Did you know that? Did you know I was miserable after you left?"

She paused and stared at me, waiting for an answer that didn't come.

I scratched my beard, staring at the Pyramid far in the distance. This kind of talk was exactly what I had wanted to avoid, I thought, pissed that I had agreed to the walk.

"Merle, what has gotten into you, anyway? I noticed it back at the house when we were eating. You're hard to talk to now. You don't need to be invisible—I'm trying to be nice to you and . . . just talk."

I stepped up and threw the rocks into the lake; they hit the water, hissing for a split second.

"Winnie, what can I say? I got some jobs, took some lumps, nothing special. I've been on the run mostly."

Winona walked over and put her arms around my waist, cuddling her head against my chest.

"Calm down, will you?" she said reassuringly. She looked up into my face. "We were lovers, remember? Not long enough really, but we were lovers. I'm just trying to understand what's going on in your head."

I looked down at her, standing ramrod straight. With my rough hands, I touched her shiny hair, hesitant at first, then slowly stroking its full length down her back. Winona pressed against me; then she settled closer.

"How come you're still wearing these dirty overalls after the shower?"

"It's all the clothes I've got."

"Really? Why?" she asked.

A few long moments passed. I had no answer for her. The dry wind hummed softly.

"Do you remember that time we took the canoe out to the island—that time after the party?"

"Sure. I thought about it this morning. I spent last night out at the Pyramid."

"Did you?" she asked. "You're lucky."

Then, unexpectedly, she laughed. "That was fun. Do you remember how afraid you were of the Kui-Qui fish, when I told you they were like piranha." I could feel her body shake in a giggle. I glanced down and she was smiling, head resting on my chest. "Making that fire after we got back from the canoe ride. I don't know why I went for all that—it was just so romantic, I guess."

Winona dropped into silence, pulling away. She crossed the sand and knelt down at the edge of the water, running her hand through the water. Behind her, shadows were hitting the upper reaches of the elephant-backed mountains. I walked up behind her, torn between wanting to touch her and wanting to bolt.

She stood up as I approached.

"Merle, where did you get that tattoo?" she asked, with more than a hint of criticism.

"I took the needle treatment in Battle Mountain. A buddy of mine was licensed, and he convinced me to do it one night."

"But why a skull and crossbones?" she asked.

"Shit, I don't know."

She sized me up from head to toe.

"You've been living hard, Merle. I don't really know what you've been doing, but whatever it is—" She hesitated. "I'm sorry. Come on, let's walk. It's too nice out to deal with all this stuff."

She strolled along the shoreline, lost in her own thoughts, and I followed behind.

She reached into the pocket of her blue jeans and pulled out a pack of cigarettes. She struggled to light one in the wind then continued walking. As she smoked, her image as my former lover vanished; now all I could see was the student, the political activist, the problem-solver, with her serious demeanor.

"How's your family?" she asked.

"They're fine," I answered coolly, although I hadn't spoken with my parents and sister since last seeing Winona.

"No big traumas about your quitting school or anything?"

"No, they don't care what I do."

Winona stopped and faced me. "That's not true. Why are you lying to me?"

"God, Winona, believe what you want to believe."

"Well, maybe Roe was lying then."

I stopped walking and looked Winona in the eye.

"She came here," Winona said, dead serious.

"You're joking. When? When did she come here?"

Winona took a drag off her cigarette, the smoke disappearing into the wind as she exhaled.

"Before Christmas. She said you'd disappeared—vanished. I guess she'd visited Reno, talked with the dean and even the police, and our name popped up during the search."

"Were my parents with her?"

"No, not when I saw her." Winona paused. "She's very beautiful."

"Cream of the crop. But she's a little crazy, too," I added, needlessly cruel. I pictured her startling hazel eyes, which matched my own.

"She didn't seem crazy to me, just anxious to see you. Why haven't you contacted them?"

"I'm living away from home now. That's it in a nut shell."

"If you'd stayed in Nixon, I could understand, but it looks like you're living hand-to-mouth to me. What are you doin' with your life anyway?"

"Whatever I want. Why do you ask? Are you overjoyed with the reservation, taking care of Nanna, being out here in the middle of nowhere?"

"I love Nanna," she said. "She's the most important thing in the world to me. Anyway, it's important to be in Nixon because of what's going on politically. You used to be able to relate to stuff like that."

"I'm tired of talking in circles," I said.

Winona laughed bitterly, stamping the cigarette out in the sand. "I'm tired of talking in circles, he announces," she said, exasperated. "Hot one minute, cold the next." She flipped her hair back over her shoulders, then glanced away angrily, saying: "You oughta go back to Cherry Creek, Merle, that's what you oughta do."

The sun was obscured by a thunderhead to the north, cooling the air.

"I think I've stopped listening."

"Go home—you're confused. You're never going to get it together until you go back and clear things up."

"Will you shut up," I shot back.

In a flash, Winona slapped my face. "No, I won't," she blurted out, pounding my chest with her fists, "because I loved you, you shit." Then her hands went limp and she burst into tears.

I stumbled away, taking long strides down the beach. I wanted to apologize, but was too confused to utter a word. This is all sentimental bullshit, I fumed.

"There's a postcard in my room," she yelled. "You get it."

I glanced back—she was kneeling near the water, her image blurred—then I set off in a run along the path through the pasture. When I got back to the Waterstone's house, I picked up my bedroll and canteen beside the back door then stepped into the kitchen. Cracker Joe was closing the refrigerator door as I entered and flashed his typical good-natured smile.

"That was a long walk. You been gone an hour."

I said nothing in response, passing into the living room. Cracker Joe followed, eating a chicken wing.

"Cracker, listen, can you give me a ride to Fallon?"

"When, right now?"

"Yea, I got work there tomorrow, and I'll lose the job if I don't arrive there on time."

"What kind of work?"

I knew Cracker Joe could tell when I was being dishonest, so my answer meant next to nothing.

"Just some humping, nothing special."

"Forget it, man. I thought we were going to party some before you hightailed it out of here. I already been to Reno. What's the big rush? Are you and sister at it again?"

"Let's party now—on the way there. Come on, Cracker, I'll make it worth your while. For the Good Old Times . . ."

Cracker wiped his mouth with his sleeve, grinning, thinking. "I never could turn you down for nothing, Merle. Anyway, it's Saturday, so let's get happy."

I told him we needed to go immediately, so he went into his room to get his things. While I waited, pacing the living room floor, I glanced into Winona's room. Nanna was sitting in her rocker. How strange old people are—so alien to everything. I waved to her, nodding, but superstitiously avoided her eyes. She raised her arm, holding something in her hand, and motioned towards me. I stepped into the cool, stuffy room, and she handed me a postcard. I nodded my thanks, fleeing the place as if I'd seen a vampire.

In twenty minutes, Cracker Joe and I were driving a steady fifty miles an hour down Highway 47. He sat low in the seat, one large hand gripping the steering wheel. The old Chevrolet station wagon had transported me home from the testing sites for two years, and the miserably cracked vinyl dash, the shoebox filled with audio tapes at Cracker Joe's side, the silver dog figurehead (salvaged from a Mack truck) screwed to the hood, were immediately familiar. God, it feels good to be off my feet, I told myself.

"Listen to this . . . old Zeppelin," Cracker Joe said, half-yelling. "It's from Physical Graffiti—their fourth album." The small speaker in the door beat visibly. "It's like religious music."

"It's too loud," I said, reaching over and lowering the volume.

I lifted a can of beer to my lips and stared out the window, my body caught between the high of the drugs we'd just shared, the fatigue deep in my bones, and my bad temper after fleeing Winona. I twirled the end of my beard silently, trying to block out the annoying rock n' roll song, letting the cocaine bring a detached order to my scattered thoughts. I had done this stuff a couple times before and never really liked it, but at the moment, I needed a change of head by any means possible.

I rolled down the window. The air seemed simultaneously cool and warm; shadows had taken over the valley floor, and on the southern horizon, footprint-like clouds changed from pink to gray. I had come to dread the desert twilight over the past year; if I had no good place to bed down, utter loneliness would set in.

I reached under my overalls and pulled out the postcard that Nanna had given me before leaving the house.

"What's that?" Cracker Joe asked.

"Letter from the folks."

"Really? How they doing?"

"Who knows," I said. Cracker Joe kept talking, but I ignored him. The front of the postcard was a black-and-white photograph of the Eiffel Tower, probably from one of Mother's many "special order, artist rendered" stationary collections. I looked at the picture:

continents, oceans, entire worlds, separated me from the famous tourist attraction. For all I knew, the Eiffel Tower was on Jupiter.

Turning the card over, I recognized my Mother's tall, bold handwriting. Taking another sip of beer and a deep breathe, I started to read but quickly stopped. My body felt out-of-kilter, the cocaine swelling my nostrils. I couldn't remember having ever received another correspondence from her. If I was to read the postcard, I would hear her voice in the written words, as if she were sitting right there in the station wagon, asking something from me in the name of the family. That I couldn't deal with, so I tossed the postcard out the window then rolled it up.

"Can I have a sip off that bottle?"

Cracker Joe reached under the seat and pulled out a pint of Jack Daniel's whiskey.

"You're going all out, aren't you?" he said, looking at me. "You deserve it though—need to get the sand and grit out of your teeth."

I took a long drink, the whiskey stinging my chapped lips, and handed the bottle back.

Then, from out of the growing darkness, a jackrabbit appeared in the lane ahead, frozen in its tracks. Cracker Joe swerved to hit the small animal, but it leapt off the highway. Cracker Joe sat up in his seat and looked in the rearview mirror.

"Son of a bitch. Did you see those pink eyes—that's bad spirits, man. Better to kill it dead when you see eyes like that. I oughta get my automatic from under the seat and go back."

"You ought to be ashamed of yourself," I said sarcastically, again rolling the window down, looking out at the growing darkness. "Poor little rabbit. Besides, what are you carrying a pistol for?"

"What for? I'll tell you what for—living in Nixon. Things haven't been easy around home. And I'm not even talking about that shit on the hill. What'd they say?"

"What'd who say?"

"Your family."

"Nothing much. Just a "Hello, how are you?" kind of card. Let's do another toot, Cracker."

"Right—you serious? Enjoy the buzz, Merle, this is good stuff. Relax a little bit."

"I've been relaxing. You don't know how much relaxing I've done. Come on, I got money, if that's a problem."

"I didn't say anything about money, Merle, why do say that? I'm glad to see you, brother, and this whole thing is on me. You're my oldest buddy, always remember that. Dealing, I'm always fucking with people about money. Here, take this and keep it."

He handed me a vial. My ticket somewhere, I thought, my tongue sliding along numb gums. I did up two ample lines off the back of my hand, then put the vial back in my chest pocket, next to the bundle of cash. A long silence passed. I watched the last blush of gold disappear from the hilltops to the east. As the strong medicinal smell of sage wafted through the station wagon, my body felt lifted out of itself, launched into a clear picture of blackness. Then I happened to glance at Cracker Joe, noticing he was upset. I had always felt sorry for my friend, taking his best interests to heart, but now I just felt annoyed by his vulnerability.

"What's wrong?" I said loudly over the rushing wind, rolling up my window. "I'm O.K. Don't worry, man," he said gruffly, phlegm in his throat. I kept looking at him, the dashboard lights giving his skin a strange yellowish sheen.

"I'm just so happy to see you. I been lonely." Emotion overcame him again, and he tipped his head down, sobbing, and seemed to lose sight of the road. I reached out and grabbed the wheel, but Cracker Joe immediately raised up and pushed my arm away.

"I'm alright. Don't worry about it."

I sat back, disgusted with my friend; he was acting like a sentimental old woman. With night closing in, depriving me of a view of the desert, I was beginning to feel like a caged animal inside the station wagon.

We passed a sign for a fish hatchery, then a historical monument for Chief Joseph and the Nez Percé.

"Where you been keeping yourself? It blew my mind when Marcos said you were around."

I looked out the window, annoyed by his questions. "I been travelin' the whole time."

"Travelin', really?"

"I don't think I spent more than a few weeks in any one place."

"I thought you went south. Went back home with your tail between your legs. The bad boy; the dropout."

"How could I be a dropout—I never started. But I did get thrown in jail," I confided deviously.

"What? Not again," Cracker Joe asked. "For what?"

"Robbery. Vagrancy. They said I robbed a house," I said, admitting the act for the first time to anyone. It did seem absurd, and I laughed to myself about it.

"Did you?"

"Yes, but they couldn't prove it. They just kept me locked up for a while."

"What happened? Did you see a fancy stereo you liked?"

"No, I was broke, busted. I didn't have anything."

An awkward moment passed, and I could sense that even Cracker Joe, who had never lived a life of privilege, didn't understand what it meant to really have nothing.

"Did you make out O.K.?"

"Twelve bucks and a roast beef sandwich."

Cracker Joe burst into laughter, slapping the steering wheel and throwing his head back. Then he started to cough and it took him a minute to get under control. Still chuckling, he began steering with his knee and leaned back, pulling another vial out of his pants pocket.

"Here, put some of that out for me. That story cracks me up. Use the shoe box top."

There was no overhead light, so I unsteadily completed the ritual of dumping and dividing in the dark. Cracker Joe snorted the lines up with a gold straw that hung around his neck. He lite up a cigarette and opened his window slightly.

"So you never went home, never saw old Papa."

"No."

"You know, I've thought about it a lot. That bastard, he worked our asses off. I hated him, but respected him, too. Remember how every morning at the shop he would talk about the job we had to do—like a pep talk by a football coach. It's before sunrise, freezing cold, nobody's listening, just standing around drinking coffee, waiting for the trucks, and, man, he doesn't even notice, but just keeps acting like some sort of commander-in-chief. He was something else. So many memories, man."

Oh! boy, here we go again, I complained to myself.

"Remember that time we found that melted rock out near the munitions dump? It was melted green, like a ginger ale bottle. Remember that? Weird. You know, Winona was telling me about some reports somebody did about the radiation on the sites. We got fried—did you know that?"

"You're fried right now, Cracker," I said to end the conversation, not wanting to think any more about the past.

"I know, man—flying."

I nodded, biting a fingernail, recalling that it had been a strange sight. We'd been dropping a load of concrete, when we came across the oddity, created by God-knows-what weapons testing. It was about as big as a car. Papa had followed us out there, and when he saw the thing, he told us to step back. He climbed up onto it, and for about five minutes he went through his inspection, quietly walking back and forth across the glassy surface. After he jumped down, he told Cracker Joe, myself, and two Army grunts to get back to the trucks, quick.

I forced my thoughts back to the highway, which was illuminated like a tunnel by the headlights. Cracker Joe put on a new tape, explaining that Winona had just given it to him as a birthday present. It was traditional American Indian music—odd sounding flutes, drums and chanting that grated on my nerves. An acrid taste welled up in the back of my mouth and I washed it down with another pop of whiskey. Rolling down the window again, my mind rushed as fast as the wind, everywhere and nowhere at once.

After half an hour, lights appeared here and there outside, then Highway 47 came to an end at a stop sign in Wadsworth. The little town was closed up for the night. Cracker Joe let the engine idle, and we stared across the street at the one streetlight in front of the post office.

"You been dating any women?" he asked out of the blue.

"What do you think?" I said.

"Well, you moved in on Winnie pretty easy."

"Cracker, what the hell are you talking about?"

"Shit, I haven't even talked to a woman in a long time. Women don't like me, unless they want something from me," Cracker Joe said, almost philosophically. "Listen, why don't we do something about it?"

I asked him what he meant. Hesitantly, he said that he had started going to the local whorehouses; he knew about a small, comfortable place in Fallon that he thought I might like. I could tell by the hint of tenderness in his normally gruff voice that he was embarrassed making this confession. I'd never paid much attention to the famous skin trade in Nevada, but at that moment I had money and simply wanted to be somewhere, anywhere, where I could sit and be left alone. I told Cracker Joe to lead the way.

On the drive to Fallon, we kept our high at a feverish pitch, and it wasn't long before my mind and body felt like a piece of laminated wood that was splitting apart. I just sat there, trying to control myself.

To the southeast, the moon rose up so big and pale that it seemed you could just grab hold of it, jump on, and take a ride. No sage or greasewood or rabbitbrush caught the eye now, only brightly illuminated fields, flat and barren.

Civilization slowly began to appear out the window: rows of mailboxes; a truck stop here, a wrecking yard there; and down long driveways, lights from small ranch houses.

"Never been to Fallon before," I said without curiosity, the fact that it was plain and ugly not worth mentioning.

Cracker Joe asked me what I meant: I was going to be working there the next day, wasn't I? I told him I'd been bull-shitting him. He told me where to get off, that he knew it all along anyway. I told him he was lying, and he responded, no, that I was the liar. We were both right, I hopelessly concluded.

I kept thinking of Mother's card, pissed that I'd tossed it. After all, I kept repeating to myself, it was my only link to anything. What would Paris be like? I wondered. I'd never visited a faraway city (or even been outside the Nevada state line, for that matter) so how would I know? I tried to recall images of that grand place from movies or photographs or books, but all I could come up with was Charles Lindberg and his airplane . . . and Fallon.

We pulled up to a four-way stop. An eighteen-wheel Peterbilt rolled through the intersection, heading north, decorated from bumper to bumper with a constellation of bright orange lights. As we moved forward, a tour bus on our left did the same. Cracker Joe abruptly put on the brakes, shouting an obscenity out the window. Seeing the bus hesitate then stop, he stepped on the gas and bolted across, the engine whining.

"What the hell are you doing?"

"I didn't do nothin', he pulled right out in front of me," Cracker Joe yelled defensively.

My paranoid eyes looked steadily into the rearview mirror. Something—and I hesitated to explore my intuition any further—was going to happen that night, and whatever it was, I didn't want it to involve the police. The thought of the police getting their hands on me made me shiver with fear.

At a sign for the King Neptune's Rock Shop, we slowed down and turned south onto Amarillo Road. My eyes focused on the broad circular driveway and open property in front of the business.

"Nice rocks," I said in a barely audible voice.

"What did you say?" Cracker Joe asked, tossing the butt of yet another cigarette out the window. He looked at me, laughing. "Aw! you're just fucked up, aren't you?"

"I said, "Nice rocks.""

"Where?"

"That place back on the corner. What did you think I said, something about getting your tocks off?"

"No, but it sounds good to me. Man, I hope Sherry's there."

We moved slowly down a quiet residential street, then approached a small sign blinking: The Rambling Rose Club. We pulled into a parking lot, which was half-filled with cars and military trucks. In the back was a complex of trailers illuminated by pink floodlights. A security guard paced around the entrance.

"Here," Cracker Joe said, dumping an ample amount of

powder on the back of his hand. "But be careful." As I bent over to take the hits, I noticed the immensity of his hands—like big, ugly tools attached to his body. I had seen Cracker Joe destroy a number of men in different fights over the years, at parties, out behind bars, in desolate, specially-chosen, locations in the desert. The nickname described the particular impact his fists had on opponents' skulls. As his chosen friend, I had used his fighting skills as a protection for myself more than once, something I wasn't all that proud of.

We got out of the station wagon. After being checked for weapons at the front door by the security guard, we stepped into the main trailer.

A woman stood up from behind a makeshift hostess table and walked towards us, saying, "Hello, cowboys, welcome to the Rambling Rose." She looked to be in her forties, with perfect red hair; her ample breasts were pushed up, then together, under a sheer blouse, which was tied in a bow above her navel.

"Hello, Joe. Can I take your jacket?" she asked directly. He stopped in his tracks at the question, embarrassed by her sense of familiarity. He clumsily took it off and handed it to her, then began rolling up each sleeve of his orange Harley-Davidson t-shirt, revealing his meaty biceps.

"I see your dressing casual tonight," she said to me, smiling. "You don't want me to hang up those overalls you're wearing, do you?"

"Maybe later," I said, the words barely escaping my thick, half-thawed mouth.

"This guy here, he's the only friend I got," Cracker Joe said.

"I see," she responded, "Well, come with me. You can meet some new friends." We followed her through a curtain of hanging yellow beads.

The room, which was surprisingly large for a mobile home,

was made claustrophobic by a low ceiling and red velvet wallpaper. A handful of men sat at small, cafe-like tables and chairs, laughing, tossing back shots. On the far side of the room, in the corner, was an open pool table. The slow refrains of a Vince Gill song floated from a juke box. "My name is Jeannie," the woman said, standing closer and talking louder. "I manage the house, so holler if you need anything. You pay me when you leave, after I find out from the girls what the services have been." She put her hand out and touched my arm. "Enjoy," she said, then walked away.

Cracker Joe and I faced each other. My energy had sky-rocketed from the last hit, my jaw floating, my eyes capturing everything in the room at once, my feet wearing electric grooves in the floor. Cracker Joe put his hands on his hips and looked around in wide, uninhibited glances. I had seen the look before and didn't like it; his expression seemed to say: *Cross my path if you dare, but I'm warning you, I don't know the meaning of the word fear.* After waving my hand in front of his face as a distraction, we took two seats at the bar.

Off to the side of the bar, near a hallway that I guessed led to the rooms in the back trailers, three women were standing on a low stage decorated by a row of blue Christmas lights, moving in a slow abstract way to the music. They were dressed in tight bras and g-strings and high-heels, and although each woman looked very different from the other, all seemed to look out into the room with the same bored, but attention-seeking, stare. It was uncomfortable to watch—simultaneously exotic and repulsive—and I turned back, staring into the mirror behind the bar, wanting to be left alone, or better yet, to disappear.

We ordered Wild Turkeys with water backs from a female bartender. She was unusually tall, almost skinny, and wore a matching black hot pants and halter top. Her large blue eyes seemed to always be looking just beyond what was in front of her. I paid with one of my century notes. I tried to get Cracker Joe to accept the same in payment, but he refused. We raised shot glasses, toasted our being together, then pushed back the shots, the liquid burning through my throat and reaching devilishly into my stomach.

"Who's your squeeze, Cracker, the redhead or the brunette?" I teased.

"Sherrie? She's blonde. She's not out yet. She's my little sweetie. We actually talk about stuff. Deep stuff."

Cracker Joe seemed pitiful, but I kept my mouth shut about it.

"You goin' back home?" Cracker Joe asked.

I breathed deeply, trying to collect myself.

"Naw."

"Just asking—'cause it doesn't seem like you're coming back to Nixon to stay with us."

"You got enough trouble there without me around. No sense stirring things up."

The bartender set my change down, thanking me with a smile and her first eye contact.

I wanted Cracker Joe to shut up—just listening to his stream of words was becoming difficult—but he kept on. "It's funny being here with you, man. You know, I couldn't get over it when it seemed like you'd be going to the university. I knew you'd be closer to us up here, but I still thought, Christ, Merle's going to be too big to speak to me now. But look how things have worked out. Here we are doing what we always did together—having fun."

The comment seeped into my mind like unwanted rainwater. "We need some music," I said abruptly. I took some quarters off the bar and walked carefully across the room.

As I made my choices, a group of skinheads from some local military base walked into the room. They were dressed in familiar scivvies and black boots, cigarette packs rolled up into the sleeves of their white t-shirts. Loud and boisterous, they walked over to the tables near our place at the bar. My Willie Nelson choice came on as I walked back towards the group.

Cracker Joe had ordered two more Wild Turkeys, and he was now off his stool, taking in the newly arrived customers with an arrogant expression.

"Whiskey River, take my mind," he sang along as I sat down, slapping me on the back.

One of the skinheads came up to the bar and stood beside me, waiting to order drinks.

"How you guys doing?" he said, smiling smartly, tapping the bar with his wallet.

"We're good—real good," Cracker Joe said, pushing his stringy black hair behind his ear. "Where you from, junior?"

The man turned and looked more closely at Cracker Joe, now more suspicious. "We drove over from the Naval Air—"

"Not that," Cracker Joe persisted. "Where'd you grow up?"

"Indiana."

Cracker Joe let out a loud, rough laugh.

The man turned away. "Can I have five Coors drafts?" he asked the bartender.

"I haven't seen you boys in a while. Where you been keeping yourselves?" she asked, noticeably more spontaneous and friendly than before. She threw her sleek brown hair over her shoulder and reached down into the cooler.

"The unit went down to the base near Vegas for some flight training. Got back last week. I sure am glad you missed us."

Twisting the tops off the beers, the woman glanced at the man and winked. I could tell that Cracker Joe was about to make a remark, but suddenly the juke box went dead and a new song—a brassy strip tune—came over the sound system. Cracker Joe quickly straightened up and lit a cigarette.

The blue lights running along the bottom of the stage were blinking now; the three women who had been on the stage stepped down and walked off, only to be replaced by four other women, three brunettes and a blonde. Each woman took her place in line, taken aback by the loud applause coming from the skinheads, who were now raising their beers in appreciation of the show.

A man and a woman stood up from a table in the corner and walked by us, seeming to ignore the revelry—the man humbly taking off his cowboy hat as he passed into the hallway. I watched Cracker Joe; his eyes were on the stage, and he seemed more subdued than moments before.

Cracker Joe turned to me, "You just go up and say, let's take a walk. You gotta take a shower. And they'll talk to you about the money." He smirked, tipping his head back to finish his whiskey, looking towards the bar again. "If you're lucky, you won't have to wear a rubber." His hands ran nervously along his pant leg—like a student about to give a piano recital—grinning as he glanced about the room.

"Go for it," I said, "I'll be here when you get back."

But just as Cracker Joe was about to move his bulk off the stool, the young man who'd just ordered the drinks stood up, and, at the noisy encouragement of his friends, pushed his chair aside and walked towards the stage. He'd decided on his pick and walked up to the blonde, who leaned over and listened to him, then stepped down off the stage. I looked closely at the woman; she was cuter, younger, than the others.

Cracker Joe went into a frenzy as he watched the two walk away together, clenching his fist and hitting his leg over and over.

"Was that Sherrie?" I asked.

He mumbled something under his breath, shaking his head.

I ordered two more whiskeys.

Cracker Joe sank the shot in a single hand motion then hunched over, taking a long, disgusted draw off his smoke.

"Cracker?"

"What?"

"Come on, look at me."

"Fuck it!"

I kept silent, methodically turning the whiskey glass in my hand, my eyes racing over the red-speckled surface of the bar. Cracker Joe took another drag, a low, grinding cough echoing in his chest.

"She'll be back," I said impatiently.

Angry and distracted, Cracker Joe crushed his cigarette in an ashtray and stood up, steadied himself, then walked up to the stage. I was grateful he was gone, but at the same time, frightened at being left alone. I eyed his reflection in the mirror. He approached the second woman in the lineup—her brown hair was a halo of curls, her hips chunky—and within a few seconds they talked away, in what was now becoming a familiar ritual. I turned my head as they approached the hallway, thinking Cracker Joe might acknowledge me before he disappeared; he did glance back, but his eyes only glared in the direction of the table where the military men were sitting.

As the minutes passed, anxiety nibbled at me from the inside out. This cocaine shit: you needed to service yourself again and again, or else you felt like you were falling off a cliff. I felt faint for a moment, but I kept my eyes closed and the feeling passed. A voice brought my attention back to the room.

"Hi. Do you mind if I sit down?" I turned and looked up, startled to see Jeannie.

"Whoa! I didn't mean to frighten you, honey," she said, laughing. She placed a small gold purse on the bar, sitting in Cracker Joe's place.

"Are you O.K.?" she asked. Looking closer, her face scowled: "No, you certainly are not." She called the bartender. "Brenda, give me an orange juice and soda water. Would you like something more?"

"Wild Turkey."

"You heard the gentleman."

She turned to me. "Wild Turkey. Maybe that's your problem—how do you drink that stuff?"

"I . . . don't . . . normally. It's my friends."

"I'm sorry, I couldn't understand you."

"It . . . is my . . . friends favorite."

"I see—a male bonding sort of thing."

I scratched my beard and rubbed my nose.

She took her drink from the bartender.

"Thanks, Brenda. Is Gretchen coming out soon?"

"I'm waiting," she said, looking at her wristwatch.

"She'll be just a sec, you wait and see," Jeannie said. Brenda shrugged, continuing to rinse glasses in the sink.

As Jeannie turned to me, she was interrupted by one of the skinheads.

"Good evening, Jeannie," he said, leaning a pool cue against the bar. "How's life treating you?"

"Just fine, I can't complain at all—and anyway, it wouldn't do a world of good if I did."

"I would really like to talk with you, one on one. I'm over at the pool table with the other guys. Got another winner's game, then I'm ready to go."

"Why, young man," Jeannie said with mock sophistication, "how can you talk to me that way in front of this gentleman?"

"This guy? Farmer John? He's nothing. Jeannie, listen, my money's talking, not me."

He pulled a wad of cash out of his wallet and set it on the

bar. "I'll take a gin and tonic," he said to the bartender in a loud voice, "and give the change to Jeannie."

"No, please, that's not how we do business around here. You keep that."

He pushed me on the shoulder; I ignored him, staring straight ahead. "You havin' a good time tonight?" he asked. He was about to touch me again, but got distracted by Brenda serving his drink.

"Brenda, wait a second," I said weakly, trying purposely to speak up to make myself heard. I reached into my breast pocket and took out my money. I unfurled the green bills in a long row, like some lucky flush I had been dealt in a card game.

"I want to buy this pilot and all his buddies a drink."

"Wait a friggin' moment," he objected.

"And here's two hundred dollars for your labor," I persisted, "And here's five, no, seven hundred dollars more. I want you to give that to Jeannie for giving us such a warm reception when we came in tonight."

Jeannie giggled to herself. Brenda took her tip and pushed the stack of hundreds down the bar towards Jeannie.

"Well, I guess the man isn't as poor as he looks," the skinhead said, crushing his lime in the tall glass. "Probably some rancher's son. Is that it? A rich daddy?"

I felt like giving the man a backhand, bloodying his nose (where was Cracker Joe?—he would have stuffed this guy in the garbage by now) but I looked straight ahead, trying to control the flood of feelings in my body, unable—I felt shy, really—to make eye contact with Jeannie.

"Darling, you've been down in Vegas too long," Jeannie said, sitting up straight, pushing her bangs out of her eyes. "Calm down and go play some pool."

"No, I'm going to—"

"I said, go and be with your friends. Don't give me any trouble, or I'll bounce your fanny out of here. We can talk later. Go have some fun. Go on now." Knowing I wasn't going to look at him, the man glared into the mirror and met my eyes before walking away.

Jeannie looked out across the room, watching the break at the table. When she turned back to me, I noticed how beautiful her red hair really was, piled high on her head, all ringlets and bows and highlights.

"Jesus, you can always tell those boys from the Midwest," Jeannie said, motioning to Brenda to return the money. "But they're good customers. The girls play up to 'em." She pushed the stack of bills back down the bar to me. "Thanks, but no thanks. I like to earn my money."

I shuffled the bills into a neat stack then absentmindedly set it next to the ashtray.

"Would you like to spend some time together?"

"Just leave me alone," I said bluntly.

"It doesn't need to take much time."

"I have no time, ma'am. I'm sorry, just leave me alone."

"I can take a hint. You take care of yourself." She got up from the bar and walked over to the pool table.

I ordered another drink, then went to the restroom and did all the powder I could stand. When I came out, Jeannie smiled at me curiously from her table by the entrance; I kept my head down, pretending like I didn't see her, and returned to my seat.

A few new customers had arrived, the room noisier than ever. Women strolled enticingly from one table to the next; one approached me, but I waved her off without a word.

I stared down the clock over the bar: eleven forty-five. I had lost track of how long Cracker Joe had been gone. What is he do-ing right now, I wondered, fumbling with the brunette on some heart-shaped bed, listening jealously for sounds from Sherrie in the next room? What a dumb bastard! The people around me, their needs and motivations, seemed dirty and meaningless. I rubbed the back of my neck, closing my eyes, words and images darting through my mind like fireworks gone mad. I began making a low humming sound, droning like an insect . . .

—A shot glass was slammed on the bar. I opened my eyes. The bartender—it wasn't Brenda, but a new woman wearing a black fishnet outfit—was laughing with a gray-bearded man. The room erupted in noise and a wave of numb sensation washed over me. I thought I was going to get sick.

This is it, I whispered under my breath, this is it—I'm gone.

I polished off the whiskey then got up and walked unsteadily towards the front door. Jeannie said something I couldn't understand. I made it out to the parking lot; the security guard said something I couldn't understand. I concentrated on just taking one sure step at a time.

When I got to the station wagon, I fumbled around under the seat, my heart pounding like an angry piston. I found a pint of whiskey and, after more blind groping, pulled out the gun. The light was dim and I held it in front of my face for a moment, making sure it was what I thought it was. Biting my lip, I touched the cold steel to my face then slipped the weapon into the waist pocket of my overalls.

I crawled inside and shut the door. Lying back on the seat, I stared at the swelling, sinking, ceiling. I closed my eyes and a deep gripping fatigue—an apathy—came over me that I had never felt before. Tired, tired, tired—the word kept echoing inside me, everything fading . . . I took a rough snort of whiskey, then another, liquid spilling out of my mouth . . .

—It was just a decision, like a light going off . . . I put my hand in my pocket, feeling the revolver close to my—

—Then a burst of yelling opened my eyes—

—Cracker Joe? —

—I heard many voices, but, yea, at the center of the screaming was my buddy—

I raised up as best I could, forcing myself to focus on the entrance to the Rambling Rose, where the bright floodlights outlined his hulking figure, surrounded by the skinheads.

Cracker had one of the men in his grips and flung him to the ground. Another landed on his back and he shook him off, bellowing, giving him the boot. Women appeared at the whorehouse entrance, huddling together. There was a flurry of threats and obscenities exchanged between the men, followed by another flurry of arms swinging, Cracker Joe standing in the middle of the fray like an injured moose surrounded by wolves.

I sat up in the seat. I needed to help my friend, but how? What was I going to do? I knew I could go out there with the gun and stop everything, but, no, I couldn't get arrested . . . no,

I couldn't, no matter what . . . Moments passed and the more I looked at the fighting, the farther away it seemed. I just didn't care anymore; he'll survive, I told myself.

But as Cracker Joe walked towards two of the men, another skinhead crept out of the shadows near a storage shed. Holding a long object in his hands, he swung and hit Cracker Joe in the back of the head, making a thudding sound. Cracker stood motionless for a second, then fell flat on his face.

There was whispering among the men, then they started dragging him off towards a truck. I was horrified! Get out and do something, my mind repeated. But after they lifted him inside, the truck backed up and the headlights flooded over me. I laid flat to avoid being seen.

In a moment, everyone was gone and it was quiet. I started

shaking uncontrollably. My body felt like it was clogged with cotton.

I pretended I was smelling a bouquet of flowers and drank from the bottle as quickly as I could, engulfing as much as my breath would allow, then more and more and more. I let go of the bottle. The inside of the cab smothered me. I couldn't use the gun right there. I leaned out of the truck door, falling onto the ground. A convulsion rose up inside me, but wouldn't express itself. Getting up onto all fours, then half-standing, I stumbled away.

There were a few moments of lucidity—a house, turning and trying to guide myself, trees, being tangled in something, a dog yapping—then my legs started running off by themselves— leaving me far, far behind—then blackness . . .

"If you'd eat some of this you'd feel 100% better . . . I promise . . . It's some meat and potato stew . . ."

I opened my eyes to a yellow pillowcase.

"Crystal, get down now. Let the man be. I'll feed you in a moment, kitten."

I stirred as my beard tickled my mouth. I turned over on my back, groaning softly, and raised up my hand—it fell like a dead fish against my face. The world was a blur that I was too weak to confront.

"Yes, there you are. I knew you'd come around. How do you feel?"

I tried to look towards the voice, but the images were painful to my eyes. There was a square mark of blue above me: I took it in, comforted. I breathed in the cool air.

"Are you hungry? You gave me a good scare there for a while . . . had to nurse you like a baby."

There was a man—an old man—staring at me.

"Good afternoon," he said, chuckling to himself. "You've been sleeping a long time."

"Where am I . . . and—" I had to stop for a moment. "Who are you?"

"Relax, just lie back. Do you feel like eating?"

The rich smell of the food filled my nostrils, turning my stomach.

"What's going on anyway?" I asked in a fragile voice.

"My name is Bill Farnsworth. I live and work here."

My head dropped back on the pillow. I was surprised to find that I was naked under the sheets. A skinny black cat jumped up and walked onto my chest, kneading and purring.

"See, Crystal is worried about you, too," Mr. Farnsworth said, smiling,

I made no response. Worried about me? I thought—why was that? I looked around the room suspiciously. It was neat and clean, the oak chairs and dresser, the yellow curtains, like antiques from another era.

My head, especially my face, ached.

"You've got a good scrape there."

My cheek stung when I touched it. "Shit. How'd I get this?"

The man laughed, standing up and putting the food on top of a bookcase. He was slightly built, bald, and dressed modestly in gray laborer's clothes. He moved in a calm, assured manner.

"I don't know how you got it. You might know that better than I. When I found you, you were out in the back lot face down, and it didn't look like you got there digging for gold. So, I would deduce that that fall might have had something to do with that shiner you're complaining about."

"Where's the back lot?" I asked.

"Where's the back lot? Maybe you took a worse tumble than I thought."

"No, I mean, where are we? Where do you live?"

"In Fallon, my dear boy. Fallon, Amarillo Street, Nevada— you understand?"

Images rushed through my mind when he mentioned my whereabouts, like the haphazard frames of an old silent film, then all I could think of was my overalls.

"I need to get dressed," I said weakly.

"Are you sure you feel up to it? You can rest as long as you like. Are you thirsty?"

"I'm thirsty—really thirsty, now that I think of it. But I need my clothes."

"I have your overalls right here. They were filthy—like something you'd pull out of a cow pen—so I washed them." I pulled at my beard, staring nervously, helplessly, as he lifted the neatly folded garment off the bureau and set it next to me on the bed.

"Your other possessions are next to the lamp. I'll leave you be and get some apple juice out of the fridge."

"Do you have any beer?" I asked, thinking of what would best satisfy my thirst.

"No, I don't. I'm sorry," he said, leaving the room.

I felt the compulsion to fall back to sleep, but some inner fear of being alone again—alone with the man—forced me to get up and sit on the edge of the bed. Then I remembered my last few minutes of consciousness the night before: how could I have survived? I asked myself, disgusted with how things had turned out. I put on my overalls and sandals, wondering where the gun had gone. I quickly grabbed my money from the bureau, then counted it, shocked to find that I'd spent one thousand dollars since leaving Nixon the day before.

Mr. Farnsworth came through the door, carrying a pitcher and a glass.

"There you go. How does it feel to be up and about?"

I took the apple juice. "Fine," I mumbled. I gulped the liquid down, then another glassful as well.

"Come on out, let me show you around. This room's for sleeping, not standing dumbfounded with your hands in your pockets."

"Wait. Do you have my blanket and canteen?"

"No, none of that."

I followed him through the living room of the small, quaint house, out onto the porch, where there was a chair and chaise lounge.

"This is my smoking chair—so don't you dare sit in it. You can lay down over there if you want." A faint voice inside of me pressed to leave, but I simply didn't have the physical strength to push through with the idea.

I lay back on the chaise lounge. Down the porch steps, a stone path crossed a lawn, passing a large poplar tree that shaded the two buildings at the front of the property. Rocks of all varieties were strewn about the yard, some lined up against the buildings, standing upright like human torsos, others stacked in piles in wood boxes on tables. When a truck passed by on the highway out front, I dimly remembered my whereabouts from the night before.

"You're a rock hound then, huh?" I asked, with a hint of admiration.

"You could say that. This is King Neptune's. Pretty famous in this part of the state," he said, pulling out a pipe, packing it with tobacco.

I wanted to talk, but laying back—resting, disappearing— was too seductive.

A minute passed; I heard the hollow, fluttering sound of

the man's lighter over his pipe; the spicy smoke hit my nostrils.

"You know, if you need to take a shower, there's an outdoor shower back behind the workshop. It's not too fancy and you ..."

When I woke up the second time I felt considerably better. The poisons in my blood, my mental disorientation, even my bruised cheek, seemed to have subsided. I stretched my arms and legs, the movement so deep and satisfying that it made me laugh.

The smoking chair was empty. I half-expected Mr. Farnsworth (what a stupid name—like a librarian) to be snooping around and getting in my business. I peeked through the screen door: no one, only the sound of the strong winds passing through the trees, and a whirring mechanical sound that I couldn't identify. I had to visit the Rambling Rose, immediately.

I left the house, re-tracing the path that Cracker Joe and I had taken the previous night. My worst fear was confirmed as I walked into the parking lot and saw my friend's station wagon. Hesitantly, I walked up and looked in the window. The whiskey bottle was on the seat, a quarter full, and it hurt me to see it. Christ, what have I done? I asked myself. I saw my bedroll, my canteen, but I couldn't bring myself to grab them—they seemed contaminated somehow.

"You need something?" a voice asked me. I looked up and saw a security guard. He walked towards me lazily, a short, barrel-chested man wearing reflector sunglasses. "You better not be drinking out here, I'll tell you that right now."

"I'm not drinking. Do you know if Jeannie is working?"

"No, I don't see her yellow Corvette. Sorry. But don't let that stop you from going inside." He laughed joylessly, as if his words were said many times a week, to too many strangers.

"Is anyone inside?"

"What do you mean, is their anyone inside? Of course there is."

"Any customers, I mean."

"No. Pretty quiet this time of day."

"I'm looking for a friend of mine. Big, heavy-set Pauite."

"Haven't seen him."

I tugged at my beard.

Just then a buzzer went off near the front door of the main trailer. "I'm being called. Remember, don't be shy."

I walked over to the hedge running along the property line between the Rambling Rose and a neighboring house, guessing that this was the yard I passed through to reach the King Neptune property. A short distance to the north, I could see the top of the poplars by Mr. Farnsworth's workshop, but my view was blocked by a tall grape arbor separating the side yard from the back lot. I expected to see the gun somewhere on the ground, but I couldn't find it.

I started walking back down to Amarillo Street. My duty was before me, clear as day: I had to find Cracker Joe. My mind mulled over the options. I could phone Nixon. I could return to the Rambling Rose and pursue the matter with Jeannie. The police could be contacted. All those things would be easy enough, if I would just pick one and do it. After all, I had to be loyal to my friend. But who was I fooling? I asked myself, empty inside, knowing I didn't have the determination or the guts to solve the mystery. Forget it, I convinced myself, what's happened has happened, end of story.

"I thought you'd be in Tonopah by now," exclaimed Mr. Farnsworth as I walked up to the rock shop. He turned away before I could respond, opening the screen door for a woman and two young boys.

"Do you have those good luck stones in your pocket?" he asked the youngsters, who both smiled—they were twins and cute as buttons—hiding behind their mother's legs.

"Thanks," the woman said, "I'll pick everything up next Tuesday, the day before his birthday. O.K. you two, say bye-bye." Both children peeked timidly at Mr. Farnsworth. He bent down and pretended he was going to tickle the boys, and they squealed happily and ran off towards the car, followed by their mother. He waved as the family drove away.

"I knew her husband when he was a little squirt. He was an All-State quarterback years ago—hell of an athlete," he said, his eyes thoughtful for a moment. "He's a jerk now, but what can I say? We're all jerks now and then."

I was looking at a heap of geodes in a rusted wheelbarrow near the front door. "Speak for yourself, Mr. Farnsworth," I said seriously.

He burst out laughing. "Well, excuse my carefree assumptions. Where did you scurry off to?"

"I just took a walk."

"Old men like me take walks, not young palominos like you." He took off his straw hat and wiped his brow, sizing me up from head to toe. Despite his leathery face, which was wrinkled by age and perhaps too many days in the sun, his eyes were sharp and engaging. "I know what most men do when they're in this part of town. What is your name, son?"

"Merle Honeycutt, sir."

"Let's go inside, Mr. Honeycutt," he said, leaning down and picking up a wooden box filled with chunks of rose quartz, setting it on a bench by the front door. I was, again, about ready to hit the highway, but I decided against it, what with the dry heat sapping my energy. Instead, I followed Mr. Farnsworth inside.

The store was a fascinating place. Large glass cases were filled with gems, hand-crafted jewelry and artifacts. There was an impressive collection of Great Basin animals and birds—an antelope, ground squirrel, big-eared kit fox, kangaroo rat, sage sparrow, and grouse—each displayed on a redwood base with a small hand-painted nameplate. The walls were covered with old framed photographs, maps, and documents from the 1800's.

Mr. Farnsworth stepped behind the cash register, putting on a pair of glasses, the half-lens teetering on the end of his nose as he looked over some papers.

"Don't be frightened by the zoo—the collection is a long-standing passion of mine," he said, keeping his eyes on his work. "Former students do the taxidermy."

I strolled around, detached and introverted, then knelt down in front of the glass case closest to Mr. Farnsworth, where a coiled king snake and road runner were frozen in action. I cringed when I saw an Indian basket, with brown, faded leaf patterns, a corn shaker, and three spoons carved from bone, set beside the animals; Biggs and Morgan would have been salivating.

"Where did you get that basket?" I asked, fascinated by how the weave of the basket was tight in the top coils, becoming larger in size toward the center and base. "Is that from Lake Lahanton?"

"Lahanton?—where did you hear about Lahanton?"

"Some friends of mine."

"This piece isn't from there. Most of what they found out there, before they began filling the area back up with water, were graves and bones. Not many baskets there, if any. Most of the pieces on this side of the shop are either Washoe or Northern Shoshone."

The cash register rang as he opened it, finishing his business.

"What do you do, Merle?"

"What do I do?"

"Yes, what—do—you—do? Or is that too complicated?" He started to laugh, then coughed. "I'm sorry, I've been spending too much time alone—I'm losing my manners."

I stood up and started examining the jewelry displayed in a

large redwood case taking up the middle of the shop, embarrassed by the man's bluntness. The case was beautifully handcrafted, with strips of onyx as trim.

"I'll ask one more time: what do you do?" I could feel his eyes staring at my back.

"I'm kind of between things right now."

"Well, I know that," he said sarcastically. I watched him pour a cup of coffee from a hot plate beside the register. "Would you like some coffee?" he asked. I passed. Then he walked around the register and stood in front of the basket I'd been inspecting.

"That basket is over a hundred years-old, about as ancient as my spine feels. They gave it to me as a gift when I retired from my professorship at the University of Reno a few years back. It's not for sale.

Do you like old things like that?"

"Yea, I guess," I said. "I just think of whoever made it—how they were able to make it so perfectly."

"Well, back then, people took care with things—they had to."

Taking a sip of coffee, he pointed to a large photograph on the wall, next to two antelope heads. "That's this property forty years ago. I had it blown up."

I looked at the scratchy, black-and-white image, the bare field and one-room shack, the skinny struggling trees.

"You've got a little more shade now."

"Yes, and it's a good thing. This was just a summerhouse then. I lived in Reno with my family, teaching, and would visit just a couple times a year."

Just then, a buzzer went off and the front door of the shop opened. A tall, curly-haired man, dressed in a flower-print shirt and khaki shorts, entered.

"I saw the petrified wood out front. Can I ask you about a couple of the pieces?"

"Sure can," Mr. Farnsworth said, stepping outside.

I looked around, my eyes inspecting small treasures, each so obviously close to this old man's heart. I was torn between admiration for his inventory, and a terrible desire to somehow desecrate it. Since I had so much money, the contents of the cash register was of little temptation, but I knew now, from experience, that the contents of the store was of substantial value on the black market. I gotta split as soon as possible, I told myself, frightened by the implications of my cruel thoughts.

I stepped over to a display made from a deer antler. There were a number of leather chokers hanging from the painted tips. I lifted off one of the hoops and examined it. It was made out of some type of animal skin, stiff, but very light and flexible; two knotted strings—the knots so small as to be almost imperceptible—were wrapped around the main cord, which had clasps on each end. I glanced back to the door; I could still hear Mr. Farnsworth talking with the customer. I slipped the choker inside my overalls, letting it slip down against my navel.

Just then the buzzer screeched again.

"You let me know if you're interested," Mr. Farnsworth said politely, giving a tired wave to the man's voice outside. "Have a safe trip." He picked up his coffee cup again, refilled it, then leaned on a high stool beside the cash register. He took a frustrated sip of coffee, smacking his lips.

"People want so much for so little. The man thinks a two hundred pound piece of petrified wood—20 million years old—big as an elephant leg—should cost the same as a dinner for four at a restaurant. Crazy tourists." He returned to the front door, pulled down the blinds, and put out a closed sign.

"Are you looking for work?" he asked.

I would have welcomed his question any other time, but with money in my pocket, I told him I wasn't.

"That's unfortunate. I have both the lapidary work and gift shop to keep track of—which is too much—and you can't depend on these high school boys in Fallon. Are you all right?" he asked. "You don't look so good."

"Don't mind me—I'm just tired."

"You oughta be—carousing with painted ladies all night."

"I didn't do that."

"What were you doing then?"

"I went there with a friend."

"Ah! Crime, or lust, by association—how sweet it is. Well, I hope your friend had a good time at least."

Mr. Farnsworth shuffled by me with a noticeable limp.

"Did you see these?" He walked over to the same deer antler display and lifted off a choker. "They're made by local Paiutes. People love them." He tossed it to me, and I caught it, pressing it against my stolen secret. "Keep that for yourself," he said. "A good luck charm from Neptune himself."

Before I could say anything, he turned and moved to the back door. He stopped momentarily, as if he intended to say something more, then, with a slam of the screen door, disappeared.

Later, we ate a dinner of steak and baked potato and salad, then sat out on the porch, watching the sunset.

"The twilight and the early morning hours, that's the best time here in the desert," Mr. Farnsworth reflected, his pipe smoke wafting my way, rich and fruity. There was a riot of pink and gold in the western sky, so dramatic that you could almost touch it: a million miles away.

"I don't mind the Rambling Rose. I was one of the few

business people around here who didn't object when they started the place. People are always looking for something they don't have, and a whorehouse is where some of them find it. I've been in places like that. None of it amounts to anything. That I can tell from the look on your face."

I felt tired and could have cared less about the look on my face. I rubbed the cat's chin. "Did you find my automatic yesterday?" I asked.

"Why do you bring up such a subject?" Mr. Farnsworth said, shaking his head in frustration. "There's more guns than jack rabbits in Fallon."

I decided to keep my mouth shut about it.

The sunset soon turned to ash, and violet shadows settled over the yard. Mr. Farnsworth sucked on his pipe, the ember illuminating his face. He snapped the fingers of his free hand and the cat pranced over and received his petting, turning in frenzied circles at his feet. I shifted in my chair again, glad the darkness was hiding my eyes.

"So you were a prof at UNR?"

"Yes, my entire adult life."

"What happened to your family?"

"Divorce. Then my daughter went back east to Princeton—I don't see much of her, or anyone for that matter."

"I almost went to the university," I ventured.

"Really? When?"

"Couple years ago."

"What happened?"

"I didn't go. I was going to be part of a special program and didn't get accepted."

"What were you going to be studying?"

"I didn't really know."

"But what was the special program?"

I hesitated, but decided to go on: "It was set up for people who had . . . records. I was given a chance that I normally wouldn't have been offered."

"Why, were your grades bad before you had a record?"

"Well, they weren't good, I can tell you that."

I wanted to see Mr. Farnsworth's face, his eyes, his response, but he just continued to methodically pull on his pipe in the dark. Then he grunted, puffing harder. "Well, one way or another, they don't make it easy to get into the university these days. And it costs an arm and a leg."

"Give me a break, Mr. Farnsworth," I said. "It's not hard to get accepted—if you play the game right."

"And you didn't? I thought you applied to the program."

"They didn't like me in the interview."

"Why?"

"How am I supposed to know? Maybe it was the color of my shirt, or my breathe. Beats me."

Mr. Farnsworth turned away, looking out into the yard.

"These things always have a reason."

"No they don't. Some things happen for no reason at all. And sometimes shit like that happens to certain people all the time, for no reason at all. That's just the way it is."

I let the silence that followed swell with the possibility of another threat, or worse, some touch of violence. After a minute, Mr. Farnsworth banged his pipe on the porch rail, then got up.

"You're wrong," he said, scratching his head. "But I haven't got the energy to talk about it. Like I just said, I like the twilight, which just passed, and early morning, so I'm going to bed. You retire when you like. Just turn off that floodlight by the shop door."

"I'll be gone tomorrow, Mr. Farnsworth."

"Fine, son. Whatever you decide. Sleep well."

"Mr. Farnsworth? How come you didn't just phone the police when you found me?"

"I'm old-fashioned, Merle," he said. "If you can do something yourself, there's no need for the police. Good night."

When I woke up the next morning, I dressed quickly, intent on leaving as soon as possible. I had had a good nights sleep and most of my strength had returned from the debacle two nights before.

I went out onto the porch. I considered leaving without saying good-bye, but decided to look for Mr. Farnsworth. As I passed the doorway to the workshop, I heard an electrical humming and hesitantly stepped inside.

Mr. Farnsworth was standing with his back to me. A hooded cutting machine droned in the corner. He bent over and slowly lifted a rock from the floor, then placed it on the workbench, which was lined with lapidary equipment.

"Mr. Farnsworth?"

He turned around and looked me up and down, wiping his hands on his pants.

"Well, what do you think of this?" He handed me the cut piece, which I recognized as amethyst; it was the size of half a cantaloupe, gray and crusty on the outside, perfectly smooth where the cut had been made, the hollow interior filled with rows of purple teeth.

"A big hit with the tourists," he said, "the Ford Escort of the rock shop world."

I handed it back.

"You look like your headin' somewhere."

"Yea. Time to go. But I did want to get the gun from you."

"What if I told you, I didn't find any such thing?"

"What if you did?"

"Why do you need it?"

"I might have to shoot something, that's why."

"Tough—all the young people these days are so tough. Well, it belongs to you, so I guess you have rights to it."

He brought down a shoebox from a shelf above the workbench and pulled out the automatic. I was startled at its appearance, not really being familiar with it. He inspected it for a moment then handed it to me. I slipped it into my overalls.

"I'm going downtown, you want a lift? Would that help you on your way?"

I declined, wanting no more assistance from the man, and not really knowing what direction I was taking.

"Suit yourself," he said, taking off his work bib. He checked a timer on the rock cutter then walked over to the door where a number of sets of keys were hanging on the wall. He rifled through them, mumbling to himself.

We walked outside and he locked up the main shop. "You sure you aren't looking for any work, Merle? I got some field work that I'm going to have to do all this coming week, and I need a strong back."

"No, too lazy, Mr. Farnsworth."

He looked at me, and I noticed, for the first time, that his eyes were blue.

"I doubt that. Where are you going?"

"I'm not sure."

"That's too bad. You have the wrong kind of determination. Good luck to you."

I shook his hand and walked across the parking lot to the highway. At the edge of the asphalt, I stood around listlessly, not even bothering to stick out my thumb when cars and trucks passed by. I watched Mr. Farnsworth walk out to an old, white Valiant, which was parked by two trucks: a red 4x4 and a half-ton flat bed. After warming up the car, he pulled up next to me, rolling down the window.

"Got your heat?" he asked.

I just stared at him with disdain.

He waved at me, grim-faced, then drove off.

"What a pain, getting old," I muttered, kicking at the gravel with my sandals.

The sun was beginning to bite with hot fangs, so I put my new bandanna on. The aluminum overhang at the drive-in across the highway was sending off an annoying reflection, so I walked up the road a bit, crossing over to the other side, where I could catch a ride west. I stuck my thumb out, hoping that by some quirk of fate I would be picked up and whisked away into something new and unexpected, where I could forget my descent out of the Black Rock. A school bus rumbled by—innocent young faces peering out in a neat row; then, uneasily, I watched a long caravan of camouflage-green jeeps and troop carriers pass, no doubt heading for the naval air station.

I turned away and looked back at King Neptune's, at the vehicles, the random groupings of rock strewn about, the lush trees, the grounds passively baking in the noontime heat. There was no telling whether the business was open or closed.

A livestock truck blasted by, leaving me in a swirl of dust and gravel.

"This shit's for the birds," I said, pacing back and forth on the shoulder of the highway, brimming with ambivalence about what to do. Put off by the heat, I walked back to the rock shop. I sat down on the back bumper of the 4x4, grateful to be off my feet in the shadow of the trees. I put my head in my hands, thinking. I had the gun; I could do something, but why shock the old man—it didn't seem fair. Then an idea struck. After a moment's hesitation, I jumped up and walked back to the workshop, understanding that now I was reaching a new level of desperation.

I went inside to the plaque of hanging keys. I rifled through them one by one, checking shapes and names, apprehension gnawing at my insides like a burrowing gopher. When I found a set of two Nissan keys, I walked back outside. The second key worked on the door of the 4x4, and I climbed up into the cab, which smelled new. I ran my hand along the dashboard, with its buttons and gadgetry, then nestled into the leather seat, which fit me like a glove. I hadn't driven for more than six months, not since my station wagon had been stolen in Orovada, and I was giddy with excitement as the engine started, smooth and quiet.

Between the two front seats was an open, plastic container filled with the remnants of someone's—the daughter's?—life. A pack of Salem Lights; breath mints; a map and hair brush; coins; two opened letters (I avoided reading the handwriting). Somehow these objects disturbed me, so I opened the door and emptied the container on the ground. Putting it back between the seats, I placed the gun inside and closed the top.

I let the engine idle, unsure of what to do. I knew I should split immediately because Mr. Farnsworth might return any minute. But my attention kept getting drawn across the street, to a dense grove of trees out behind the drive-in, where two red flags were blowing in the wind . . .

I waited for Mother's voice to come at any moment. Happy to be alone, but nervous, I peeked out from my hiding place behind the monument in the middle of the park, back towards the noisy festivities on Main Street. People were everywhere out there. I crouched down, leaning against the stone base of the monument, toying with my snow cone. Tipping my head back, I drank the last of the precious grape mush, the juice spilling down my chin and shirt. I tossed the cup out onto the lawn, wiping my shirt the best I could.

I wondered what Rowena was doing at that moment. She had smiled mischievously at me when she was excused from the breakfast table that morning, running off to practice her baton twirling out in the front yard. Later, just before we drove into Cherry Creek for the July 4th celebration, she entered my room dressed in her sequin outfit, but I'd ignored her, staying pinned to the wall, listening to my radio. I'd no interest in watching her show-off.

I was burning up from the sun and stood up. I considered running into the shadows of the trees at the far end of the park. I slowly read the words—Dwight D. Eisenhower—on the bronze placard, and raised my eyes up and took in the tall, uniformed figure looming above me. He reminded me of the bossy men Papa took orders from in Mercury.

"Merle? Merle, if you're there, come here immediately."

I froze inside. Papa would certainly hear about it if I ran off again, so I decided it was best to just give myself up right then. I slowly stepped out from behind the monument, sheepishly keeping my head down. As she quickly walked across the lawn towards me, I cringed.

"I don't need this, young man. Do you hear me?" she said, kneeling down in front of me. She touched the stains on my shirt, shaking her head; although I could tell she was angry, she seemed too distracted to fully express her feelings.

"Merle, listen to me, you know why we're here today. It's a special day for your sister. You're in deep trouble if you wander off again. Let's go back—and you stay right by my side." She put her hand on my shoulder and led me back towards the celebration on the crowded street.

We walked out of the park, onto the dirt lot next to Granger's Merchandise, and I stayed by Mother's side. I leaned this way and that, peeking curiously, waist high to the bodies bumping into me. A merry-go-round and pony ride had been set up; a clown in a red-striped suit and floppy black shoes stood on a platform, speaking into a loudspeaker; a man twirled pink balls of cotton candy in a push cart; and stuffed animals hung from booths, where people lined up to throw darts, toss coins, and pitch baseballs.

"Mother, can I have a soda? They're selling them right there," I said, pointing to a nearby booth.

"No, you just had something." She paused, distracted. "Come with me," she said, turning away. She seemed to ignore me for a moment—was she going to abandon me in this crowd?—but then she turned back, grabbed my hand, and we walked away from the amusements, over to the edge of the crowd.

I stood there with nothing to do. Everyone around me was up to something, talking cheerfully, smiling, eyes glancing everywhere at once, but Mother seemed different. I watched her, worried. She wore a white summer dress with a red belt; her hair—which was thick and always shiny—fell in a ponytail. She began looking in the purse hanging from her shoulder, frowning, placing her wallet awkwardly under her arm as she rifled through her possessions. She finally pulled out a brush, put the wallet back, then, unclasping the pony tail, began brushing her hair. She turned her face to the hot sun and seemed to leave the situation, dreaming, taking her time as she stroked and stroked. I impatiently glanced back at the green park and the bed of flowers under the cottonwoods.

"Where's Rowena right now?" I asked, tugging at Mother's left hand. "Has the parade started?" She pulled away and put her brush back in the purse, looking back at the street with new determination.

"Don't worry about her. She's going to be just fine, you wait and see. The band sets up on Euclid Street, then comes down Beacon and turns right onto Main. But look at the people—you can't even see the street from here. Let's move south, where there's some room."

I began to follow her, but our way was blocked by three women wearing long dresses, their old wrinkled faces shaded by identical straw hats.

"Good afternoon, Mrs. Honeycutt," said the small woman standing in the middle.

"Hello, Mrs. Pack," Mother said, hesitating, then putting her hand on my shoulder.

"It's must be a special day for your very talented girl."

"Yes, it is."

"We sure have missed you at the Sunday services, Mrs. Honeycutt. No one has seen hide nor hair of you lately. I hope you're not avoiding us."

"Dear, I wouldn't lose any sleep over it. I'll bake some bread for the August sale—you can depend on it. Excuse us."

We pushed forward, the women stepping back in confusion as we passed by.

Just then the low muffled sound of the band could be heard from up Main Street. Mother grabbed my hand and we walked quickly towards 3rd Avenue.

We moved past the last of the booths, out into an open area near rows of parked cars and trucks. Three men in soiled blue jeans and t-shirts walked towards us. One of the men stumbled to the ground awkwardly, laughing uncontrollably as he listened to his friend's loud, joking remarks. The man looked up as we approached, his wild eyes staring at my mother. She bumped into me suddenly, trying to make a path around the men. I kept watching the man who had stumbled, he was on his knees now, and he took off his cowboy hat, smiling with his mouth open.

"Am I dreamin' or is this heaven?" he shouted out for everyone to hear. He started walking on his knees towards us.

"He's drunk, Merle. Don't mind him," she said, averting her eyes and giving the man her shoulder as we walked by. "Crude piece of filth. Merle, don't you ever be like that."

We stepped between the parked vehicles and came out onto 3rd Avenue, then began winding our way through the crush of people. I kept my head down, listening as, time and again, Mother apologized and stepped between this person and that. Finally, we made it to street-side, and Mother nestled me in front of her, facing up Main Street towards

Beacon Road. The street was empty and the sound of the band had stopped.

"Oh! come on," Mother said impatiently. I turned and looked up into her nervous face. "Where in the world is your father?" she asked. "I knew he wouldn't get back from the air show in time."

A few minutes passed as the crowd stirred restlessly in the afternoon heat. Murmurs of music and cheering floated on the air, only to disappear into another silence. Then Mother shook me by the shoulders. "Papa's here. I can see him coming down the street. Go tell him where we are, Merle, but hurry up."

I hated standing and waiting for Rowena, and gladly darted away. For a moment, I thought of escaping to the park again, but I finally saw Papa a good distance down 3rd Avenue (he was walking Buster, our Weimaraner) and broke into a run towards him.

"Papa, Papa!" I yelled out, running up and putting my arms around his waist. "Did you see the big bombers?"

"Stop it, Merle!" he said. "Where's Mother?"

Buster recognized me and began wiggling happily, then let out a yelp. "Quiet," Papa told the dog. "Has everything started?"

"No, something's wrong. But you can hear the band."

"They must be coming then." His square, clean-shaven face was caught in a scowl, eyes brows pinched together; he surveyed the street.

"You take the dog, son."

"No, Papa, I don't want to." I stood back and crossed my arms in resistance.

"Don't argue. Come here, Merle. Stand here." I edged forward re-luctantly. "Buster has been with me all day in Las Vegas. He'll obey you. We have to hurry or Mother will throw a fit."

Placing the leash in my hand, he saw me handling it weakly, so he knelt down in front of me, saying, "Be stronger. It's just like at home—the dog will obey you but you have to control him. Don't let him push you around."

"There's too many people, Papa. I don't want to."

Papa abruptly grabbed the leash, wrapping it around my hand. "Come on," he said, setting off towards Main Street.

Buster followed his master immediately, and I stumbled along as best I could, trying to keep from falling down and being dragged along. We pushed our way through the crowd, to the spot where Mother was standing.

"Bob, why did you bring Buster?" she asked angrily.

"Because I had to. He couldn't stay in the station wagon, it was too hot."

"You could have left him home to begin with—there's thousands of people here. Merle, honey, squeeze through here so you can see your sister. Buster, you be a good dog now."

Booming noises came from up Main Street, then piercing gunfire. Turning the corner, three Indians on horseback charged down the street, screaming, waving bows and arrows, hooves cracking on the asphalt. As they galloped towards us, a large group of cavalry pursued them at high speed, firing rifles at the outnumbered renegades; more cavalry followed behind, riding upright and carrying American flags.

The crowd roared its approval, clapping and whistling. Although Buster remained obediently still during the loud spectacle, after the riders passed he began barking at another dog directly across the street. I pulled back on the leash, rubbing the dog's head, trying to distract him, but the barking continued.

"Buster, stop. Sit down," I heard Papa say.

"Bob, take the dog, for God's sake. Merle can't handle him," Mother complained.

"He's gotta learn sometime," he answered.

But the blaring horns and drums of a marching song caught everyone's attention, and as Rowena appeared from around the corner, the sun catching her red, sequined leotard, I heard Mother say, "There's my girl." Buster kept barking, but it didn't seem to mat-

ter now; I just held on tight as I could, the leash pinching my hand.

My heart beat uncontrollably as I watched my sister standing down the street, so small and vulnerable, stepping in time, baton twirling at her side, envious at how brave she was to perform before so many people. As the band began filling in behind her, she began prancing from one side to the other, the baton resting on her forearm; then she stopped, sent the stick flying into the sky like a satellite, grabbed it when it came back to earth, then continued her walk, smiling to the applause. The band moved in perfect formation behind her, playing songs that I'd heard before at the air shows.

Buster became more aggressive on the end of the leash as the band moved closer, barking and snapping at his enemy across the street. I gave up on controlling the dog, keeping my eyes on Rowena, who had all eyes upon her. Her baton twirled from hand to hand, under the leg, over the shoulder, faster than I'd ever seen at home. The applause went up from the crowd again, and she moved forward once more, pushed by the rolling beat of the snare drums.

Somehow, amidst all the noise, people, and excitement, I thought my sister might see me, acknowledge me, but I saw that she was lost in the performance and had no idea where I was. Everything seemed to be moving closer, crashing louder, and the only thing I was aware of was the pain of the leash around my hand. I pulled the leash with my free hand, trying to relieve the pressure.

Rowena came down the middle of the street, kicking one leg into the air, then the other. I didn't want to see her face up close. Then she turned and angled towards us.

Wanting to disappear, I let the leash unravel from my hand. Buster burst out into the street, barking. I turned away as quickly as I could, pushing past another small boy, but someone grabbed me from behind by the neck—

The blast of a truck horn brought my mind back to the grove of trees, the red flags, King Neptune's. I panicked, not knowing how long I'd been daydreaming. Gunning the gas pedal, I backed up the truck, then pulled out to the highway, given a lordly view of the blacktop in the tall-standing cab.

A once-forbidden idea crept into my mind, making sense: go talk to Roe, she's the compass. Go ahead, get rolling.

"Listen, I don't care what Pattie says," the bartender's voice boomed. He rubbed the back of his neck impatiently, his back turned to me and the empty room.

I stared at the collection of fighter squadron decals covering the wall behind the bar, seeing whether any new additions had been made.

"You tell her to get her ass down here if she still wants a paycheck. No, no, no, she can look at the schedule. Do it, pronto."

He put the phone down. Like any experienced barkeep, he sensed a thirsty customer close by and spun around on his heels. "May I help you, good sir?" he asked happily, setting a drink napkin in front of me.

"Sure. Give me whatever you have on tap." I had a mean thirst from the seven-hour drive I'd just made.

The man, who I didn't recognize, turned away, whistling to himself. He was short, with dark curly hair, his body thrown out of proportion by an enormous stomach, which peeked out from under his short-sleeve shirt.

"Is Dwayne McGriff around?" I asked.

"He sold the place."

"Really," I said, surprised, "when did he do that?"

"About two months ago." He walked over and placed the beer in front of me. "Moved up to Oregon. I'm the new manager, my name's Cal. You going to Vegas? I've never seen you here before."

"I'm visiting family here in town."

"Good, it's nice when I meet locals who aren't making a pit stop on the Gambler's Special. What's your name?"

"Merle Honeycutt."

"Well, Merle, it's a pleasure to serve you. We've got some Merle on the jukebox, so enjoy yourself. Excuse me, I have to make a phone call. I'll be right back."

I examined the decals again: 34 TAC FTR SQ RAMS; SKY CRANES; DEATH ANGELS; HEAVY LIFT RUN COMPANY, lost in memories of uncountable evenings at The Thunderbird, drinking and carousing and wasting time with the crew. It was the only bar in town, and you were in for a bad time if you frequented it without being fiercely loyal to the military and happenings at the test sites. Cracker Joe's ghost haunted every square inch of the musty place, with its plain, unexceptional furnishings of jukebox, television, pool table and military memorabilia. I sipped the beer, trying to enjoy it, but gagged reflexively at the flavor. I pushed the suds away. Sitting in this place, alone, drinking, suddenly seemed like a betrayal to Cracker Joe, which put me in a bad mood. I left money on the bar and went outside.

I drove slowly down the gravel road, which was lined with a succession of empty lots and plain storage buildings. A young girl darted across the road on her bike, her long ponytail bouncing behind her. She jumped a wooden ramp over an irrigation ditch and disappeared behind a hedge of dusty oleanders. I've seen that before, I said to myself.

The road winded up a hill and met Deacon Lane, where I pulled over to check out the view of the town below. Here was Cherry Creek, where there was no creek, let alone any fruit trees; only a thousand people, living mostly in mobile homes, with not much to enjoy but the clear blue sky, miles of creosote, an occasional coyote.

To the east, across Interstate 95, was the only reason for the towns existence: the Wallaby Air Force Base, which branded the distant valley floor with its matrix of runways and control towers. Wallaby had been our entrance into the test sites with Papa and the Shelby Construction crews. Our trucks would pass through the checkpoint gates and proceed five miles northeast to Mercury. After joining up with Department of Energy personnel, we would set off for the designated spot of the next underground atomic explosion, providing concrete and steel for the deep tunnels that the explosive device and monitoring cables were placed in.

What did it mean that I knew this town and its surroundings like the back of my hand? Not much, really. I knew about the old remnants of the Eternal Youth Nudist Camp and Utopian Society, which had been built by a wealthy evangelist, Avery Bilkes, a mile up Deacon Lane. Down in the wash, on the northern side of the high school football field, there were always diamondback rattlesnakes to kill in summertime. Forty years before, on a hillside just outside of town, people had frequented the Atomic View cafe, eating burgers and sipping malts at scheduled blast times listed on the front door, waiting for the quick blink of light, then, moments later, the tall burgeoning clouds to form over the Pahranagar and Timpahute ranges. There was a ghost town, Needlepoint, up the canyons, with a large rock in the town square, which my buddies and I had pelted with hundreds of beer and tequila bottles, the shards of glass collecting in piles, blushed purple by the desert sun. I also knew, having just passed by the location coming into town, that our old house off Highwater Street had been torn down and replaced by nothing, just large stacks of sheet metal and lumber.

Mother had asked a thousand times: "Why does anyone live in this God-forsaken place? People were drawn to other places by a great river, a holy mountain, fertile soil, thriving business, but why Cherry Creek? Just people with accidental lives." I had never understood her meaning before, but now it made sense. It was absurd to be tied by fate to this forgettable place. I had just driven down Main Street, and nothing—not Stowe's Wrecking, not the Clean Scene laundromat, not the row of American flags in front of Granger's "Best In The West" Merchandise, not the sheriff's station, not even the Dwight D. Eisenhower Park—had changed.

I checked the digital clock on the dash: four-thirty. It was an in-between time, I thought, realizing that I was a stranger who knew nothing about my family's schedule or whereabouts. I decided to try Mother first.

A mile northwest out of town, on Pahrump Road, I pulled off at a white stucco building. Just before I'd left for the university, Mother had leased these offices—which were very respectable by Cherry Creek standards—for her growing consulting business as a lobbyist in the Nevada State Legislature.

Mothers's jade-green Acura was parked in front (in that instant of recognition, I felt I'd returned home), along with a long, black pickup truck and horse trailer.

Inside the building, I checked the register—Citizens for Nevada First, Suite 210—then went upstairs, but the door was locked. I knocked, waiting anxiously, staring down at the cactus garden in the foyer.

A stranger opened the door.

"Can I help you?" the man said, his cold eyes running me up and down.

"Yes, I'm here to see the president—Evelyn Honeycutt."

"And who should I say is calling?" he said in a slow suspicious drawl.

"I'm her son, understand? Tell her Merle's here."

He looked at me a moment longer and I could see a note of acknowledgment in his critical gaze.

"I'm sorry, come on in," he said, stepping back and opening the door wide. "She's in back. Give me just a second." He was a tall man, with a handsome, square chin, informally dressed in a red jogging suit and sneakers. As I stepped inside, he walked to the back of the large suite of offices.

The air was warm, humid-feeling, the curtains closed. I looked this way and that, trying to take everything in at once. Behind a receptionist's desk, there was a view of a conference table, chalkboard, and video equipment in an adjacent room.

As I would have expected, it was all very professional, organized, well-decorated, if you could deal with the brown and gold color scheme. I smirked as I checked out the large, framed prints of London, Kyoto, New York, and, yes, Paris, along with the obligatory shots of the state capital building in Carson City.

I heard voices coming from behind one of the doors in the back—I assumed it was Mother's sharp voice that countered the man's words. I felt like a bull in a China shop, smelly and repugnant, and tried to calm myself down by sitting on the couch.

There was a martini glass on the table in front of me. The glass stood at attention, half full, sweating droplets of moisture. Whose drink was it and why was it poured? I had my suspicions. Off to the side, on a table beside a lamp, there was a framed picture of Roe. She was striking a pose, hands aloft, pirouetting; I had never seen her hair like that, or the outfit, and I assumed it had been taken in my absence. I remembered Winona's comments about Roe visiting Nixon. I would have paid all my money to see that.

A door opened at the back of the room. Mother stepped out, dressed in a yellow pant suit. She was turned away at first, making a remark to the man, then proceeded to walk my way. Her fine hazel eyes captured me like an x-ray.

I stood up.

"Merle, why do you surprise me like this?" she asked, shaking her head. Then she stopped in the middle of the room. I could tell she was shocked by my appearance. "You've changed," she said, folding her arms. "I hope it's only skin deep—that you're not really as different as you look." She came up and embraced me, and I kissed the hesitant cheek she offered. She seemed to have gained a little weight.

"When did you arrive?"

"About an hour ago."

"I ought to take you over my knee and whip you, but we have a guest. Even a tattoo I see."

"Yea. Listen, I just thought I'd drop by before going up to the house. I can leave if you want."

"No, don't be silly. Do you know Bill?—of course you don't—this is Bill Davenport. Bill, my son, Merle."

We shook hands.

"Where you coming in from?" Mr. Davenport asked.

"Fallon."

"Where is Fallon, anyway? I've heard of it."

"Up by Reno."

Mother kept staring at me, tears coming to her eyes.

"Evelyn, are you all right?" Mr. Davenport asked.

"Sure, I'm just surprised, that's all." She turned away, taking a tissue from the box on the desk. I knew she would regain her composure instantly, and she did. "We were just finishing up," she said, dabbing her eyes. "Two lobbyists from Carson City came by at three o'clock to discuss our chances of winning the Flaming Gorge Initiative in Las Vegas. They left just a few minutes ago."

Mother stepped over and picked up the martini glass.

"Bill, could you do something with this? It's still cold."

He took the glass, sipping from it as he moved to the back of the room. He stopped at a bookcase and began rifling through some mail.

Mother stared at me deeply, then glanced at her bright-red fingernails.

"Bill, I think we're through for today," she said, keeping her eyes on me. He immediately put down the mail, then picked up a cowboy hat and prepared to leave.

"You got a letter from the rancher's association," he said. "I left it under the paperweight."

"Thanks," Mother replied, gratefully touching his shoulder.

"I'll mosey along. Orders from the boss," Mr. Davenport said politely, putting on his sunglasses. "Listen, native son, don't stay away so long next time."

"I'll see what I can do," I said as he left.

Now that we were alone, Mother immediately started giving me the cold treatment. She walked over to the reception area, checked a calendar, then turned off a blue-screened computer. She moved to the back of the room, picked up the glass Mr. Davenport had left behind, then disappeared through the door.

I was half-tempted to leave, but sat down instead. She came back in a moment, carrying a soda.

"Do you need anything to drink?" she asked.

"No. Just had something at The Thunderbird."

She placed her drink on a coaster and sat down on the couch across from me.

"Who's your new gentleman friend?" I asked cautiously, wanting to interrupt her concentration.

"What business is it of yours?

That "gentleman friend" is the president of the Tri-Valley Growers Association, and gives me lots and lots of business. I'm their lobbyist at the capitol. If you had been around, you probably would have seen him quite frequently at one shindig or another."

I didn't want to talk with her like this. "Mother, I'm heading up the hill." I stood up from the couch. "How's Roe and Papa?"

"Why ask me? Go find out for yourself—you like surprises. You don't deserve my description of our circumstances."

She sat back in the chair and spread her arms out.

"Do you like how the office is decorated?"

"It's alright. Must be a dream come true, huh?"

She looked at me with an exasperated expression. "Do you know I can hardly recognize you with that beard. You look like a tramp on the rails."

The house was some distance away. I took Pahrump Road up and over the ridge west of town, where the two-lane stretched across a juniper-covered valley. Red Pepper Canyon, where my folks had bought property and built a home three years before, was at the end of that valley, twelve miles to the north.

I had been raised in two places: in Mercury, in military housing on the test site itself, up until I was eight years old; then, later, as a result of Mother's complaints about life in Mercury, we moved to the mobile home in Cherry Creek. When I was about twelve, Papa announced that he had purchased some property in the mountains outside of town, so throughout my adolescence, the family would drive up to Red Pepper Canyon on Sundays—the only day of the week Papa didn't work. Most of the time we would stop at the property line and eat a picnic lunch off the hood of the station wagon. If I didn't have to accompany Papa on a quail hunt, I would flee as quickly as I could and take the dogs and hike up into the stands of pinion pine, hoping to find colored rocks and the dried remains of scorpions.

At the end of the valley, I reached Starlight Pass, where the grade became steeper and the road snaked east.

The gate for Red Pepper Canyon appeared off the right side of the road a mile beyond. After opening the gate, I took a dirt road through a boulder-filled riverbed, then out across an open field. A landing strip had been graded down the middle of the expanse. I figured Papa must have purchased the other forty acres he'd considered buying for so many years.

At the southern end of the field was a low storage shed, with Papa's Cessna 240 Constellation nearby. A windsock hung motionless on a pole. I noticed someone kneeling under the wing of the plane and stopped the truck. Being some distance away, I couldn't make out the person, so I turned down the runway to see who it was. It had to be Papa.

The figure didn't change position as I moved closer, and I stopped the truck once I pulled up in front of the shed. It was my father, and, knowing this, I froze up inside. I opened the door and got out.

He looked up at me once then continued attaching a cable between the wingtip and an anchor set in the ground.

I walked across the asphalt.

"Hello, Papa. I'm back," I said.

Kneeling, eyes squinting, he grappled with the cable. He was dressed as I'd always known him to be dressed: in baggy, gray work pants and shirt, with a blue windbreaker. He stood up, dusting off his pants. Although he seemed thinner and his hair had turned salt and pepper, I was struck by how much his body was still like mine.

"Is that you, Merle? Pretty fancy vehicle you got there." He put a pair of pliers in his jacket pocket.

"It doesn't belong to me."

"Where's the station wagon?"

"You don't want to know." As he tested the cable with his hand, I asked, "When did you put the runway in?"

"About a year ago. It doesn't make any difference now—it was a big waste of money."

Papa walked to the front of the Cessna, touching the propeller as he passed, and knelt down to connect the cable on the opposite wing.

The mountain air was cooler than what I was accustomed to, and I felt naked in my overalls, with no shirt. I walked over to where Papa was working.

"Some pretty bad winds come through here, I bet."

Papa looked up at my face. He was about to say something, but held his tongue, continuing to stare at me.

"Let me help you." I stepped over and put my hands on top of the hollow aluminum wing. Papa took the loose cable and easily hooked it to the anchor.

"Good," he said, pulling a rag out of his back pocket and wiping his hands. "You're right, that plane will blow to the end of the canyon if I'm not careful."

"How much you been going up?"

"Not at all."

"How come?"

"I haven't wanted to, that's why." Papa reached into his pocket and pulled out a cigar and began to unwrap it.

"What have you got to say for yourself?" Papa asked, putting his lips to the cigar, wetting the tip.

"I don't know."

"You don't know? Where did you go? What did you do? Read me your journals, Ceasar."

I didn't know what he was talking about and he knew it. He took out a box of wooden matches and lit the cigar.

"Sometime you tell me what you did," he said. "You see, I also never went back. When I was young like you, I left, just like you did, and I came here to Nevada. That was 1957. But I never went back to Pennsylvania, that's the difference." He paused for moment, and since I was speechless, he gave up on my responding and walked over to the shed and locked it, then walked off towards the road.

"Hey, Papa, where you going? It's gettin' dark. I'll drive you back," I said, walking beside him, gesturing with my hands to get his attention. "We'll go in the truck."

"There's plenty of light," he said, shuffling away, his gait slower, more mechanical, than I remembered.

It was useless getting him to come with me, I thought, disappointed. I passed him on the road, beeping the horn, but he continued walking without responding, puffing the cigar.

When I got up to the house there were lights on near the side gate and up on the second story. There was a tractor, concrete mixer, and a pile of wood near the garage door, and it seemed the property around the house was as undeveloped as two years before.

I pulled in next to Roe's Trans Am and got out. I walked up to the gate and heard exactly what I expected—a dog's bark, loud and wailing. It bellowed at me from inside; I smiled, shouting out, "You dumb-ass dog," shaking the top of the gate. I was surprised that I didn't hear more barking along with that lone canine voice. I stood on my tiptoes and looked into the patio. A Rottweiler jabbered at me from inside; I couldn't recognize the dog's face.

I knew how Papa trained his dogs, so there was no sense in entering at the gate. I went up to the front of the house—in the valley below there was a smattering of lights from Cherry Creek; the test sites were invisible in a blue-black void. I checked for and found the key that was always left behind the swinging sofa on the front porch.

I opened the front door and went inside, immediately turning on all the lights in the living room, then went to the kitchen and did the same.

"Roe, guess who's back," I announced. "You up there?"

It felt so good to say her name again, and I bounded up the stairs. I passed by my room and walked softly down the carpeted passage to the light under Roe's doorway. I expected to hear music, even her voice, but there was nothing. I knocked on the door, then called her name again—nothing, silence.

I opened the door and was greeted by musty air. The light that had given me hope was only a reflection from outside, so I switched on the room light. There was a disordered upheaval of Roe's possessions lying all around: clothes piled in the corner, a bed leaning on its side against the wall, a saddle placed on top of a box of books, a mobile of dance slippers hanging from the arms of a coat rack. On a small table was an opened box of old black and white photographs; I looked them over quickly, discovering that certain shots were of Mother when she was a young girl. I went over, parted the curtains, and opened the window to let some air in. I stood there, faced by my distorted reflection, feeling confused and alone.

I went into my room. I turned on the light and sat down in a well-worn chair—the one with the cowboy faces etched in the red leather cushions; the one the next-door neighbors had given me when I was a boy in Mercury. I sat there a long time, expecting Papa to walk in the back door. But after a while, when nothing happened to catch my attention, I leaned back in the chair and fell asleep.

Sometime later, I heard my name being spoken.

"Merle . . . Merle, just lie down on the bed if you're tired."

I started, looking up at Mother. She laughed warmly. "Merle, my God, it's me. Honey, you look exhausted," she said, touching my forehead. "Take a shower if you want."

I rose up and rubbed my face, still astounded at being home.

"Where's Roe?" I asked.

"She's in San Francisco, Merle."

"What's she doing there?"

"She finally made it to the mountain top: she's dancing with the San Francisco Ballet. She moved there last fall." Mother was still dressed in her office clothes. I could tell by the way she was standing that she wanted to change into something more relaxing. She undid a hair clip and let her hair down; it was still as blonde as when she was a young woman.

"What did you expect, that everything would stay the same?"

"Why didn't you tell me at the office?"

"We talked about other things at the office. Merle, how am I supposed to give you a summary of the past two years? That's not possible, so don't expect it. If you'd been the least bit interested, you would have been here."

For a moment, Mother seemed young to me again, but in the simple act of stepping out of her high heels, and bending over and picking them up, she aged before my eyes.

"I think I'll take a shower," I said.

"I'd recommend it. And, if it's possible, scrub that gruesome tattoo off," she said.

"If you don't like—"

"I'm just kidding, honey. But you're so thin, Merle."

"I've still got an appetite though. You got anything downstairs?"

"You know I do."

"Where's Papa?"

"He's out in his office."

"I saw him down at the air strip when I was driving up."

"And?"

"He wanted to walk all the way back. I was expecting to meet him here, but I guess I dropped off."

Mother became more serious. "I guess I couldn't have expected him to explain things. Your father isn't working now."

"Isn't working? What are you talking about?"

"There was an accident at the sites and two men were killed. It was an explosion of some kind. He's responded poorly to the whole thing. He's depressed—clinically depressed—and he's been off work from the trauma. It's hard to explain, he just isn't himself anymore."

"So he's just staying at home? Who's running the crews?" I asked, trying not to sound as alarmed as I felt. After all, Papa had worked on the Shelby Construction crews for over thirty years.

"Jim Peel."

"That guy? He's a fucking idiot."

"Merle, stop that. You're not working there—"

I interrupted her. "When did all this happen?"

"The accident was over a year ago. He did all right for awhile, then everything started going downhill. When he tried to go back to work, he just couldn't do it. He was worried, slow.

"And he's seeing a psychiatrist. He's going to Las Vegas for that."

I shook my head. I couldn't get out of the chair.

"Things happen, Merle."

"Well, when is he going back?"

"I don't know, maybe he'll never go back."

"What? Is he going to retire?"

"I don't know, Merle—he may have to. It's to the point where Shelby doesn't want him back now. I have to talk to his attorney."

I felt flushed, guilty.

"He's living out back now."

I paused before answering. "I'm going to see what he's up to. I'll shower later."

I followed Mother downstairs. She introduced me to Natasha at the kitchen door, explaining how the dog was a grandson of Romulus, one of my favorite dogs growing up. I stepped out onto the patio and got acquainted with the dog, kneeling down and letting her catch my scent. Mother turned on the patio light, and I could see the young bitch had her grandfather's handsome shoulders and mouth.

I was about to ask about the kennels, but Mother went inside. I watched her through the window. She stood at the kitchen sink, washing dishes, a phone to her ear.

I walked out to the swimming pool, which was empty. Lounge chairs were stacked beside the diving board. I saw the light on in Papa's room, which was located off the garage. In back of the pool, behind Papa's room, were the barely identifiable remains of a kennel, with half the fencing collapsed. Natasha sniffed the ground near a yucca, her attention caught by something in the darkness.

What was I doing back home? I asked myself, stroking my beard repetitively, listening to the electric gossip of the crickets. The moon was rising over a gang of pinion pines. I breathed in the crystal-clean desert air, which was so pure I felt like I was taking the entire Great Basin into my lungs. I looked at Papa's room again. The door was partly open, so I went over and tapped on it.

"Papa?" I asked.

"Who is it?"

"It's Merle."

"Come in. There's nothing stopping you."

I carefully stepped inside. The pungent smoke from Papa's cigars thickened the air. He was sitting in a chair in the middle of the room, apparently doing very little.

"Sit down, Merle," he said, pointing to a matching chair under the window. It was piled with books, newspapers, and candy bar wrappers. I cleared the stuff away and sat down.

"You need a maid."

"I need a lot of things."

"I was joking."

"Were you? It was a bad joke then; either that, or something's wrong with me—could be one or the other."

I glanced around the room as he spoke, trying to maintain my calm and composure.

He stirred in his seat. "Merle, would you get my knife? It's on the floor near the bed."

"Sure," I said, surprised at the request. I retrieved the bone-handled knife from beside the unmade bed, handed it to him, and returned to my seat. He pulled a cigar out of his shirt pocket and patiently began to clip the tip.

"From the old blueprints, I didn't realize this was going to be a room," I said, trying to make conversation.

"It wasn't meant to be originally," Papa answered. "The garage was going to extend out to the wall you're sitting up against, but I changed things." I was hesitant to ask why he had changed things, and just sat back, watching and waiting. He struck a match, and after repeated puffs, lit the short black cigar. He leaned over and picked up an ashtray off the floor, which already contained two half-smoked stogies. Smoke burst out of his mouth as he sat back, curling like ghosts towards the ceiling.

"I've been seeing a psychiatrist," he said unexpectedly. "That's a Doctor of the Mind. He say's that I'm in what he calls a life-stage. Everything I've done, everything about me, it's all up for grabs. Fifty seven years-old and everything's up for grabs—how do you like them apples?"

"Who's this psychiatrist?" I asked curiously, surprised at how philosophical and verbal Papa was being, suspicious of it.

"Dr. Pfund. I see him on Thursdays. A funny guy—a young man, actually. He asks me things."

"Do you like to be asked things? I don't."

Papa looked at me, dead serious, turning the cigar in his mouth. "Depends on what's being asked."

Suddenly the screen door banged once, then twice. Mother was outside, struggling with a platter of sandwiches. I jumped up to let her in, but she used her knee and swung the door wide. "Here take this. I'll get some drinks," she said. I gave Papa one of the plates of food, but he just set it down on the same spot from which he'd retrieved his ashtray. Mother returned with soft drinks for each of us.

"Bob, eat something. You know I don't get to the kitchen much, so appreciate it when I do. You're going to starve yourself to death."

"Don't worry. I'm taking a smoking break."

I sat back down in the chair and sipped my soda. Mother stood still, half looking at Papa, half scouting the room, surveying its disorganization. She wore the same expression when she had first seen me in her office that afternoon. For a brief moment, it seemed that she was tempted to clean the room up (maybe dismayed that I was seeing its condition) then decided against it, keeping her eye on Papa, who said nothing and stared out the screen door.

"What do you think of Merle being home, honey?"

"I'm glad Merle's alive. Since Roe's been gone, I've been lonely."

Mother paused and smiled faintly, shaking her head. "Were there enough pills?" she asked.

"Sure, but it doesn't make any difference," Papa said, speaking out the side of his mouth.

"How's your headache?"

"It hurts."

"Dr. Pfund's secretary phoned. The next appointment is canceled. Who knows why—she said sweetly that he wouldn't be available to see patients next week."

Papa stirred in his seat, tapping the cigar lightly, then twirled it in his mouth. His foot tapped repeatedly.

"I've got to go make some more calls for the fund raiser tomorrow. Merle, I'm having some people over for a get-together at four o'clock."

"You won't want to be part of that event, believe me," Papa said. "Maybe we can fly up north tomorrow."

"No," Mother snapped, "don't by silly, Bob. Why do you keep talking like that? I'll bring a truck up here and tow that Cessna away if you keep that up. Do you hear me?"

"Turn on the television, please. I want to see the news."

Mother ignored him and turned to me.

"Your father shouldn't be operating any aircraft—is that clear, Merle? The psychiatrist agrees with me."

"Wasn't on his list of adult living activities," Papa remarked.

Mother kept at me: "He shouldn't be going up, period."

She looked around the room again, exasperated and tense, but still determined to get her point across. "Just be responsible— both of you."

Mother left, leaving the room in an awkward silence. I took a bite of sandwich. Then Papa started to laugh, a shrill, haunted laugh that seemed to have nothing to do with me.

"Merle, will you turn on Channel 22 for me?" he asked, settling down again. He made no attempt to look at me as he made the request. In the past, I'd never known a man to be more strong-willed and less likely to depend on others than Papa, but now he didn't seem capable of doing the simplest things for himself. I got up and switched on the television.

"I like knowing the weather," he said, putting his cigar down then standing up. "What storms are moving through. It's very important." He disappeared into the bathroom. When he'd finished and shuffled back to his seat, he said: "Your mother has lots of ideas, Merle." He turned and looked straight at me for the first time. He said nothing, but kept scrutinizing me, until I became intimidated and spoke up.

"She always has," I said, casting my eyes down to the plate in my hands. "You two aren't spending much time together are you?"

"That's pretty obvious," he said, taking a long, noisy gulp of soda. He retrieved his cigar. "But that's what I've been learning: people only talk about the obvious—nothing more."

He sighed, keeping the cigar in his mouth, picking his fingernails.

"How long have you been off work?"

"Be quiet, shhh," he demanded, turning his attention to the television. He listened to the weather report for a minute. "Perfect skies," he said, smiling.

"How long have you been off work?" I asked again.

"Too long; way too long. I'm a professional patient now," he said ambiguously. A long ash on his cigar dropped to the floor and he scattered it with his foot.

I stood up and walked over to the window, separated the curtains, and stared out into the darkness. I wanted to say something about myself, about the last two years, but my memories were like a baffling jigsaw puzzle that didn't fit together.

"What do you think about Roe?" I asked.

"What do I think about her? We haven't had much contact from her, so I don't know."

"You haven't talked with her?"

"I don't think we know where she is."

"What do you mean?"

"I don't know the whole story. She moved and things happened. I don't know, ask your mother."

"I came back to see Roe."

"Well, you're in for some disappointment."

"I know she's in San Francisco."

"That's right. Somewhere, doing something. We got a card with a picture of the Golden Gate Bridge."

Natasha pawed noisily at the screen door. I was about to let her in, but in a stern voice Papa told the dog to lie down, and she immediately obeyed.

"What happened to the kennels?" I asked.

Papa wouldn't answer. I asked him again, but he remained silent, so I got up and walked out into the backyard, restless and disoriented. I couldn't imagine being around my parents any longer, so I went out and got in the truck and took a moonlight drive down the valley into Cherry Creek.

My starting point had to be The Thunderbird, the nerve center of town. The parking lot was crowded with cars and trucks as I pulled up. Inside, jukebox music—George Straight—swamped the room, which glowed in a red smoky haze. I stuck my hands in my deep pockets and strolled over to the bar, fitting into the reverie like a bee in a familiar hive.

"Hi. What'll it be?" the female bartender asked.

"A tall coke." No sooner did the words leave my mouth, than the woman, who was a cute blonde with dimples, began glancing at me.

"Do I know you?" the woman said, grinning and tipping her head. I recognized her immediately—it was Julia Templeton, one of Roe's high school friends, who was also a dancer.

"Yea, but you might not recognize me."

She kept looking at me, but couldn't make a connection.

"Merle Honeycutt," I said.

"Oh! My god!" she squealed, her eyes opening bright. "Merle, what are you doing here? I haven't seen you in so long." She came around the side of the bar and hugged me.

"Look at you! You used to be, like, such a square," she said, looking me up and down, to my embarrassment. I remembered Julia from many visits to the trailer, and from more than one glance out a station wagon window, in some parking lot outside a gym, or fairgrounds, or convention center, where she and Roe had performed. I couldn't remember her skills as a dancer.

I watched her as she went to get my drink. She was a doll, with a full lazy swing to her hips, and from the far end of the bar, she glanced back at me and smiled, as if savoring some unexpected memories.

The room was humming and soaked with alcohol. A group of ranch hands at the bar rolled dice for drinks; a fat man, wearing an Impeach the President t-shirt, leaned against a pinball machine; a crowd of old rhinestone queens took up the tables in the middle of the room, smoking proudly, putting on makeup; and above it all, a Clint Black video on the far wall.

"Here you are!" Julia said, pushing the soft drink towards me. "Can I get you something with a little more wallop. It's on the house—to celebrate our meeting!"

"Sure, a Wild Turkey. What the hell," I said spontaneously. I noticed that two Pauites were playing pool in the corner, keeping to themselves. I looked at each man's face, but didn't recognize them.

"I heard about Roe," she said, placing the shot glass in front of me. "I'm so proud of her, I can't stand it."

"She escaped," I said in a low voice. I raised the whiskey and took a careful sip—it spread like venom in my mouth and I set it back down.

"More than that, Merle. I mean, come on, going from Cherry

Creek to San Francisco—with all the things going on there—it's, like, so great. She really deserves it. She danced more intensely, and better, than all of us put together."

She turned and poured a customer a drink, then continued.

"You know, before she left, she came by my folks place. We hadn't really been that close for a while: boyfriend stuff mostly. But we talked about everything—and I mean everything." Julia dumped an ashtray and wiped it with a towel. "But, Merle, she seemed down. You know Roe—come on, you know better than anybody how moody she was and the problems she's had—but it was something different. She didn't even seem like she wanted to go; like she couldn't comprehend what it meant to leave."

I didn't say anything, handing her a ten-dollar bill.

"Keep the change, Julia."

"Well, thank you, Merle. What have you been up to?"

"Nothing."

Somebody was calling Julia from behind the swinging door in the kitchen. She looked at me and rolled her eyes.

"Don't let me keep you," I said.

She gave me a sweet, curious smile. "Don't make a stranger of yourself. Anybody I know from the old days is important to me. I work Mondays and Tuesdays. And say hello to Roe when you see her. But remind her that I was always a prettier Giselle than her, O.K?"

I said I would, then moved away from the bar, leaving the whiskey. I leaned against the wall, watching the pool players. One of the men was real good and methodically went about clearing the table. After the game, they put their sticks on the wall and went back to their pitchers of beer. I was about to take the next game when they got up and walked out of the bar. I followed right behind.

As they were crossing the street I called out, asking them if they knew, or had seen, Pete-Pete Kramer. They were unresponsive at first and suspiciously quizzed me about who I was and why I wanted to see him, but after I strung a few quick anecdotes together about Breckenridge, they told me he lived in a trailer by the cement plant near the freeway.

I drove down the hill, located the trailer in a field strewn with dilapidated construction equipment and cars, then parked. I put the gun in my middle pocket, out of fear that something unexpected might happen.

As I approached, I could hear loud music inside.

"Pete-Pete?" I shouted out as forewarning. As I stepped onto a small wooden porch at the front door, a dog howled from inside. Lights went on and the music was turned down, the dog told to shut up.

"Who's there?" asked the voice inside.

"An old friend from down the block."

"The block, huh?" the voice asked.

Pete-Pete peeked out of the door. "Honeydipper!" he said in a grim voice. He opened the flimsy screen door. "What's happening, man?" he said. He slapped me on the shoulder, his hand like a vice when I shook it.

"Saw some injuns' at The Thunderbird. They told me you were here."

"Glad they did. Man, this is too much, come on in."

The trailer was a shambles of dirty dishes, clothes and dog hair, and he scrambled self-consciously to clear a chair for me.

"Still on the sites?" I asked.

"No, bunch of cutbacks, and you know the first to go. Want a beer?" I passed. Pete-Pete went to the refrigerator and popped one for himself. He was a slow-moving man with a thick horseshoe mustache, his muscular upper body overwhelming his wiry legs. Around the collar of his t-shirt, I could see the edges of the tattoos on his chest and back.

"Where you been? Everybody thought you were dead."

"Almost—been hanging out up north."

"Any trouble?"

"A little bit—couple weeks worth."

"What about you?"

"Mr. Clean."

"Do you know what happened with Papa?" I asked bluntly.

Pete-Pete looked at me, surprised, I guessed, that I would ask about such well-known news involving my own flesh and blood. "That was a bad scene, Merle," he said. "Two men died—you didn't know them. A gas explosion right near the surface of the tunnel—blew the guys to bits. Richey—do you know him?—Don Richey—he was in charge, and he didn't know what the fuck he was doing. It was out near the Dead Horse Mountains. Remember where that small bombing range used to be out there?"

"Yea. But where was Papa?"

"He wasn't there."

"Why wouldn't he be there?" I asked. The idea seemed preposterous, knowing Papa's compulsive style running the crews and drilling operations.

"He was away on business or something. I never got the full low down. Don't you know all this? He ended up arriving after the explosion. I only saw him a couple times after that. How is he?"

"He's different. Screwy in the head."

"Really? Too bad," Pete-Pete took a sip of beer then looked down at the floor. "Even though he's a maniac, I respect your dad."

"He felt the same way about you, minus the respect," I said, and we both laughed.

"Pete-Pete," I asked, "can I talk to you straight about something else?"

"I guess, Honeydipper," he said, standing up and putting on a Doobie Brothers tape.

"No, I mean, I don't know your current scene—"

"Right. Don't worry about it, shoot."

"I have a truck that I want to get rid of."

"You want to get rid of it? Let me think about what that means."

"I have a new Nissan truck, in mint condition, that I want to get rid of."

"You don't want to sell it?"

"No, Pete-Pete, I don't own it. Can I get rid of it in Las Vegas?"

"I don't know. I'll have to think about it. There's some people I can talk to down south, but it's not a sure thing."

I hated, yet expected, his response, knowing that I would have to sit and wait for the deal to be done. It might not work out, I thought to myself, because I didn't want to stay long in Cherry Creek. But still, I wanted to avoid getting caught with the vehicle, while adding to my cash savings.

"Check into it as soon as possible, if you can. You'll get a big cut."

"You're damn right I will," he said gruffly. I told him to phone me at the house, and he got up and wrote down the number.

"You remember Cracker Joe's buddy, Jimmy Thomas?"

"Yea, I think so. Had a busted lip—that guy?"

"Right," Pete-Pete answered. He finished his beer then smashed the can with his boot, tossing it into the corner of the kitchen. "Nine years for armed robbery."

"Breckenridge?"

"Right."

"That's too bad."
"Yea, well, he's a dumb fuck anyway."
"Lots of dumb fucks around."
"Right—you're right. Like you and me."

I woke up the next morning with Natasha licking my face. Someone had opened the door of the truck and let her in, and she was taking advantage of my helpless position sprawled across the seat. I covered my face with my hands. "Get away, Natasha," I commanded, and the dog backed off.

The previous night, when I had returned from visiting Pete-Pete, I couldn't bring myself to enter the house and sleep in my room, so I bedded down in the truck. I'd slept in fits and starts and now felt like a total wreck.

I sat up and saw Papa walking towards the side gate. Natasha nipped at his hand as he reached up and pulled the latch, disappearing behind the green, cinder block wall. Had he been watching me sleep?

I got out of the stifling truck, guessing it was mid-morning. Up in the higher altitude of the Spring Mountains, the sun felt like it was ten feet away, and I could tell the day was going to be blistering hot. I needed a shower in the worst way, so I walked into the patio.

Everything was quiet. I saw Papa's door was open, but I felt too grimy and sleepy to talk with him, so I went into the house, got some orange juice from the refrigerator, then sat down with Mother in the living room. She was sitting on the couch, her feet tucked under her legs, papers spread all about, adamantly making a point to someone on the phone. I sat back in the soft leather chair, put my hands behind my head, and stared out the large windows at the cloudless blue sky.

I felt no connection to the house after my long absence, and, knowing that Roe was gone, had no curiosity about our upstairs rooms. When Mother got off the phone, she laughed to herself; she was distracted for a moment, tempted to make another phone call, then looked at me.

"Where have you been?" she queried, picking up her address book.

"I slept in the truck."

"Are you hung over? You look terrible."

"No, I'm not. I just didn't sleep very good."

"Of course you didn't, you were sleeping in a truck. You have a nice bed upstairs, you know. I made it up for you. You may feel like a stranger here—being gone for so long—but you don't have to act like one. Good Lord, what a strange young man you are. Where did you go last night? I made you something to eat."

"I went into town."

"After talking with me for just five minutes?"

"After talking with Papa, I didn't feel like talking to anyone."

Mother collected her papers and put them in order. "Yes, he's having his troubles, there's no doubt about it." She didn't look at me as she said this, but paged through her address book, jotting notes with a pencil.

"What happened to the dogs?" I asked, finishing my orange juice.

"Well, Romulus died, and that was it."

"And that was it? Since he's been out of work, you'd think he'd have more time for stuff like that—the dogs, getting this place together."

"One would think so, but he just lives inside himself now.

The only thing that exists on the outside is flying, and that's more fantasy than reality. He talks about it, listens to the weather, reads the magazines and reports."

"What a retirement," I said, shaking my head, putting the glass down on a side table.

"He's not retired," she said, pointing out a doily I could put under my glass. "The doctor told me it just takes time to resolve his grief."

"Have you met with the doctor?"

"Once, but that was enough to know."

"Papa doesn't have the fire to go back to the test sites. He's too slow now."

"You have to hope that he will."

"It's hard to get that fire back once you've lost it."

"You have to hope, Merle."

"Well, I'll leave that to you."

There was a long pause.

"Yes, I'm sure you will," she said finally. Slouching down in the chair, I could feel Mother's diamond-hard gaze, but it didn't keep me from looking out the window. The clock on the mantle above the fireplace ticked and ticked. Since she was staring at me, I twisted the ends of my beard, knowing it would bother her.

"What happened, honey?" Mother asked in a softer, more intimate voice.

"About what?" I asked, sitting up slowly and crossing my legs. Mother put her hands behind her head, tightening her bun with a lacquered comb.

"With school—what happened with school?"

"I knew you were getting to something."

"But wasn't that our plan? That's what the phone calls and inquiries and applications were all about, wasn't it? Did you ever go to Reno? Did you interview for the program?"

"Yea, I did," I answered nervously. I got up and went to the kitchen for more orange juice.

When I sat down again, Mother reassured me, saying it was understandable why I was struggling to communicate. I wanted to tell her the truth—how admirable, to simply tell it like it was—but as my mind recalled meeting Cracker Joe two years before, and, prior to the interview, the three days of ferocious partying at the casinos, strip joints, and friends' homes, I knew I would have to be deceptive.

"Yea, I went to Reno. I arrived with my pockets stuffed with all the lists that you'd given me for this and that. I didn't really know what I was doing."

"O.K." she said, waiting, spinning a bracelet on her wrist.

"It was colder than a son of a gun. I don't know if you remember, but it was the end of the drought—that winter that broke all the records. Well, by the time I got up there a storm had clamped down on the Sierras and Reno was up to its knees in snow.

But after I went and saw the school, I decided I didn't want to go there."

"Why not?"

"I just didn't think I could do it?"

"You mean the class work, the studying?"

"Everything."

"I don't understand. What exactly was it? There must have been something specific that you didn't like. Was it the atmosphere of the campus, or the students, or the quality of the food in the cafeteria, or what? I had talked with a Mr. Wiskerson a number of times. He seemed like a very informed gentleman."

"He was an asshole."

"Please don't talk like that, Merle. I'm your mother, not a drinking buddy."

"Well, he was."

"Maybe you just weren't ready for college. Maybe you

should have gone to school down here first. Gone to Sundance Junior College or a trade school."

"I've had enough of vocational training, Mother."

"I didn't mean that."

"Just forget it. I'm not cut out for it."

"It just seemed like such a great idea, sweetheart: studying something new. Doing something different than working with your father. Being independent."

I got up and walked over to the front window, taking in the fifty-mile view of the desert below. I had ants in my pants so I opened the door and stepped outside. As the warm air enveloped me, I stretched and scratched my stomach for a minute.

"Merle, would you come back in here. The air conditioning is on."

I stepped back inside. "Papa says that Roe is missing," I said, taking my seat, trying to sound as nonchalant as possible. "Is that the latest scoop?"

Mother stared at the granite fireplace, momentarily lost in thought.

"Your father says all sorts of things these days."

"But is it true?"

"In a sense, yes. She hasn't kept in contact with us about her new address." Mother got up and poured herself a cup of coffee and returned to the sofa.

"She went to San Francisco almost exactly a year ago. Then she started at the Academy and we talked on the phone a couple times."

"Didn't you go and help her get settled?"

"No, it was a very bad time. I had commitments at work and your father was ill, so she flew out to the coast."

"So no one knows what she's doing?"

"She wrote us a few times. But then—Oh! I don't know,

about four months ago—many weeks passed where I heard nothing from her. Naturally, I got worried and called her apartment, but the phone was disconnected. Then I talked with Jean Atwater, the director of the Academy, and she also indicated that Roe's participation had become spotty. Mrs. Atwater didn't know where she was staying. I sent letters, but they were returned."

"Have you gone to see her, to check what's going on?"

"That's what I wanted to talk about—I thought you might do that for the family."

"What? What's this "family" stuff supposed to mean. You mean, do it for you, right?"

"No, that's not it. We're all concerned. I'm going mad with worry about her situation, but we can't go."

"You won't go. You're as afraid to go as Roe was."

"Oh! stop that. Your father has been almost suicidal at times; I couldn't leave him."

Mother set her coffee down and disappeared out of the room. I could hear her footsteps upstairs and in a minute she returned with a letter in her hand.

"I want you to look at this and tell me honestly what you think. It's the last thing she wrote to us." Mother leaned over and handed the letter to me.

> *Early Some Morning*
> *Dear Deserters,*
> *The rains have come to an end, the fog lifted. Rain, rain, rain, rain, rain that I thought would never stop or leave me alone. All the other people, in the streets, in the buildings, thought the same way too, I believe, though I never asked anyone. My feet go in a new direction every day. Like Nijinsky, but for the People, not animal dreams. Like Ballanchine, but for the oppressed, not the anorexic. Like Morris, but for the*

hungry, not the classical. Like little Merlin, but for a new man, not a boy. I'm glad to say, it's all ended. Finished. Go it alone, have no fear, it can only be springtime there. Go it alone, have no fear, it can only be nighttime here. Fly on, without a care. I dare, dare, dare, you. I dare, dare, dare, me. Never was a good writer. Could only use my feet. To whisk me away.

Roe

Little Merlin! I read the whole thing over again, but no matter how hard I tried to think straight, it wasn't any clearer the second time around. It was more like crazy poetry, or diary stuff, than a letter.

"What do you think?" Mother asked.

"I don't know what it means, do you?"

"It's a cry for help. She needs us."

"She needs us? She needs you—the letter was sent to you. I was out of the picture."

"But you're not out of the picture now."

"Oh! Yes I am. That's business you should have taken care of. You're the one who's primed her for her day in the sun, not me. I've been an observer all these years."

"You're sitting here in this living room."

"Forget it, Mother."

"You think about it, Merle."

"I have—no dice," I said vehemently.

The phone rang and Mother answered it. I got up and walked out the back door. The cool shade of the covered patio brought a tingle to my skin, protecting me from the harsh, white glare in the yard. Mother's voice—now clear and happy—echoed from inside. Well, I stood my ground with her, I thought proudly, still confused and worried about Roe's circumstances.

I walked over to Papa's room. The door was closed, so I

knocked: no answer. I tried the door: locked. I stepped around the corner and peeked in the window. He was lying on a bed against the far wall, his back showing. There was no reason to wake him. I stared at him for a minute, identifying with his sorry condition; the fact of the matter was, I had no more purpose in life than Papa did.

I looked around at the shameful condition of the backyard. The idea of forgetting myself in some hard work sounded good, so I set about putting the place in order. I swept the long adobe-tiled patio; pulled the tumbleweeds out of the swimming pool; stored the concrete mixer around the corner of the building, then moved piles of bricks, lumber, and bails of wire out by the unused kennel; picked up dog shit; and rearranged a pile of moss rock around five struggling, misplaced rose bushes. Two cawing blue jays, and a turkey vulture circling overhead, kept me company during my labors.

In an hour I worked myself into a breathless sweat. Then Mother emerged from the house, carrying a tray of food. She walked out to where I was standing, rake in hand, by the swimming pool. Shading her eyes, she smiled.

"What's gotten into you? It looks great."

"Keeping myself busy—nothing else to do but talk."

"Don't want to indulge in that, heaven forbid.

Here's a sandwich, a drink, and some potato salad. I'll set it on the diving board. With all the people coming for the fundraiser, I was so embarrassed about the state of affairs out here. Thank you.

I have to go see whether Papa needs any lunch."

"He's sleeping."

"Well, he's always sleeping. You have to wake him up, or he'll literally sleep all day."

"Good luck," I said, sitting down to the food and drink. I watched her pull out a key and open the door, then disappear inside. I ate the lunch voraciously and felt extremely tired afterwards. I still seemed to carry the damage of that night in Fallon in my bones and muscle. Still uncomfortable hanging around the house, I walked up the hill, to the northeastern corner of the property. Here the pinion pine gave way to a ridge of granite boulders. I picked my way through the rocks, coming to a point where I had a view of the desert, then sat down, ducking out of the wind. Cherry Creek, the Wallaby Air Force Base, the Pallaquat Mountains, seemed to disappear before the sheer vastness of the sky. I breathed deeply. I couldn't help it, but for a minute all I could see was Roe's face peeking at me, appearing, then disappearing, fragments of an image in the clouds. I hadn't actually seen her in so long that I had no lucid memory of her features, her expressions. I missed her terribly—or was it something totally different that I missed, something I just didn't understand?

Suddenly, there was a sharp blast to the north. It took a moment, but I spied the jets, little triangular specks moving steadily across the sky: F-18 Hornets. They were well past the Amorgossa Mountains, probably moving southwest towards Death Valley, then Los Angeles. Papa would love this, I murmured; he always used to say, "Those birds fly at twelve hundred miles an hour, and, folks, that's fast." The jets disappeared in a minute, leaving long creamy trails of exhaust.

I lay back into a comfortable groove in the rock, turning on my side with my hands underneath my head. The wind touched the back of my legs and I could hear it whipping by above me. That day at the university . . .

Maybe everything would have been different some other registration time, some sunny, blue-skied spring day when I hadn't seen Cracker Joe and hadn't met Winona for the first time and when the sidewalks weren't iced over. But that day, as I crossed the commons, no one seemed to be around—the storm the previous night and the lousy road condi-

tions had kept everyone home. So there I was, checking out the statue of William Stanton, the founder of the School of Geology, half-expecting the Founding Fathers to come walking down the steps of the tall, dignified buildings I passed by.

I was lost and freezing cold, so when some students walked up the library steps, I followed them inside to get warm and find directions.

That spooky library silence greeted me. Students stood in the aisles of books, examining titles; others sat at tables, talking in low voices. One guy was sleeping, and his coffee had spilled all over the papers near his face. The only decoration on the pale green walls was a large clock above the entrance. The librarian asked if I needed help; I nodded, yes, and was told how to get to the Student Administration building.

When I finally arrived at the Admissions Office, Special Studies Section, I was about an hour late. I couldn't believe I was that tardy.

The office was like school offices always are: ugly brown linoleum, metal desks, oak chairs, and fluorescent lighting that made everyone's face look pasty and half-dead. There were three men and one woman ahead of me, so I waited another hour for their interviews to finish, pacing around, coming close to dozing off, reading magazines, thinking about Winona, and worrying about Mother's expectations.

Finally, a short, middle-aged man came up to me, asking me my name, introducing himself as Mr. Wiskerson. He verified our meeting then asked me to follow him to his office.

"Please sit down, Mr. Honeycutt."

"Thanks, sir."

"Terrible outside, isn't it?"

"Sure is."

"Unfortunately, the weather in Reno is miserable most of the year. In summer, it's very hot."

"I'm from Nevada, sir."

"Yes, I know, I've been looking at your file—your background. I was curious, why did you drop out of high school?

"I didn't like school."

"Can you tell me why similar problems wouldn't exist now, and lead to your dropping out of our program?"

"No. Nothing specific. That was then and this is now. I'm different."

"How are you different?"

"I don't really know how to answer that, sir."

"Fine. Did you know this was going to be an interview today?"

"Yes, I did sir."

"You look . . . disheveled. Your shirt is dirty, and, if I'm not mistaken, you exude a slight odor of alcohol. Are you aware of this?"

"I'm sorry, I should have spruced myself up a little bit more."

"For future reference, this is not the way to present yourself at an interview of any sort."

"You're right. I apologize."

"Do you need some water?"

"No thanks."

"The Special Studies Program is unique in this state, where there is no great opportunity, or sympathy, for individuals with your background. I'm sure you know this. However, we are committed to providing a decent education to everyone. But we also have to be very careful who is accepted, and who isn't accepted, into the program. We will have no crime on this campus.

How long were you at Breckenridge Detention Facility?"

"Six months."

"Why were you there?"

"Haven't you talked with my mother about all this? Or looked at my records?"

"I've talked with your mother many times. She is a very persuasive woman, but she won't be attending the university, you will."

"Why did you go to Breckenridge?"

"Drunk driving and aggravated assault."

"Tell me about why you were sentenced?"

"I told you why."

"I want you to explain the circumstances."

"Whys that, sir?"

"It's important that you be able to reflect on your experiences and demonstrate an awareness of your actions, and what you've learned from them."

"Listen, I like history a bit, the desert, how things work, and that's why I want to go to school. To learn something, maybe get a job that I like. That's it—nothing special. I'm smart enough."

"I'm sure you are. If you were to attend the university there is a student group we would like you to be a part of, and a probation liaison with State Corrections that would meet with you on a monthly basis."

"I don't know about that. I'm not here to apologize for anything."

"Would you commit to meeting your responsibilities?"

"People would know my background then."

"That is not our intention."

"No, but what am I supposed to think about that? Can I use the restroom?"

"Young man—Merle—I'm asking you a question. Unless you're having a medical emergency, you don't ask to go to the bathroom in an interview after being asked an important question."

"I'm not going to be pointed out here—like, there's the guy who went to prison. Forget that."

"Yes, I know, I know. But no matter what your feelings are about the situation, you will have to abide by the minimal amount of monitoring—but let's go on to other matters. Tell me about your family."

"Can I go to the bathroom?"

"Oh! It's an emergency then?"

"Mr. Wiskerson, to be honest, this isn't going the way I thought it would. I may be a disappointment, but I'm leaving. Adios."

"Yes, Mr. Honeycutt, I see how this might be hard for you. Your decision is, perhaps, not such a bad idea. Good-bye. I'll phone your mother *myself, so don't be concerned. The lavatory is the third door on the right."*

When I returned to the house sometime later, the fundraiser was in full swing. I tried to slip through the backyard, with the intent of visiting Papa, maybe staying in his room throughout the event, but Mother spied me first.

"Where did you go?" she asked happily, setting some boxes in the trash on the porch.

"I took a walk up on the ridge and fell asleep."

"I wish I could say the same. I've been running like the wind getting the house and lunch in order. Go upstairs and shower—"

"No, I'm going to see Papa."

"Merle, don't be silly. I laid some clothes out for you."

I relented and went upstairs and cleaned up (I decided, however, to continue wearing my familiar, though soiled, overalls) then came back down to the gathering.

With her political and business connections, Mother knew a great many people, and all of them seemed to be converging on the house. The living room was filled with some fifty guests, and who was the first person I saw? Bill Davenport. He carried a big plate of food and was chewing on a piece of corn. With his well-groomed hair, blue eyes, and fancy cowboy boots, he was a handsome fellow, there was no getting around it. He smiled at me, but I pretended not to see him. I turned to a buffet of cold cuts and salads on the kitchen table, then began building myself a sandwich.

I looked out the window to Papa's room. His door was open, which I interpreted as a positive sign that he was up and about. I couldn't imagine him joining in the festivities and planned to go see him at my first opportunity. I nudged my way through the kitchen, finding a spot in a corner of the living room opposite from Mr. Davenport, near a portable bar that had been set up near the fireplace.

Mother rushed by carrying a tray of champagne glasses, rolling her eyes in mock exhaustion. She was attractive in a beige pantsuit with a turquoise necklace and bracelet. I watched in awe as she worked the room, seeming to communicate, with a nod, a handshake, an exclamation, with every guest she passed.

A balding man in a white linen outfit stood next to me. He contentedly stirred his drink.

"Quite a bash," he said, smiling. "Evelyn always has the best get-togethers."

"I didn't know she had so many friends."

"Well, some are friends, some are enemies, and some are biding their time before taking one of those two positions. What is your affiliation with this group?"

"I'm Evelyn's son—an enemy."

"Oh! I see," he said, chuckling. "I hope I haven't been indiscreet. My name's Arthur Bilet. I'm an arts and entertainment critic for the Las Vegas Sun. It's very nice to meet you."

We shook hands.

"And your name?"

"Sorry—Merle Honeycutt."

"What do you do, Merle?" he asked, taking a bite from the skewered cherry in his drink.

"Not much right now. I've been away, traveling, and I just got back a couple days ago."

"Where did you go?"

"The northern part of the state."

"Did you like it?"

"It was O.K."

"I can't stand this state. Too dry, too barren. I'm from Vermont originally, where there are streams and beautiful trees, not this sandy surface to everything. How is your sister?"

"You know her?"

"I've seen her perform and written some reviews of performances in which she has danced."

"To be honest, I haven't seen her for quite a while."

"I was just wondering how she had fared. Things are unpredictable at larger ballet companies."

"She was very excited about going, I think."

"Oh! I'm sure she was. No doubt about it. But what the young dancer finds is that these larger companies, especially one with San Francisco's reputation (and I say this as a way of reflecting general opinion about the company's performance—I have my doubts about their level of excellence) just chew dancers up and spit them out. Everything is for the sake of reputation, new productions, fund raising, and little for the careful development of a dancer's skills."

"That's too bad," I answered ludicrously.

Mother hugged a new arrival at the front door, causing a lively crescendo of voices. Many people were crowding the bar, so Mr. Bilet and I stepped away. I finished my sandwich and set the plate down on a table.

"I did think your sister had great potential as a dancer," Mr. Bilet went on. "All the fine points were there: the stature, grace of hands, a physical intelligence which couldn't be denied. I wish her the best. If you see her, tell her to give me a call to say hello. I try to follow the careers of people from this area who excel in the arts."

"No problem. I don't know when that will be, but I'll let her know."

"This fruit concoction is feeling very good soaking into by brain. I think I'll get another. It was a pleasure talking with you."

After Mr. Bilet took his leave, I surveyed the room. Mother was busy in the kitchen, so I slipped out the front door, passed around the corner of the house and entered the side gate. The blinds were drawn in Papa's room, the windows open; silence greeted me after I stepped through the open door.

"Papa," I said in a careful, understanding tone. "It's Merle."

He wasn't in the room, or the bathroom. A gust of wind through the windows twisted the curtains violently, sending a sheet of newspaper floating around the room like a gigantic leaf. I could feel Papa's presence around me, as if he had just left the room, leaving a faint impression of himself in the air.

Where'd he go? I wondered, concerned, checking the room for clues. At a younger age, as an obedient son and worker, I would have possessed an intimate knowledge of Papa's room and the status and whereabouts of all his possessions. I tried to instantaneously regain that familiarity as I began to inspect the mess around me. I noticed a few things laid out in some semblance of order on his bed: a tube filled with papers; an open metal box, with a leather eyeglass case beside it. Printed on the case: Whitney Flight Services. *The airfield!*

I bolted out to the truck and sped down the hillside and, sure enough, there was Papa standing near the tail of the Cessna. Driving down the runway, I remembered Mother's warnings; approaching the plane, I stopped the Nissan and jumped out.

"What are you doing, Papa?"

He carried a backpack to the front of the red and silver aircraft, opened the small door to the cockpit and dropped it inside.

"Papa?" I asked again.

"What, Merle? What do you want? I thought you were enjoying yourself at the party."

"You're changing the subject."

"What subjects are you—"

"You're not supposed to be flying," I insisted.

He turned to me; his eyes had a bit of the old, determined fire I knew so well. He stepped up to me, shoulders square, feet firmly planted.

"Do you want to take a ride?" he asked.

"It's not safe."

Papa put his hands on his hips, laughing, shaking his head as he looked up at the sky. "Not as many things have changed as you think, son. Now, you're welcome to come along for a ride, but if you don't want to, just skedaddle."

He disconnected the ground cables at the end of each wing. Then he stepped up into the cockpit and, after a couple of stutters, the engine roared, the spinning propeller catching the sunlight.

No, I told myself, he's not going to do it! I ran over to the truck and pulled it over and parked it across the runway, directly in front of the plane. I looked to my left, out the driver's window. Behind the blurred motion of the prop, just a few feet away, Papa stared at me from inside the cockpit. In that moment, if he'd moved the plane forward, I imagine he could have killed me.

Then Papa got out of the plane, disappearing, and as he did, I slid over to the passenger side of the truck and got out too. I found him pushing the tail of the Cessna so that the plane aimed west, instead of north. As I watched him slowly, one step at a time, move the aircraft, I understood that he was going to do whatever it was that he needed to do, with or without my, or Mother's, approval. When he was through and about to get back inside the Cessna, he waved to me, beckoning me inside. I wasn't about to let him go up into the sky alone, so I climbed in.

I had never been inside a plane before. The seat was small, snug, and I followed Papa's example in putting on the seat belt and shoulder harness. He jotted a note on a piece of paper after looking at the instrumentation, then put on his sunglasses. I could feel the vibration from the purring engine in my butt. My palms started to sweat; what if Mother was right?

"You need to move the truck. When we return, it'll block the runway."

"All right, you win," I answered. I got out, and by the time I had moved the truck and climbed back inside, Papa had repositioned the Cessna.

"Are you ready?" Papa asked.

"Yea, I guess," I said with mock confidence, "but don't worry about me—are you ready?"

"Of course, except my mouth is dry; my mouth is always dry from medication. Here we go."

As Papa slowly pulled out a large knob in the dash, the r.p.m. of the engine rose to a high whine and we began to move forward, bouncing slightly, gaining speed—the pinion pines passing by faster and faster—then, as we got closer and closer to the dirt road, Papa pushed the steering wheel up and the Cessna lifted off . . . Like some crazy carnival ride, the ground dropping away, falling away, the plane smoothly climbed up over the hills west of the house.

I loosened my hands a bit and looked at Papa. He stared straight ahead, eyes concentrating, licking his lips.

"You like my beard?" I asked, looking down hundreds of feet, trying to distract myself.

"That's not a beard, that's just something that's growing on your face, like a weed patch," he said, matter-of-factly, keeping his eyes on the sky. He reached above his head and pushed a red button, then checked what looked like an altitude meter.

"Thanks a lot," I said, chuckling to myself. "Where are we going?"

"Just a short flight out over the Amorgosa, then we'll do some dive bombing practice on the way back."

I chuckled again; I could tell Papa knew I was afraid and was playfully taking advantage of it. I took a minute and looked around, almost dizzy from the radical view out into the blue void. There was nothing, except down below, way down, the white desert, spotted with green and black, fenced in by the immense, bending horizons. And fundamental to it all, buzzing out in front of us like a mean lawn mower, the engine.

"I've never been up in a plane before."

"Neither have I," Papa answered, glancing over at me and lowering his hands on the steering wheel, smiling.

"Mother's a trip, isn't she?"

"A trip?"

"Her parties. There was a million people in the house. I stood there talking to this guy—a journalist or art person or something, I don't know—and he talks the whole time about Roe and her dancing. Where does she find these people?"

"You got me. What did he say?"

"He was worried about how she would do in San Francisco. Do you think he's right."

"You can bet it won't be Cherry Creek."

"How come you sent her there alone?"

"That's your mother's job—helping her adjust."

"She said she couldn't—she was too busy taking care of you."

The plane entered a wind pocket, bucking up and down. I grabbed a handle on the door, helplessly looking outside, and glanced at Papa.

"You can't see it, but you sure can feel it," I said.

"Yea, let's go a little higher," Papa decided, tipping the steering again, "and see if we can get out of this." The turbulence continued for another couple minutes, even though we gained altitude, then finally stopped.

"Look out your window—straight down," Papa said. I saw the long rectangular runways of Wallaby Air Force Base, and closer, nestled in a cluster of buttes, Mercury. The test sites spread out as far as the eye could see: dry, anonymous, covered with scars.

"Seems funny that I spent the better part of my life out there."

"Do you miss it?"

"I miss the men—especially the men who died; maybe I should miss other things, but I don't."

We suddenly swooped down, my eyes, my insides, lurching out in front of me.

"The military air space starts pretty quick, so we need to change direction," Papa said. We descended in a half circle, until we finally leveled out, heading due south. In the far distance, another aircraft was visible momentarily, then disappeared into a streak of clouds. With Interstate 95 directly below us—cars and trucks moved along it like blood in a vein—we headed in the direction of Cherry Creek.

"Do you want to fly?" Papa asked, glancing over to me. "You want to take the yoke?"

I laughed and tugged at my beard. "No, you go ahead."

"Don't be afraid—it's very simple really. There's lots of room for error."

"Famous last words—no thanks."

"You haven't changed much, son—still gutless as a paper bag."

I let the comment pass, too excited to be angry.

"Papa, what happened in the accident anyway?"

"A chemical explosion."

"Where?"

"A storage area. The men shouldn't have been there. If I had been working, they wouldn't have been."

"Where were—"

"It was all my fault. The crew had no real supervisor and were just following stupid orders from headquarters. It was a mess; an ugly God damn mess."

"But where were you?"

"I didn't go to work that day."

I had never known Papa not to go to work; every word out of his mouth made me more and more curious.

"But the men could set their watches by you."

"You're right—I worked every day, on the dot."

I looked at Papa. He seemed distracted suddenly. Maybe it was wrong to have brought up the accident while we were flying.

"It must have been terrible. Let's not talk about it," I said.

"It has to be talked about. That's what the doctor says: the truth will cure you—slowly. I was with your mother on the twenty-seventh. She had arranged some meeting in Carson City with a lawyer—we were going to get a divorce."

I had no mental template for what he had said, and just let the words sink into my mind.

"Jeez, really?"

"I was in the office of a divorce lawyer the day my men died. As it turned out, it didn't happen."

"Divorce . . ." I said, my words coming to a halt. Shaking my head, I looked out at the clouds migrating across the sky. I didn't know why really, but the word was disgraceful, humiliating. "After being together so long—"

"Why are you so shocked, you of all people? It happens all the time. Why, you divorced yourself from the family, didn't you? Roe has divorced herself. No papers were signed, but still, it's the same thing."

"No, it isn't."

"Wait," Papa said abruptly, wiping some spit from the corner of his mouth. He looked to the west, glancing at his wrist watch, then flipped a switch on a panel to his left. "I don't want to get distracted."

"From what?"

"From where we're going."

"Where's that?"

"Home. We're going home."

"Good."

Down the long narrow valley, Cherry Creek was becoming more and more visible, turning from a shadow on the desert floor into a child's toy land of intersecting lines and miniature structures. Then Papa sharply angled the plane to the east, laughing to himself strangely; I let him laugh, too preoccupied with my own confused thoughts to bother with him. Cherry Creek was suddenly lost from sight beneath the fuselage as the Spring Mountains came into view. With our elevation dropping, the mountains rose up, as if pushed by an invisible force.

"Are we getting close, Papa?"

"The house is over there. You can almost see it," he said, pointing down below. And, yes, I could see the house (an orange square against the gray hills) and it made me aware of how isolated its location really was. In our approach to the airfield, I expected Papa to fly west, past the house, then position himself for the runway in a turn south. But he held his course along the eastern side of the mountain range, the house becoming more and more distinct. Down below, the shadow of the plane was cast on the ground, in hot pursuit of itself.

"What are you doin', Papa?" I asked, with a hint of desperation. The plane dropped precipitously, bringing us flush against the mountainside.

"We're going home, that's all. Just going home," Papa said, as if revealing a secret to me. With short, subtle hand movements, he moved the steering back and forth, as if practicing.

"Papa, watch it," I said.

We came straight at the house (you could see a few people standing on the porch) then, fifty yards away from the front door, the Cessna gained just enough altitude to pass by over the rooftop. I looked over at Papa as we circled away. He was smiling, eyes steely, sweat on his brow. Maybe Mother was right, I thought, he was crazy. He brought the plane back around, heading again in the direction of the house.

"Come on. Stop!" I yelled, gripping the seat. He didn't respond, but I could see him breathing heavy.

This time there was an audience of people on the porch. The miniature-like guests were waving and pointing at us. I wanted to hide. Papa jerked the yoke back and forth, the plane tipping dangerously right to left. Then we roared by the front of the house like a circus act entertaining a Standing Room Only crowd.

Flying off over the mountains, Papa said sarcastically: "O.K, we've attended the party. We still have plenty of fuel, so where do you want to go?"

"I don't care," I said in disgust, staring out over the test sites. "You're the boss, Papa."

Hours later, when we came back up the road from the airstrip, the only sign of the fund raiser was Mr. Davenport's truck and horse trailer. Natasha greeted us at the side gate, wagging her tail and groaning with pleasure at our appearance. It was nearing twilight and deep shadows were cast down from the hillside above the house, the temperature cooler than the previous day.

"You handsome dog," Papa said nonchalantly, as if he were returning from the grocery store. The "dive bombing" must have had some significance to him, but it was hard to say exactly what. He staggered through the gate, and I followed behind, then he disappeared into his room without a word. I glanced at the back door of the house, guilty and intimidated; lights were on inside, but the curtains had been drawn over the kitchen window. Soft bossa nova music could be heard. There was a high-pitched shriek of laughter, followed by another. My thoughts simmered: Mother together with that man—it was humiliating for the family; either Papa didn't hear or he didn't care.

I went inside. The kitchen was piled high with plates and cups and leftovers. I poured myself a glass of water and was gulping it down when Mother walked in from the living room. She began preparing two gin and tonics, giving me a cold shoulder.

"Where's Davenport?" I inquired.

She dropped ice cubes into each bubbling glass. She turned towards me. She looked tired, relaxed, maybe a little drunk. "Out on the porch. Why do you ask?"

"I don't know. I don't want to disturb you."

Mother gave a messy laugh. "Well, it's a little late for that consideration."

"Listen, that wasn't my idea."

"But I asked you specifically—"

"He was going up one way or the other. What was I supposed to do, tie him up and take his keys away? He's my father. I was just trying to keep track of him."

Mother sipped one of the drinks. "He doesn't know what he's doing."

"Yes, he does. More than you think."

"My son, the shrink."

Just then, I could have slapped her on the side of the head. I finished the water, my hand shaking.

"Don't you think that went a little over the edge?"

"Yea, it did. He's angry at you."

Mother sipped her drink. "That's nothing new."

"Where's the letter from Roe?"

"Why?"

"I want to read it again and show it to Papa."

"It's upstairs, in my desk drawer. By the way, some man gave you a call—actually he called three times—this afternoon. He said it was about personal business, and that you would know what it was all about. He didn't leave a number."

"O.K. Anything else?"

"Yes, I want to talk with you later."

"Later?"

"When Bill leaves."

"Is he leaving?"

"Of course he's leaving. It will only be a few minutes."

Mother returned to the front porch and I went upstairs. I found the letter in her desk, then sat down on the bed and read it many times, confounded, hypnotized, by its ambiguous meaning. Maybe Papa shouldn't see it, I thought; then again, maybe he should. I stared at the large poster on the wall: *Monet at Giverny, 1896: Scenes from the Garden, New York Modern Art Museum*, my eyes swimming in the dreamy purples and pinks. I put the letter in my pocket and went downstairs.

I was about to leave out the back door when I heard Mother's voice call me. I went back into the living room to confront her.

"Bill just left. Are you hungry?"

"Yea, I am."

After turning off the music, Mother went into the kitchen and brought me back a plate of ham and baked beans.

"Would you like a beer?"

"No."

"I don't see you drinking like you did before."

"Haven't had much of a taste for it." She popped a soft drink at the wet bar and handed it to me.

I sat down on the couch and ate my food, chewing slowly, listening to the crickets outside. Mother poured herself another gin and tonic, then curled up on the couch. She took the pin out of her hair and shook her head.

"Was it a success?"

"The fund raiser? Absolutely, especially the air show."

I kept eating, a smirk on my face.

"I had never gone flying before, ever. When you're up there you realize that Cherry Creek is just a little cluster of cracker jack boxes in this wide-open desert. It was weird. You should try it sometime."

Mother laughed, almost snorting. "That's all I need: a reminder that Cherry Creek is a set of cracker jack boxes in the middle of nowhere. This good-for-nothing place."

"Don't worry, Mother, the house stood out like a real mansion. You should be proud."

Mother's attention focused through a haze of drinks and fatigue.

"Mansions. Pride. Why, you don't even know what you're talking about. I lived in a mansion when I was young, or at least it was a mansion compared to this stucco lodge. Just think: eight bedrooms, three fireplaces, chandeliers in the dining room, stained glass everywhere, a stream in back. It was up on a hill, overlooking the steel works. That was in my hometown, Bethlehem, in Pennsylvania.

It was a beautiful, beautiful place, especially when it snowed. I wish you could have seen it in the snow."

"It sounds like a fairy tale," I said.

"It was a wonderful place."

"No, I mean it seems like that place—Bethlehem—never existed. It's like Cinderella or something."

"The house isn't in the family anymore, honey."

"What family?"

"You never met them."

"I know that."

"Everyone's deceased. There's no use going back. It's sad. It would be—I mean, it would have been—nice for you and Roe to have seen Bethlehem."

I got up and put the plate on the kitchen sink, then came back to the couch.

"No grandparents, uncles or aunts—just the four—the three—of us, up here on the hill. It's kind of strange. I know Papa was an orphan, but what happened to your family?"

"Merle, dear one, I don't want to talk about that right now. Please, I can barely think straight."

"Is that what those photographs upstairs were about?"

"Yes. I found those in an old suitcase. Why are you suddenly so interested in family history? Frankly, it surprises me."

"Because you're always bad-mouthing Nevada, talking about better times."

"Nevada deserves to be bad-mouthed."

"Then leave. You could divorce Papa and leave. Wasn't that the plan anyway?"

"What in God's name has gotten into you? Don't ever talk to me like that." I thought she was going to cry, but she just rubbed her forehead, eyes down.

"You could have at least told me you were going to get a divorce from Papa."

"But we aren't getting a divorce, that's what's important. Anyway, you weren't around." She sat up more erect, pushing her hair out of her eyes.

Just then the phone rang in the kitchen. Mother got up to answer the call. "Merle, it's your suitor, whoever he may be." I stood up and took the receiver. Mother returned to her seat. I turned and looked out the kitchen window.

"Hello?"

"Merle. Pete-Pete."

"Why you phoning here so much, man?" I said in a muffled voice.

"Because, motherfucker, you asked me to do you a favor. Am I wrong?"

"What's up?"

"I got something going."

"The real thing."

"The real thing. We gotta talk."

"I can't right now."

"When then?"

"I don't know. You gonna be around?"

"Yea."

"I'll come down tonight."

"O.K. And one other thing, get a new receptionist at the house. She's a bitch."

"Fuck you," I answered, then slammed the receiver down.

When I returned to the living room, Mother asked me who I had been talking to.

"Just an old friend," I said, intent on changing the subject.

"That's what I was afraid of," Mother said in a calm, resigned voice.

Her remark shamed me because, if I was honest with myself, she was right in insinuating that I was getting into trouble, again.

"Afraid your little boy is a recidivist?"

"I suppose. Aren't you?"

"Mother, there's nothin' to be afraid of now. Once a jailbird, always a jailbird."

She stood up and walked out onto the porch. It was dusk and a soft, lavender impression of the sunset out west reflected in the eastern sky. She walked back and forth pensively, then, after a minute or two, came back inside, standing by a tall, potted cactus.

"I think you should leave, Merle."

"What are you talking about?" I took a quick sip of soda, feeling flushed.

"Leave! Vamoose! Go live with your friends in town."

"It's like a tomb here anyway."

"Yes, it is," she continued. "I don't know what you had in mind in coming back. I think you just wanted to see Roe and be a little boy again. Well, she's not here, so you'll have to fend for yourself."

I crushed the can in my hand and put it on the coffee table, where it teetered.

"Maybe I'll just be Papa's roommate."

"You won't like that for long, believe me. What you need is a future, something to do."

"Give me a break. If I do anything, it will be what I want to do." I stood up. "I got one thing to say before I go: You should practice what you preach. Just try that for once. So long, Mother, see you in two years."

I walked out of the house, slamming the kitchen door.

I went over to the window of Papa's room and looked in: again, nothing but a dim figure on a bed against the wall, illuminated now and then by the fitful glare from the television. There was no sense in hanging around, so I got into the truck and drove into Cherry Creek.

I stopped across the street from The Thunderbird and turned off the engine, still fuming at Mother's remarks. I wanted to go inside and lose myself in the alcohol-soaked gloom and noise of the bar, but the front of the place was flooded with members of a softball team. There must have been ten of them, all wearing gold and black t-shirts and caps—from Sandy's Muffler—slapping each other on the back, fresh from a summer league game. The group put their arms around one another, swaying back and forth, then let out a cheer in unison and burst into laughter. Two other trucks pulled up, and another team in red uniforms jumped out and marched through the doors with the gold and black. Forget it, I thought, there won't be a seat in the house.

There was no alternative but to go straight to Pete-Pete's place.

As I rolled down the bumpy driveway to his trailer, I noticed there was a pack of cars parked at random in the nearby field. A party was not a good place for doing business, so I pulled up a good distance away and turned off the engine and headlights. I rolled down the window, watching the shadows of the visitors cast chaotically on the curtains, listening to the raucous guitar sounds. I would have been more comfortable if Cracker Joe had been along; shit, where was my friend anyway?

A man suddenly burst out of the trailer door, moving fast, but clumsily. Walking towards a car, he bent over and put his hands on his knees and began tossing his guts. Two other men appeared, laughing, throwing beer cans at him. When he finished, he yelled something at the sky then stumbled to a car. The car lurched forward and began skidding in a broad circle around the field, the engine whining like a frightened pig.

Fuck this scene, I told myself. I started up the truck and backed up the driveway, grateful to be free of the place.

The truck needed gas, so, with nothing to do, I stopped at a station on Main Street. I watched the attendant go about his work, stroking the tip of my beard. I pulled the letter out of my chest pocket and set it on my lap. Then I counted my money, keeping it between my legs so no one could see. My total stash: almost two thousand dollars. Biggs must still be furious—and looking for me; he wasn't a man to take financial losses lightly.

The side mirror was splattered with mud, so I checked the glove compartment and floor for something to clean it with. I couldn't find anything useful, but ran across a CD under the passenger seat. It was one of those classical music affairs: the Berlin Philharmonic this, by Johann that, playing the Fourth whatever. The attendant tapped on the window, so I paid for the gas and asked him to clean the mirror.

After he finished, I played the CD, daydreaming as I listened to the rising then crashing interplay of violins and horns and drums. This was Roe's kind of music: made in another place and time. How someone could dance to it I could never understand. Having never set foot on a dance floor—not in school, not in the cotillion classes Mother tried to schedule, not in a bar—all dance seemed like a miracle to me.

A van beeped behind me. I started and looked in the rear-view mirror. The horn blasted again, so I quickly moved the truck a ways up the street and pulled off to the side.

The street was desolate. Some Saturday night, I thought irritably, turning the music off. Looking north, I could see Granger's Merchandise, a squat black building beside the trees of the Dwight D. Eisenhower Park, the scene small, insignificant.

I picked up Roe's letter and turned on the inside light.

Like little Merlin, but for a new man, not a boy. I examined the phrase, analyzing it again and again. What was she saying? Was it an insult? A secret communication? Maybe the whole thing was a cry for help.

As my fingers tapped the steering wheel, a plan slowly dawned in my mind. I had the wheels and the money to accomplish it, and, deep down, I just couldn't face Red Pepper Canyon again.

I put the letter back in my pocket.

Pulling out onto Main Street, I headed for the on-ramp to Interstate 95.

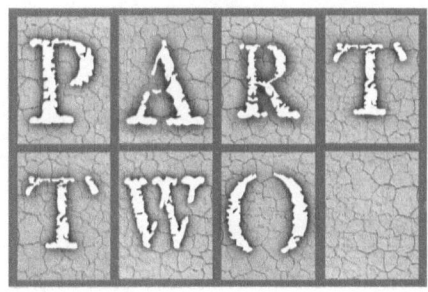

PART TWO

The black man at the toll booth was chewing gum fast as a squirrel working on a nut, and when I handed him the five dollar bill, he burst into song: "It's gonna be a bright (bright), bright (bright), sunshiny day." With a push and a slap, his hands working with the precision of a blackjack dealer, he gave me back my change. "And you have a nice day, baby," he said, sending me on my way up the skyway of the bridge.

There were three California Highway Patrol cars parked at the end of the toll-booth complex, and I drove by slow and invisible. After merging, and more merging, I slowly moved up onto the bridge overlooking a sprawling bay.

To say I was exhausted from the trip would have been an understatement, because, except for a cat nap along the highway just before sunrise, I had driven all night, working my way back up the flat belly of Nevada, climbing over Tioga Pass, then crossing the San Joaquin Valley into the dense urban stretches in Livermore, Castro Valley, and Oakland. I kept at the driving for one reason only: fear of turning back.

High winds snapped at the truck as I crept steadily along the bridge. The crush of traffic looked like a mass exodus from an unknown emergency behind me. I had never seen so much water, even at Pyramid Lake. To the north, there was a large island and, alone and barely visible, a smaller one, with a backdrop of green headlands, a tall mountain farther in the distance. The sky had been swept clean of clouds by the wind, and white caps rioted across the surface of the brownish-purple water, which seemed to be churned from its depths. A single, lonely yacht struggled with the elements. On the other side, the bay bent away to the southern horizon. Two immense container ships—their sides covered with foreign words I couldn't identify—moved towards a row of tall cranes in some shipyards.

Just past the middle of the bridge span, the traffic moved through a tunnel on an island. Coming out the western side, what I assumed to be San Francisco came into partial view, with a great wave of fog overwhelming most of the skyscrapers. The fog seemed to huddle in just one place, as if the city were stuck in a cold, in-hospitable season all its own. I remembered one of Mother's old photographs—a framed picture in the trailer: a bright blue sky, a red-fronted Chinese store, a family of tourists, with cameras, cross-ing a street, and in the background, a monument. If she could only see me now, I thought, proud, but frightened.

At the end of the bridge, the tall skyscrapers and billboards crowded around and I held tight to the right lane, taking the first available exit, which curved down to street level. It was only when I began confronting the merging buses, the bread trucks, the flocks of well-groomed pedestrians, and the fact that I didn't know where I was going, that my fatigue hit me square between the eyes. I made a few turns, nervous as a cat, just trying to flee the traffic, and found myself up a little hill, underneath the massive underbelly of the bridge, near where the bay ended and the city freeway began.

I parked, then opened the window: the traffic hissed by overhead. The tall bridge supports stood at attention, running in a row down the hillside and out into the bay. I wanted to get out of the truck and take a walk in the worst way, but the air was chilly and damp.

I pulled out Roe's letter and looked at the address: where was 197 Pacific Street, anyway? I toyed with the letter, folding it back and forth, lost.

Then—something at the truck window. I turned my head, startled, as a woman stared at me from outside, so uncomfortably close I could almost feel the breath from her ugly, toothless mouth. She was a miserable sight: matted hair, greasy clothes, a tomato-like face. Her mouth was moving, saying something, but I waved my hand violently at her—away, get away, go. To my relief, she turned and shuffled down the street. Then I saw there were others—bums, drunks—emerging from a row of shrubs at the base of a billboard. One by one, they stumbled out, dazed by the morning light, glancing at me apathetically before moving down the hill.

I started up the truck, made a U-turn, and drove west into the heart of the unknown city.

I bought a city map at a gas station and, with the help of an attendant, I identified the location of Pacific Street and began my trek towards what was called the Marina District.

I went north on a wide one-way street, the traffic moving in fits and starts through a series of stop lights, the storefronts, coffee shops, and warehouses, all a blur. Black men in army fatigues grouped in the doorways of many of the buildings, smoking, while others wandered, without concern, through the stalled traffic.

I drove across a main boulevard with trolley tracks, then came to a large plaza lined with old government buildings from the turn of the century. A beautiful, domed building took up the western end of the square.

Rising up a hill, I passed through a crowded neighborhood of shops and laundries, all Asian. A small corner park was filled with men and women, just like the folks I had just seen under the bridge; they were cloaked in blankets and sleeping bags, some huddled together, others horizontal on benches, like gray cocoons waiting for the damp air to lift, and the warm sun to bring life to their tired bones. A policeman talked and laughed with a woman in a wheelchair. She was holding three rabbits in her lap.

A block up the street, a tangle of stalled cars beeped like barking dogs. Biding my time, I watched the action around the newspaper stands, where women—and men—and, I guessed, exotic variations of both sexes—were dressed so outrageously they would have made the Rambling Rose ladies look like spinsters in a nursing home. They moved about, prancing, flashing smiles, marketing themselves to the stalled drivers.

I continued up the street, eyes straight ahead, eventually rising over a hill with a view of the bay. Out west, over the neighborhood rooftops, I could see the massive suspension towers of the Golden Gate Bridge (even I knew the Golden Gate Bridge!) rising out of the fog like four spoons sticking out of a bowl of whipped cream. Carefully checking the map and the street signs, I finally arrived at Pacific Street. I turned left, followed the addresses west a mile, then parked.

It was cool and breezy when I got out of the truck. I rubbed my arms for warmth, immediately feeling like a fish out of water. The neighborhood around me—fancy three-story homes, yards filled with blooming shrubs, quiet rows of shiny-leafed trees—oozed money, unlike the neighborhoods I had just passed through. A woman in a BMW convertible beeped her horn—without knowing it, I was standing at the end of her driveway—and I jumped aside and let her back out to the street. She was talking on a car phone and didn't pay me any mind as she drove away.

I had better make myself scarce, I decided, and walked off in search of Roe.

197 Pacific Street was only a short distance away: an old,

white house with a shingle roof, surrounded on three sides by taller residences. I walked up the steps and rang the doorbell.

A tiny window opened in the middle of the front door.

"Yes."

"Is Roe Honeycutt there?"

"She doesn't live here anymore."

I put my head down, thinking.

"Do you know where she lives?"

"No. Why?"

"I'm trying to find her. I'm her brother. I'm passing through town and this is the only address I have."

"Where are you from?"

"Nevada."

"And what's your name?"

"Merle."

"What's your sister's birth date?"

I had to think for a moment.

"March 4, 1978."

There was a pause. "Just a minute," the voice said. The door opened and I found myself in front of a small, gray-haired woman wearing a yellow dress and apron. She wiped her hands on the apron. "I'm sorry for being so suspicious, but you can't trust anyone these days."

"No problem at all."

"Roe did mention her family in Nevada. She did, I remember. However, I don't know where she's living now. She used to rent the house in back. I still have some boxes of her things that she left with me. Tell me, dear, have you talked with her?"

"No, we kind of lost contact and got addresses mixed up."

"That's a shame. She was a lovely girl—but a little hard to get to know and unpredictable in paying the rent. I ended up telling her to leave."

"So you don't have a clue about where she might be?"

"No, I don't. You might try the ballet, they may know something."

"Could I see the boxes that she left?"

"No, there in storage. I couldn't let you in back there. However, if you come back with Roe, I'd be glad to."

"All right. Well, I'll be heading on. What's your name?"

"Mrs. Spitz."

"Well, thanks, Mrs. Spitz. Could you tell me where the ballet is? I don't know my way around town very well."

She gave me directions down Gough Street, back to the domed building I had just passed, which she indicated was City Hall.

"Did anyone ever tell you how much you look like Roe," she said as I was leaving.

"Yea—I don't see it much myself."

"It's your eyes. There's no question. That's the only reason I opened the door for you."

I said good-bye and went back downtown. The San Francisco Academy of Ballet turned out to be a modern four-story building with gold railing up the front steps, not far from City Hall.

Although I had accompanied Roe and Mother on many ballet excursions growing up, I had never seen anything as fancy as the Academy. The entranceway opened out into a large registration area with gray marble floors and life-size color photographs from Swan Lake covering the walls. At the far end of the room were two bronze statues of male and female dancers, set before a glass wall radiating the outside light. The subdued hustle and bustle of scores of dancers filled the high-ceilinged hall.

How exactly was I supposed to find Roe? I wondered, taking my place in line at the registration counter. I was a dog without a scent to follow. One by one, the dancers checked in and climbed a nearby stairway leading to the second floor. I quickly moved to the front of the line, where an Asian woman greeted me.

"Hey, listen, I'm trying to find my sister, Roe Honeycutt. She's a dancer here."

"Is she a student? I mean, we have many different types of dancers. What is her affiliation?"

"She's part of the ballet. I was supposed to meet her here."

"You know, I don't have her name on the computer, but my info is only related to the ballet class starting up on the second floor.

You're probably going to have to talk with Jean Atwater, but she won't be back until three o'clock. She's the administrative director, and knows everything about everything."

A security guard, sitting on a stool behind the reception area, sipped coffee and glanced at me, wearing a blank mask of authority.

"I was supposed to meet her at the class."

"The eleven o'clock class?"

"Yes. Do I need to pay?"

The woman laughed.

"No, but visitors aren't allowed at rehearsals without special passes."

"Can I get one?"

"Again, Ms. Atwater would have to approve that. The class will be over in half an hour."

I scratched my beard and stared at the woman, feeling the impatience of the dancers waiting behind me.

"I'm sorry. I think you'll have to wait," she said.

"Yea, I guess so." I stepped aside and wandered over to a bench at the base of the stairway and sat down. Son of a bitch, I whispered under my breath, suddenly obsessed by the desire to see Roe in class, dancing, unaware of my presence.

"Excuse me, can I slip in here?" a voice said. I looked up. It was a black man, with a shaved head, a medallion hanging around his neck.

"Sure," I said, scooting over to the end of the bench. He sat down and began rifling through his exercise bag. "I just love these overcast days, don't you? All gray and dreamy," he said. He was very handsome and stylish. "It brings everything, and everyone, closer together, don't you think?"

"I just got to San Francisco, so I don't know much about it."

"What brings you here?"

"Family."

"That's great. Most of the time, it's just the opposite—escaping family."

I heard what the man said, but paid him little attention. I noticed that the security guard had disappeared into an office, and the receptionist had turned away, so, without hesitating, I sneaked up the stairs to the second floor.

I walked along quietly, listening to the muted sounds of a piano, a voice giving directions, the patter of feet. I set off down one hallway, past an elevator and a set of windows looking down to the first-floor rotunda. A male dancer in red leotards emerged from behind a door, threw a towel over his shoulder, and rushed by me. I realized I was moving towards the dressing room and backtracked, walking down another hallway. The sounds of a ballet class became louder and louder as I went along. I peered in the glass window of a door to my left: a group of dancers taking barre, heel-toe, heel-toe, a teacher clapping her hands. Roe wasn't there. I moved to another door and looked inside: a circle of dancers sat on the floor, talking amongst themselves, legs stretched out, hands reaching to feet, faces bent to the floor. Nothing.

At the end of the hallway, I came upon a rehearsal hall with an expanse of floor as big as an auditorium stage. This has to be it, I figured. There were no doors to the rehearsal space, just one large entranceway, and I kept close to the outside wall, peering in. The dancers, perhaps twenty of them, had taken their respective positions across the floor. A teacher walked back and forth before the group; he stopped and demonstrated a sweeping arabesque with his arms outstretched, then stood upright again, continuing to talk. My eyes flew from one dancer to another, checking faces, bodies, outfits. God damn it! I murmured.

"Young man?"

I turned around. It was the security guard. He was a young guy himself, skinny, with a pale complexion, his uniform covered with meaningless names and insignias.

"You aren't allowed on this floor without a pass," he said. "You didn't get a pass downstairs, did you?"

"No, I didn't. I'm trying to find my sister."

"Whatever. I don't know what you're trying to do. We get all sorts of people in here off the street. You're trespassing. Come with me."

I gave one last glance into the rehearsal area. The class pirouetted in unison, turned, then moved three steps forward on point, like so many flamingos, the instructor voicing his approval.

The security guard took me to a nearby elevator.

"A little dream factory of beautiful ladies, isn't it?" he asked, as we descended to the first floor.

"One of them is my sister, sir."

"Sure, and one of them is my wife. Give me a break. You homeless guys follow the students in off the street all the time. This isn't a peep show."

"How long have you worked here?"

"What's that have to do with anything? You just shut up."

I did. I kept quiet, eyes down. I knew only too well that it was smart to let guards have their way; they were the same everywhere: guns, shiny badges, into every dirty little secret.

The elevator doors opened and we stepped out into the lobby. The security guard told me not to frequent the premises again or he would call the San Francisco Police, and I replied that I would be returning in the afternoon to meet with Ms. Atwater. He added that it was a free country and that I could do what I liked, but that I would pay for it. I ignored the man and walked outside.

The sun had finally come out! The fog had broken into pieces and was floating across the sky like a flotilla of ships. A bus pulled up to the curb, discharging riders onto the already crowded sidewalk. I stood there, a stranger to everyone, with hours to kill. Did I really think Roe was going to magically appear for me in that dance class? What an idiot I was.

I started walking aimlessly down the sidewalk, feeling that if I stopped too long at any one point I would fall asleep in my tracks. I came to the main boulevard again, and watched the green and yellow streetcars clank by for a few minutes—the asshole words of the security guard ringing in my ear—then decided to get something to eat.

I stopped at a little place, Café Dodo, and turned out to be the only customer. I took a window seat and ordered a hamburger, fries, and coffee. Across the street was a liquor store and laundromat and three boarded up storefronts stamped with lease signs. Trash was strewn everywhere in front of the buildings. I watched the comings and goings at the liquor store. It was a circus out there, no doubt about it, but what was a spectator like me supposed to do?

My meal was served and I devoured it in no time. Sitting back, the sun shone through the window, warm and sultry, and I felt dangerously tired. I must have slumped down and closed my eyes because a voice said, "Don't go to sleep in here, buddy!" I started and looked over at a heavy-set man behind the cash register. He was wearing a dirty white apron.

"There's no loitering in here. Period."

Loitering? I just ate a meal! I pointed out to myself, too tired to confront the man. I apologized, paid for my food, and stepped back outside. Turning the corner of the building, I accidentally bumped into the black man I had seen at the Academy.

"Oh! Excuse me," he said. "Well, we meet again." He was wearing a light maroon-colored jacket and carried a leather bag over his shoulder. Earlier, when I was sitting beside him, I hadn't realized how tall and broad-shouldered he was.

"Sorry about that," I said, "I was daydreaming."

"I'll never forgive you," he teased, smiling, his teeth very white and even. "What are you up to?"

"I just had a burger for lunch."

"You didn't eat in this roach palace, did you?" he asked, motioning to the Café Dodo.

"Yea."

"It's a dump in there. If you want a truly great burger, try The All-American on 18th Street in the Castro. They have the best." Then he seemed distracted, tipping his head to look down the boulevard. "Here it comes. I've got to catch this trolley or I'm going to be in deep doo-doo with my significant other. I'm Terry. What's your name?"

"Merle Honeycutt."

"Honeycutt? Is that so? I—well, no time for other stories. I'm off. Bye-bye." Then, after letting a taxi pass by, he dashed across the street and boarded at a concrete island, waving to me as the trolley rolled west. Weird guy, I thought, he acted like an old friend; he probably just took class.

I happened to glance between the tops of two surrounding buildings, catching a glimpse of the City Hall dome in the distance. I didn't know the time and felt the pull of my responsibilities towards my sister, so I decided to head back.

After walking down a long alleyway, I found myself standing

at the eastern end of the square that I had driven through that morning, surrounded by government buildings and museums and libraries. I walked across the square, through a patchwork of trees and lawns, sculptures and fountains, then stopped at the street fronting the City Hall. I gazed up at the magnificent gray dome topping the structure. Nearby, a little community of bums and tramps hung out under the trees, huddled around shopping carts, sleeping inside cardboard boxes.

I stared at the rough-looking crowd, my eyes settling on a man leaning against a tree trunk. He was eating food out of a container with chopsticks. He looked up at me, mouth full, and told me to sit down if I wanted to, that there was nothing to be afraid of. I knew that, I told him, and sat down on a bench. He asked me if I wanted anything to eat, and I said no. I asked him for the time, but he didn't know it; he asked around the encampment, but the answer remained a mystery. "We goin' be late for our appointments today," a young woman said, with a slurred Southern accent, strumming a three-string guitar.

I sat down, listening to their murmuring, exclamations, complaining, and laughter, the welcome sun faintly warming my face. A crowd of pigeons surrounded a sea gull and fought for a pile of popcorn. I tried to think of the time again, my obligation to Roe, but fatigue got the best of me. I curled up on the bench and closed my eyes, guitar chords repeating . . .

When I woke up, City Hall was looming above me. I went through a momentary disorientation, then sat up and rubbed my face to come to my senses.

Then I noticed the police cars and vans parked on the street. A group of police, wearing bright orange jackets, were entering the encampment under the trees, making declarations and gesturing for attention and obedience. Some of the people quickly got to their feet, hands raised, fearful and timid; others kicked back, familiar with the law enforcement ritual, gesturing and complaining from their reclined positions. My thoughts went in ten directions at once, ending up with one conclusion: I couldn't get taken in, no matter what.

I was on the far side of the trees, closer than the others to the lawn and fountain at the center of the square. I needed a Pyramid to climb, but only buildings surrounded me. I stood up and walked back from where I'd come, my heart traveling to my throat. I got twenty or thirty feet from the bench when I heard a voice, a whistle, and bolted. I ran to the nearest street, made a clumsy, skidding turn, then ran north, through a stop sign, left then right, pushing through the people, running, running, until I couldn't go any farther. I finally ducked into a small store.

I tried to catch my breath, head down, pretending to page through a magazine. I waited a good five minutes, then peeked quickly out the doorway, back down the street: I seemed to be out of danger.

"You look too long now. You read sign?"

I looked towards a high-pitched voice in the rear of the narrow room, which was lined with a mess of magazine racks. There was a small Asian woman standing by an old-fashioned cash register. On the wall behind her were three cheap oil paintings of John F. Kennedy, Clint Eastwood and Marilyn Monroe.

"You buy now or go."

I didn't say anything, but kept staring at her from my spot near the door. Her words were so impersonal. Why did she talk to me that way? I kept my eyes fixed on her. I tugged at my beard.

I didn't mean to be scaring her; why was I so small and insignificant in her—in everyone's—eyes?

"How can I run business, make living, with people like you," she said, her voice more shrill.

But I wasn't listening. I had turned back to the magazines and happened to catch a reflection of myself in a wall mirror. I looked myself over—perhaps in the same way that this woman observed me, the security guard observed me, my parents too, and, soon, Roe. I realized I would never be trusted, never be respected, the way I looked.

The woman began to push a buzzer, which went off by the door. She pushed it over and over again.

"You hear? I call police. Not afraid to call police."

I looked in my pocket, pulled out a ten-dollar bill, then walked back towards the woman. She stepped back and barked out some foreign words to someone in the back of the store. I put the money on the counter and turned to leave. She remarked politely: "You take magazine now. Two magazine."

Out on the sidewalk, I stopped someone for the time and found that I had ninety minutes before I was due back at the Academy. I had come in a circle, because, within a block, I found myself at the corner park that I had passed that morning on the way to the Marina. The woman in the wheelchair was still there, sound asleep with her three rabbits.

I turned west and walked out of the Asian neighborhood, finding a street lined with clothing stores and bookstores. Passing by a row of young men leaning against a brick wall, past an adult bookstore, past the Adam's Apple bar, the Whipping Post bar, the Little Tahiti bar, I was constantly stared at, with looks that seemed to promise love, hate, whatever. The whole place, from top to bottom, was fags. I had never seen anything like it.

I finally found a hair salon with women in it, and went inside and got the full treatment: a haircut and shampoo, the removal of my beard, and, after some convincing from the help, a face massage. When I came out of the place, my head felt light as a feather and fresh as a mint in the afternoon breeze. Next, I found a clothing store and bought a pair of khaki pants, a turquoise t-shirt, shoes and socks, a jean jacket, and just to complete my metamorphosis, a pair of expensive sunglasses. Outside on the sidewalk again, I dumped the plastic bag holding my overalls in a trash bin. Walking back towards my guidepost, City Hall, mindful of the time, I wasn't so much a new man as a charlatan, dressed to spy in new and unknown territory. Anyone from Nevada would have split their sides laughing at me.

I arrived back at the Academy and asked for Ms. Atwater. I had hoped to see the security guard—to check the effectiveness of my new identity—but shifts had evidently changed and a new guard didn't notice me. I was told to take the elevator to the administrative offices on the third floor.

On the way up, I looked at my metallic reflection in the elevator door: my cheeks and chin stood out white as a baby's butt.

I explained my purpose to Ms. Atwater's secretary, and waited a good thirty minutes before being asked to step into her large office.

"Hello, I'm Jean Atwater."

"Pleased to meet you, ma'am. I'm Merle Honeycutt, Roe Honeycutt's brother." We shook hands and sat down in two high-backed leather chairs in front of her desk. Large colorful posters, announcing the current ballet season, lined the wall.

"What can I help you with?" Ms. Atwater asked. She seemed a woman of supreme confidence, well dressed in a maroon business suit, with short, black hair, a pair of glasses hanging from a chain around her neck. I thought, this is the woman Mother always wanted to be.

I was nervous and hesitant for a few seconds. "I would like your O.K. to see my sister, Roe Honeycutt. She's one of your dancers."

"Do you live here in the city?"

"No, I'm from Nevada, just passing through town."

"Would you like some tea?" She got up and stepped over to a tray on a table beside her desk. "I have caffeinated or decaf."

I declined. She served herself and sat back down.

"The truth of the matter is," she said, holding the cup with both hands, sipping, "we don't know the whereabouts of your sister."

"Really? Well, that's a drag."

"She isn't on good terms with the Academy right now. There was a major production some time ago. She was scheduled to dance and ended up disappearing for reasons we aren't aware of. It was a critical juncture in the production and caused more than a few problems. I had many meetings with Roe in the weeks and months before her disappearance, and I corresponded with your family, but I couldn't stop the bleeding. She was a wonderful dancer, but she never quite fit in here—and certainly never met our high expectations of her."

"Where'd she go?"

"I don't know. She left me a letter, saying she was leaving, but no one has seen her since. Evidently, she has changed her address, because we have had letters returned. I notified your family, and called, but nothing seemed to come from it. Things like this, though troublesome from our point of view, do happen, and we felt your family had the matter well in hand."

"I guess we didn't," I said, shaking my head and looking at the floor, reaching for a beard that was no longer there. "When did all this happen?"

"Let me see. The Paul Taylor piece premiered in March—about six months ago."

"This was everything she dreamed about. I don't understand it."

"She was a brilliant talent, but—how do I put it?—she had another agenda. What she learned, she learned quickly, then her head was turned by things outside the company. What those things were, I can't really say."

I stood up. "Well, I won't waste your time. Thanks."

"Have you thought of contacting the police? I don't mean to be alarmist, but they may be able to provide some practical information."

"To tell you the truth, Mrs. Atwater, I don't know what I'm going to do. I have to think about it. It was real nice of you to meet with me though."

She stood up and shook my hand.

"I'm sure everything will work out. Good luck, young man."

I returned to the truck, which had a ticket on it, and drove back to Mrs. Spitz's. It was late afternoon and, even with my new jacket on, the air seemed chilly now that the fog had rolled in again.

I rang the doorbell at Mrs. Spitz's. She opened the portal.

"Yes?"

"Mrs. Spitz? It's me again, Merle Honeycutt. Do you recognize me? Could I have a word with you?"

She opened the door.

"Yes, young man."

"I thought you might have been scared with how I looked before, so I cleaned myself up a bit."

"It serves you well. No sense in looking less than your best."

"Mrs. Spitz, I went to the Academy, just like you said I should do. The director there doesn't know where Roe is. She isn't dancing anymore, and they don't have any more idea about where she's at than I do. I was wondering whether you would re-consider me looking at Roe's stuff. There may be something there, some clue, that would help me know where she is. I know I have no right to be asking."

"You wait here a moment," she said, disappearing behind the closed door. She came back a minute later and asked me to follow her around the side of the house. At a gate at the end of the driveway, we met a tall, skinny man with bushy eyebrows, who was holding a rake.

"Mr. Honeycutt, this is Gustavo. He's my gardener. He'll help us with Roe's things." I said hello, and he greeted me with a nod of the head. I followed them along a narrow cobblestone path, back to a lawn between the front and back house. Knowing that I knew he was there as a watchdog and protector, the gardener went about his business of raking leaves near an arbor covered with large pink flowers, glancing at me occasionally.

The back house turned out to be a little cottage that looked as if it was a remodeled version of a stall or shed from earlier in the century. It was surrounded by five tall redwood trees.

"How long have you lived here, Mrs. Spitz?"

"Forty-seven years. It belonged to my late husband's family. They developed the property after the 1906 fire."

"How long did Roe live here?"

"About a year, I would say, but my memory is unreliable." She seemed older, more frail, now that she was standing outside in the lush colors of the yard. We moved slowly across the lawn; she took my arm as we climbed the steps of Roe's old abode.

"Now, it's going to be musty in here," she said, opening the door and stepping inside. "I don't think anyone has been in here for a few months. Oh! I smell a cat. There must have been a window left open."

The entire cottage consisted of one white-walled room, furnished simply with a double bed, desk and chair. The walls were bare, except for an oil painting next to a corner fireplace. In the rear, near a back door, was a small kitchen and bathroom. The rooms were in perfect order, except that the kitchen window had been left ajar and there was cat shit on the kitchen floor. The condition of the kitchen put Mrs. Spitz in a worrisome mood, and, over repeated apologies, I told her not to worry on my behalf.

"Roe's things were left in here," she said, opening the closet door. "You'll have to pull them out yourself."

I lifted two small boxes from the closet then dragged out a larger, heavier plastic container.

"I don't know what you're going to find in these things, Mr. Honeycutt."

"I don't know either, to tell you the truth."

"I'm going to go get Gustavo and tell him about the kitchen. You go ahead now, don't mind me."

"Thanks. Do you need help with the stairs?"

"Now, please, I only have one foot in the grave, not two. I'll be back in a few minutes."

I pulled up a chair from the desk and went to work inspecting the two boxes, filled with excitement, anxiety, and dread, all at the same time.

The first was packed tight with a stack of white, pink and beige leotards, ankle warmers, towels, and jeans—nothing of value to me. My heart sank a bit.

The second was half-filled with compact discs and papers. I had never heard of the titles or artists: La Canciones de Cuba; The Genius of Perez Prado; La Orquesta de Amor, featuring Cachao; The Birth of the Mambo, Arturo Sandoval and Chocolate—Together; Afro-Cuban Rhythms—Invade the Night, and a stack of others. I tipped the box on its side and slid the compact discs onto the floor, then lifted the odd assortment of papers out. There were handfuls of old fliers, advertisements for a benefit dance performance by the Raging Feet Dance Collective; blank forms from the

U.S. Naturalization and Immigration Office; pages of typed schedule information; scraps of faded pictures of dancers—they wore big baggy pants and were bare-chested—taken from the San Francisco Examiner; announcements about a new location for Raging Feet; a post card written to "Mi Amor" from Havana, written in Spanish (except for an English postscript in the lower margin, "P.S. for your loving eyes to interpret"), signed, "Jose Luis". What was all this about? None of it was of any interest to me, and didn't seem to be of any relation to Roe, except that these were her damn possessions! For the first time, it sunk into my thick skull that Roe was leading a life I knew nothing about. I had assumed she was waiting for me—the star from Cherry Creek I knew so intimately—when she really lived in another world.

I heard the sound of a door close in the front house and became aware of the time. I hurriedly fingered back through the paper materials; I needed any lead I could get my hands on. I folded one of the advertisements for the new dance collective location and put it in my jacket pocket.

I waited, expecting Mrs. Spitz to appear in the doorway, but there were only voices from the yard. I continued on, opening the big plastic container. It was like delving into a dirty clothes hamper, nothing but a pile of jeans, blouses, and underwear, but then, at the bottom, I found a small package addressed to: Evelyn Honeycutt, POB 1128, Cherry Creek, NV 89377. Well, what was I going to do, I asked myself, kneeling down with the package in my hands. I examined it again. It was perfectly wrapped, with no return address. What the hell, I thought desperately, then tore the box open, feeling like I was climbing into the past and, once again, making Roe's privacy my own. The box contained a simple pair of white ballet slippers wrapped in crepe paper, with nothing else, no note or explanation, nothing. This is odd, I thought, and, unexplainably, tears came to my eyes. I tapped the hard, but silken, toe ends with my fingers, pleased by the touch; they were like two animals that had been hibernating together. I was immediately sorry I'd unwrapped the package.

Then boots pounded the steps and Gustavo entered the front door with a shovel and bucket. He acted like I wasn't there and went directly to the kitchen to clean up. I put the slippers back in the box and placed it back in the container with the clothes. I got up and checked throughout the cottage—in the closet, under the bed, in the dresser of drawers—for any more of Roe's possessions, but the place was empty. I put the boxes back in the closet and went outside.

Mrs. Spitz was at the base of the steps, weeding.

"I'm all finished," I said.

She rose up with some difficulty.

"Did you find anything of importance?"

"Not really, mostly clothes and things."

"That's unfortunate."

"There was some information about a dance company that I'm going to check out tomorrow."

Mrs. Spitz peered at me, and I think she sensed my stirred emotions. She slowly bent over and picked up the little pile of weeds, then put it in a trashcan. By now, the sunlight was fading, the yard engulfed in shadows. There was a faint scent of the ocean in the air that I had never experienced before, and it sent a chill through my bones. A fluffy orange cat, with an odd square head and bulging eyes, meandered across the lawn. Mrs. Spitz saw the cat and muttered something under her breath.

"The fog is setting in again," she said, rubbing her arms.

"Is it always like this in the dead of summer?"

"Always. That's part of San Francisco's charm; it's a world of opposites. You'll learn that soon enough. If you think you're going to be invited to a polite dinner party, you'd better bring your dancing shoes."

I shook my head, smiling innocently, not really catching her meaning.

"What do you have planned for the evening, Mr. Honeycutt?"

The question came as a bit of a shock, because I hadn't thought about it. What was I going to do, alien that I was?

"I haven't really planned anything just yet, Mrs. Spitz."

"You're welcome to stay back here, if it suits you. I know you're new to the city, and places are so expensive nowadays."

"No, I can find a place." I couldn't believe my ears. Why would she trust me, of all people?

"Oh! Don't be silly. I like you—more than your sister, if the truth be known. I'll have Gustavo make up the room and leave a light on for you. Would you like to come inside and have something to eat?"

"No, Mrs. Spitz, I wouldn't put you out. I'll find some place to eat."

"Whatever you like. Union Street is two blocks north of us. You'll find many restaurants there, although you'll pay a pretty penny."

I thanked her again and said good-bye, walking out to the front of the house. What a funny old woman; and what luck! Although I didn't really know my whereabouts, there seemed no reason to drive two blocks to Union Street, so I took off walking.

I meandered up and down Union Street three or four times, enjoying the salty air and all the fancy people shopping at all the fancy stores. After a while I got tired of being on my feet and, safe in my disguise, stopped at a restaurant named Pompeii. It was an elegant spot, all white linen and golden light, and up to the rafters with customers. There wasn't any seating in the outdoor section near the street, so I took a stool at the bar.

If only someone from Nevada could see me now, I thought, filled with pride, noticing there wasn't a cowboy hat in the room.

A man dressed in a tuxedo played jazz piano in the corner. Waiters moved back and forth between the tables, the kitchen, and a large brick and brass oven. I was tempted, very tempted, to have a beer and a shot of Bird, but the thought made me nervous in the stomach, so I ordered a soda to avoid complicating a good time. Drink in hand, I swiveled in my stool to get a better view of the room, but knocked into a woman who was standing beside me.

"Sorry 'bout that," I said.

She slid onto her stool without responding. She seemed taller than I was, and wore a yellow silk jacket, short black leather skirt and heels, and a t-shirt with "The Cure" printed across the front. I felt like I was crowding the woman and turned back to the bar.

She looked into her purse and pulled out a long, thin cigar, which she lit with a wave of her hand. Then she ordered something called a Campari and soda.

"Can I have that ashtray," she asked, pointing to my right.

"Sure can." I pushed it over to her.

She and I seemed to be the same age, in our early twenties. I wanted to say something, but was tongue-tied. I stared straight ahead at the collection of fancy-shaped bottles above the bar.

As the bartender passed by, I asked, "Are we near the ocean?" He didn't hear me. He lifted a tray of glasses and disappeared into the kitchen.

I took a sip of pop, smelling the woman's perfume inside the cigar smoke.

"Do I know what?" she asked me.

"I was talking to the bartender."

"Oh."

"Well, you probably know. Are we near the ocean?"

"Are you talking about the bay? It's all around us."

"Right, the water. Can you walk to it?"

The woman raised her eyebrows, grimacing and smiling at the same time.

"It's a long walk—about a mile. If you go up the street to

Fillmore, make a right, then go straight, all the way to the bay. Don't walk too far though, you'll get wet."

"Thanks. I knew I was close. My nose keeps picking up the scent."

She took a delicate puff off the cigar; lowering her hand, there was a pink lipstick print on the tip.

"I'm visiting from Nevada," I risked.

"Oh! are you."

She looked impatiently out to the street.

"And what do you do there?" she asked.

"Well, I'm not working now, so not much."

"That's too bad."

"This is such a great street, isn't it. People going everywhere, doing things. What are you doing tonight?—I mean, you look all dressed up and ready to go."

"I'm going to the Warfield to see The Prodigy."

"Can't say I've heard of 'em, but it sounds interesting."

"Oh! They're very interesting, believe me."

She quickly put out the cigar and stood up as another woman approached the bar. They kissed on the lips then turned and walked away. I watched them linger on the sidewalk outside. I admired—craved—the women's legs, which seemed as tall as the parking meters. It'd been so long for me, it was almost painful to feel the sparks in my groin.

After a plate of spaghetti and meatballs at the bar, I left Pompeii's and followed the woman's directions down Fillmore Street. The street came to an end at a large lawn area that fronted the bay. A jogger, accompanied by a dog, ran by, breathing and footsteps fading away in the darkness. The moisture from the nearby water touched my face, so I crossed the lawn and came to an eddy of large rocks. The bay, which I had seen panoramically from high on the bridge that morning, now settled before me, a damp, black enveloping presence. I tiptoed down into the rocks, finding a place to sit, feeling like I was in the company of crabs.

The beauty at the restaurant—who was I fooling? Winona?— too much history. Who did I have? Not a soul. The Rambling Rose, that's all. My prospects were shitty. Maybe they'd always been shitty.

I crossed my arms to fight the chill, listening to the lapping tide. This evening would be a whole lot better with Roe, I thought longingly, or Cracker Joe. A row of lights shone from across the water. I didn't know where those lights came from, or who lived near them; there was nothing but the bay, rising, subsiding. To my left, like a dark gargantuan ocean liner, was the Golden Gate Bridge, miles wide, connecting two bodies of land to the north and south. A fog horn groaned, a seagull angled by . . .

Crash, sleeet, crash, crash, sleeet, crash, sleeet, crash, crash, sleeet, crash, sleeet, crash, crash, sleeet, crash, sleeet, crash, crash, sleeet—

—I was used to a lot of loud noise growing up, what with being on the test sites, going to the air shows, using heavy equipment, but nothing prepared me for the sound of the twelve rows of machinery in the low-ceilinged Production Building at Breckenridge. The machines just roared, then echoed, then the echo fed on itself.

I was usually on Aisle C, with Stupid John and a couple of other guys, all serving time for weapons charges. I didn't do any of the technical work in making the license plates, not knowing anything about the machinery and not having a long enough sentence to be sufficiently trained in its operation. Stupid John, who had a much longer sentence, acted as my supervisor, telling me when to do this and when to do that, mostly mindless grunt work using a dolly to move stacks of metal to shipping and receiving.

That particular day, I had been standing around, watching him repair a linchpin in the stamping press feeder. Every once in a while he would press a button and send the machine into violent gyrations.

A prison guard moved close to us, gesturing, yelling over the noise,

151

"We'll be having visitors in a few minutes. Some state officials. Be on your best behavior and stand up straight." Stupid John and I nodded to the guard, interpreting the message in each other's eyes. As the guard turned away, Stupid John put his hand to his forehead in a mock salute and stiffened his shoulders upright for a moment.

Sure enough, in a couple minutes, the visitors showed up on the work floor, the volume of noise obliterating their arrival.

Two Breckenridge prison officials, dressed in shirt and tie, were leading along three outsiders: a middle-aged man and woman, and a younger woman, who was carrying a notebook. They were surrounded by four prison guards. They moved slowly, aisle by aisle, the officials pointing out things, the outsiders nodding in response. The older couple talked to a guard, but the younger woman looked around the building, interested in something else.

I faced the stamping press, but secretly kept my eyes on the group. Stupid John knelt down in front of the machine, smiling to himself. As they came to Row C, they stopped at our work place—why, I didn't know.

"Gentlemen," one of the officials announced. We turned, hesitantly, obediently, and faced the visitors. This was the first time in five months that I had come face-to-face with someone outside the prison system (except for the weekly visits from Mother and, occasionally, Roe), and I was embarrassed. I looked towards them, but made a point of keeping my eyes unfocused.

"These people are from the Carnegie Institute in Washington, D. C. They're studying new programs in the state prison system. You men are a part of that. They're going to be asking you some questions, so answer them." I looked down at my feet, wishing I was out in the recreation yard or in bed.

When I looked up, my eyes met those of the young woman. I could feel it immediately, and I knew she could feel it too: we were attracted to each other. Her skin was fair and sunburnt, and I could tell she felt a long way from home; maybe even a bit lonely or frightened. I tried to pry my eyes away, but all I could do was stand there, dumb and numb, an animal in a zoo, and return her curious, wide-eyed gaze. As each of the outsiders dispersed to talk to different inmates, she came up to me, accompanied by a guard.

"Hello, I'm Fran Schroeder. How are you today?" she asked, smiling, glancing at the press, then moving closer so we could hear each other.

"Fine," I murmured.

"What's your name?"

"Merle."

"I know this is unexpected and that I'm interrupting your work, but we wanted to see what you do here in the manufacturing section."

Her face turned serious, avoiding the intimacy of looking directly at me. I didn't say anything. I was obvious she'd said her lines a hundred times before.

"Tell me about this work area."

"I don't know much about it. I haven't been here long," I said. "What is Washington D.C. like?"

Her eyes narrowed suspiciously, then, business-like, she smiled and answered, "Washington is very hot this time of year—hot and muggy. So . . . what do you do here?"

"We make license plates. There's nothing magical about it."

"What kind of training did you get?"

"Forced training."

"Was it adequate?"

"No."

"Do you like—"

"No."

She opened her notebook.

"If you don't mind—"

"No."

"—I would like to talk in more detail about the program you're in." She made a few quick pencil strokes. "Now, please, tell me—"

"Don't fake it."

"What are you talking about?"

"*You know what I'm talking about. Shit, it's torture for me being face-to-face with you. Can't you at least leave me alone.*"

She looked at me more seriously. "*I would appreciate it if you would keep this on the level. Now, please, give me——*"

"*No.*"

"*I don't mean here. I have an office.*"

"*Ma'am, I don't want to talk.*"

"*You can be interviewed there,*" *she went on, trying to be upbeat.* "*If not now, some other time. I know it can be very difficult just opening up to a stranger in this environment.*"

I stepped over and picked up a wrench from a tool kit on a metal table. "*Forget the whole thing,*" *I said, looking at her, pleading for understanding with my eyes.*

"*But it's mandatory,*" *she said.* "*Do you understand? It's part of my job, and yours.*"

Part of my job? I thought, grimacing.

"*When would you like to . . .*"

"*No, I won't,*" *I said, more to myself than to her, then, above all the noise, I yelled out,* "*No*", *and waved the tool, knowing exactly what would happen. The guard immediately stepped between us, motioning to the other guards with his hand.* "*No, never,*" *I repeated, weaker this time, as the woman stepped back. Then I was grabbed, disarmed, and led away.*

The next day I slept deep until noon. Mrs. Spitz greeted me when I emerged from my hibernation in the cottage, serving me coffee on the back patio. We had a polite conversation—after I made a couple of brief references to Nevada, she told me about a wonderful summer she had spent in Capital Reef National Park,

Utah, when she was a young girl of ten—then she offered me lodging for the duration of my visit. I accepted her offer then said good-bye and went out to the truck.

I roughly identified the address of the Raging Feet Dance Collective on the map. It was located on the southern side of San Francisco, quite a distance from the Marina, so I set off again down Gough Street, past City Hall, and, after zigzagging through a herd of buses under a freeway overpass, I connected with Mission Street.

The farther south I drove, the bluer the sky became, the warmer the air. Suddenly, every second person on the street seemed like a Mexican. Mothers pushed baby carriages in front of the fruit markets, young children at their sides; some teen-agers, wearing baggy khaki pants, white t-shirts, and wide ban-danas low on their foreheads—I had seen the same fashions at Breckenridge—listened to a boom box in front of Quick Donuts. Thirty or forty men huddled around a bus stop, killing time.

When I reached 20th Street, I parked the truck. Checking the addresses, I realized Raging Feet was a few blocks east, so I set off on foot through the lunchtime crowd. I passed a row of small shops, little horse-shaped piñatas and girl's dresses hanging in the doorways. Music and Spanish lyrics pounded from scratchy speakers in the second floor windows.

The neighborhood became noticeably more rundown as I walked along, the sidewalks dirty and littered, graffiti covering the walls, security bars decorating doors and windows. At 362 20th Street, I found a plain, two-story building with a brightly colored mural on the front: on the first floor level, a scene with peasants working in some corn fields, guarded by soldiers; and on the second story, a background of fire transformed into a group of angels rising up to heaven. In the window was a sign: Raging Feet Dance Collective—Cultural Center and School.

I walked up the steps and went inside, more skeptical than hopeful. I entered a large, sunny room with a desk and chair against one wall, and shelves filled with boxes and books along another. The place was deserted, except for noises coming from down a hallway.

"Anybody here?" I called out. "Hello?"

I heard the sound of footsteps. A woman appeared, dressed in baggy pants, sandals, and a tight leotard top. Her hair was thick and black, with streaks of gray. She sat down at the desk, grinning happily. "Sorry, I'm not being a good receptionist today. What can I do for you?"

"I'm looking for Roe Honeycutt. I'm her brother."

The woman nodded as I spoke, smiling again.

"I thought she might be here."

"Yes, she is. She's in the studio in back."

I stared at the woman dumbly, unable to believe my ears, and for an instant my parents came to mind. "She's in back, you said?" I finally responded.

Standing up and walking towards me, the woman said, "Yea, let's check. We might catch everyone on break. The company has been in rehearsal all day. Come on."

We entered a corridor and passed two young children, both sitting at a low table, drawing, surrounded by scattered toys. The building was much bigger than it appeared from the street and we continued back past some makeshift dressing rooms, offices, and a kitchen. We came to a door and the woman carefully opened it and peeked inside. Evidently, everyone was still on break because she opened the door wider and let me through, saying in a low voice, "She's over against the far wall."

It was a dimly lit rehearsal space and I shyly stepped inside, trying to catch my bearings amidst the twenty odd dancers fanned out across the floor in front of me.

Then I heard my name called out.

"Merle!"

All heads in the room turned as a woman ran towards me. Was it Roe? I asked myself. Yea, it was her all right, but—her hair! Shit, what had she done to her hair?

She threw her arms around me. "What are you doing here? What a surprise! I knew you'd find me."

I was speechless, grinning like a fool.

She turned to the others in the room. "Everyone—I would like to introduce my kid brother, Merle. He's visiting from Nevada." There were smiles and nods all around. I scratched my chin, sheepishly glancing at the floor. The dancers attention turned back to their work, and Roe led me over to two folding chairs set against the wall.

"When did you arrive?" she asked, reaching over and touching my face.

"Yesterday," I said.

She looked much the same: strong, but slender, with mysterious green-flecked eyes and clear, healthy skin. In fact, her beauty was more vivid now that her brown hair was cut short.

"Who gave you the crew cut?" I asked, tempted to scrub her scalp with my knuckles. She turned her head for display. The only remnants of her once glorious mane were four long braids entwined with red material that fell down her back like little tails.

"And look at your tattoo," she said, laughing, pulling up the sleeve of my t-shirt. "You look so hip."

Then from the far side of the room a man began clapping his hands, calling the dancers to attention. He walked to the center of the floor as the dancers stirred, taking positions, loosening up.

"Merle, where are you staying?"

"Guess—Mrs. Spitz's."

"What! You're kidding?" She shook her head. "Listen, I'm in

rehearsal until five o'clock. We have a big performance tomorrow and I'm really, really busy." She reached for her exercise bag under the chair and pulled out a pencil and paper from a small purse.

"It's all right. I'll wait."

"No, it's not worth it. I have all sorts of things to do. Just come to my place around six o'clock, O.K.? Here's the address and phone number. The neighborhood is south of Market Street. It's called SOMA, for short. Just ask anybody for directions."

She handed me the paper. She looked into my eyes and for a moment the dance studio and San Francisco disappeared and we were back home in Cherry Creek, hiding in her room.

"Have you missed me? Tell me the truth."

"Yea, sorta. It's been too long, Roe."

"I guess you can say that. Or maybe not long enough," she said, with a strange smile.

She gave me a kiss on the cheek then turned and bounded across the floor to take her place in the center of the dancers, facing the dark-haired man, who was instructing the group. I stared at Roe's leotard, which was covered with red spots, as if she had been splattered with blood. She stood among the other dancers, who were dressed in baggy cotton shirts and pants, like a sacrificial lamb.

I walked out of the building and sat down on the steps, stunned. The sun settled on my shoulders like a cloak, the first real heat I'd felt since arriving in San Francisco. I just closed my eyes and soaked it up for a few minutes. I felt a detective's satisfaction at knowing Roe was alive and dancing, but the rest of the business—her appearance, the dance company—did nothing but arouse my suspicions. But she still loved me; yes, it seemed from her eyes, her words, her touch, that she still loved me.

Walking back to the truck, I decided to phone Mother and Papa as soon as possible, to tell them of Roe's whereabouts. It was better to do it now, I warned myself, than wait until later in the day when Roe might change my mind. I found a quiet phone booth at the back of a laundromat and left a message on the answering machine in Cherry Creek, giving Roe's address and phone number.

I felt hungry as a wolf and walked back to Mission Street to find a place to eat. I stepped inside a little hole in the wall, where mariachi music blared from a jukebox. An old woman and man were standing behind the counter, a hand-painted menu on the wall above their heads. I looked over the items as best I could: birria, chimichangas, menudo, lengua, lomo soltado, flautas, mole. What was all this stuff, anyway? I didn't have any idea what to order, so I walked out and went back to the truck, where I sat for awhile, pondering what to do. Why couldn't Roe have just come with me? I wondered. No, she was dancing—some things never change. But what kind of dance was it? It wasn't ballet, that was clear.

I was tempted to go back to Ms. Spitz's and bide my time, but I didn't feel like facing the traffic again. I did, however, want to tell her about Roe's circumstances at some point. Then I remembered the man in front of Café Dodo and his recommendation of a hamburger joint in the Castro, wherever that was. Why not?—I knew of no other place to eat or visit. I asked someone on the sidewalk if it was close by, and was told it was within walking distance. So I locked up the truck and set off, keeping in mind my commitment at six o'clock.

After seeing Roe, I felt free-spirited walking west on 20th Street. I crossed a couple intersections and climbed up to a park that overlooked the city to the north. Palm trees lined one side of the park, running downhill into a sea of rooftops. Far in the distance was a chess set of downtown skyscrapers.

The air was perfectly still, the sky clear and blue. For the first time ever I understood what Mother's postcards and photographs were all about; and the miracle of it all was that it was me who was taking in the sights. What would it be like, I wondered, to actually live in a place like this?

I sat down on the lawn and savored the view for a few minutes, picking a piece of grass and chewing on it. Below me, on the next level of the park, two men played Frisbee. The grass was covered with sunbathers—all men. There must have been fifty of them laying face down on their towels, in rows, motionless, as if drugged by the heat. A bad throw sent the Frisbee flying up near where I was sitting. After getting up and tossing it to a smiling man wearing some nut-huggers, I set off down the steep sidewalk. Following the directions I'd been given, I turned west on 18th Street and walked up to The All-American.

I took my place in line in front of the restaurant, feeling like I had stepped into another world. Everywhere there were fags. The couples on the street?—not men and women holding hands with the usual affection, but men; the clerks changing clothes on a mannequin in a storefront window?—men; the waiters in the café, as well as the customers standing in line?—men. I had the impulse to just run away, looking at everything around me with disdain, but I decided to go ahead and eat first. There was one woman in the place, and just as I spied her, she picked up her order and walked out the door . . .

"Honeydipper?"

I opened my eyes slightly, but continued to pretend I was asleep.

The voice came again from the window in the cell door, "Honeydipper. Don't tell me you sleepin' good. I know you awake. Listen to me."

I remained motionless. But I knew by the high-pitched, nervous voice that it was Eddie, messenger boy from the laundry rooms in the Apex Building.

"Listen good, I ain't got much time. Jerome don't want you to transfer out. Hear me, Honey? Jerome don't want you goin' nowhere. And he'll follow you to New Beginnings, and even outside, if you do."

I felt like getting up and spitting into the little hole where the voice came from. With my half opened eyes, I could see the toilet, the small sink, against the wall. My body tightened like a coil.

"Honeydipper. At four o'clock in the recreation room, there's gonna be party-time. Be ready to party."

There was a moment's pause. "I hope the airwaves are clear, Honeydripper. Jerome sent me. I'm gone. "

"Can you pass me the ketchup, please?"

I looked up from my food, disoriented for a moment.

"The ketchup, please," a man sitting next to me requested. His hair was stylishly blonde, but with black roots; he was dressed entirely in white, except for a purple shirt, with a number of gold chains hanging from his neck. I handed him the ketchup.

"Thank you so much. The fries here are so big, you need to drench them in this stuff."

I looked down at my half-eaten burger, the untouched fries, then out the large window that opened onto the bustling street. I felt irritable, like I should have just been a good courier and returned to Biggs on King Lear.

"Can you believe how popular this place has gotten?" the man asked.

The man had set a bouquet of flowers and a small gift box between us on the narrow table. Who was he giving these gifts to, I wondered cynically, one of the men who leaned out of the second-story window across the street, chatting and laughing, surveying the action below?

"Are you having a bad day?"

I scratched my chin and glanced at the man. He was like a flower himself, all clean bright colors, smelling sweet.

"Why are you talking to me?" I said, annoyed, but trying not to be rude.

"I don't like sadness."

"So? I don't like you."

"Why?"

"What difference does it make?"

"You find me disgusting, don't you? I know I'm ugly to you."

"I didn't say that." I pushed my plate away.

"I know—you said you didn't like me."

A loud, boisterous group of men walked by the window, all dressed in black leather vests, small biker hats, and cowboy chaps. They moved along confidently, as if they owned the street. As they walked away, the whitish butts of two of the men were visible.

The man must have noticed that the black-clad group caught my eye.

"I much prefer white attire," he said philosophically.

I would have preferred to be alone.

"Here," the man said tenderly, "please accept these from me." He held out the bouquet for me to take.

I stood up, avoiding the man's eyes.

"I'm serious. They're for you," he added.

I'd had enough, so I zigzagged through the tables to the front door and burst out onto the sidewalk. I stood there for a minute, thinking, then went back inside. I walked up behind the same man in white, tapping him on the shoulder.

"Did you say those were for me?"

"Yes, yes, I did. Of course. It's my pleasure." He pushed his chair back and turned towards me. He saw me glance at the bouquet and instantly reached over and handed me the flowers. "Won't you sit down?"

"No," I answered, quickly walked out.

Gustavo was pruning a tree in the front yard when I arrived back at Mrs. Spitz's house. He greeted me with a wave of the hand and pointed to the back yard, so I walked through the gate and found the old lady sitting on the patio, drinking tea, writing a letter.

"Good afternoon, Merle, if I may call you that."

"Sure, Mrs. Spitz. Here, I brought you these flowers."

"Why thank you. I love carnations and baby's breath. Did you get them at the stall on Union?"

"No, in the Castro part of town."

"You don't say," she said, looking at me curiously. "I'll be right back."

She rose into a half-cocked position and went inside the house. She returned carrying the flowers in a fluted crystal vase, along with a drink. Setting the vase down, she offered me some lemonade.

"Thank you," I said. "I found Roe."

"You did? How wonderful. What is she up to?"

"She's living—how do you say it?—south of Market, and dancing with a new group."

"What a good detective you are. I'm so glad to hear it— sorry to hear that she left the ballet company, but glad that she is safe and sound." As Mrs. Spitz took a sip of tea, I noticed the cup shaking. I observed for the first time how her hands were badly disfigured, with fingers knotted like tree bark. "Is she happy?" she asked.

"I don't know. I could only talk to her for a few minutes."

"She's a nervous one, isn't she? It isn't my position to say, but Roe always seemed to be either coming or going. Why, I've spent more time with you in two days than I did with her in a matter of months.

"You know, I just can't get over those flowers. Thank you so much, you're precious to bring them."

The side gate clanged shut and Gustavo pushed a wheelbarrow across the lawn to the side of the cottage, where he dumped some cuttings into a large pile.

"Isn't the garden just beautiful the way he takes care of it?"

"Yea, it is," I said, gulping the drink down. "None of these plants grow in Nevada, it's too hot and dry."

"That's a pity. Fuchsia and rhododendron are so grand."

I set the glass on the table.

"Mrs. Spitz, could I get Roe's boxes from you? I want to give them to her this evening."

"Of course you can."

"She may need some of that stuff."

"Certainly. Why didn't she arrange to pick them up herself?"

"I didn't ask her about it."

"Maybe you should have. I know you're quite the faithful brother, but it's her responsibility."

I smiled bashfully, glancing through the wide patio windows into the kitchen, as if I hadn't heard her remark. It embarrassed me when she talked like that.

"Before I forget, please ask Roe to call me about the arrangement for the rent. She owes me eight hundred dollars. She left so quickly that we never resolved certain details."

"Eight hundred dollars. Really?" I asked, sucking on an ice cube.

"Yes, really. Believe me, it's a lot of money for a retired person."

"I'll ask her to give you a buzz," I assured her.

Evidently San Francisco could not decide what season it was, because by the time I loaded Roe's boxes into the truck and drove across the city, the weather had turned gray, cold, and blustery. I got lost for a good while, confused by the one-way streets, but finally found Roe's addresses—48 Albion Place—just off Folsom Street.

Albion Place was really just an alleyway, and as I pulled into it, a black man stood up, waving his hands, directing me like a highway flag man.

I drove a short ways down the alley and another black man emerged from behind a dumpster, running alongside the front of the truck, pointing with his hands, leading me. I slowed down— was this some sort of trap? The man ran ahead of the truck and stopped, pointing to a parking space. Since the alley was narrow and confined, I pulled in at the man's encouragement. I was afraid I might be robbed, so I opened the container between the seats to give me access to the gun. I turned off the engine, waiting for the two men to make a move. One man yelled out to the street, then hurried away. I decided to take my chances and got out.

Before my feet could touch the ground I was being talked to.

"It seem funny, real funny, what I am. But what a man to do? Black man still need to work. Black man's soul gotta be healed somehow. My time's gone. I need a favor, that's what I'm askin'."

"What do you want?" I asked, glancing at Roe's boxes in the back of the truck.

"Didn't I find you good parking? Didn't I? That a gift from the Heavenly Father in this town."

I looked the man over. He was broken-down before his time, moving nervously, as if insects swarmed under his skin.

"I'm hungry, man. You unnerstan'? Everybody ain't got what they need. Black man's soul needs healin'."

I turned away and checked the money in my pocket. I pulled out a ten dollar bill and gave it to him.

"Thank ya kindly. Thank ya ever so much. You a healer."

"What's your name?"

"Edgar. Edgar Lords."

"I'm Merle."

"It's mighty fine. Mighty fine."

"Some business you got, Edgar."

"Man gotta think for hisself in this day 'n age."

"You know where 48 Albion is?"

"There only one place people live 'long here. That's 'cross the way in those studio. See the second flo' there?" He pointed to the lights in the building.

The man agreed to help me carry Roe's belongings. While he pulled the boxes out of the back of the truck, I leaned across the driver's seat and closed the container.

After I identified myself to a man on the security phone, we were let inside the building. I wanted to tell Mr. Lords to get lost, but he moved the boxes with such enthusiasm, humming to himself, that I left him alone as we took a freight elevator up to the second floor.

It opened up to a long hallway with steel doors every fifty feet. Music pounded from behind one doorway at the end of the hall to our right. From the other direction, a door opened and a man waved at us—it was the same man I had seen directing rehearsal at the Raging Feet Dance Collective. Mr. Lords and I lugged the boxes down the hallway to the open door.

"Just set them there," the man said, pointing to the floor outside the door. We did as he said, then I faced him: "Hi, I'm Merle, Roe's brother."

"Jose Luis," he answered, quickly shaking my hand. He was about my same height, with handsome brown eyes and a neatly groomed goatee. His hair, on top, was combed straight back into a pony tail, then cut bald to the skin on the sides of his head. He gave the impression of continuously being preoccupied with, or aggravated by, something. Music and bright lights leapt out of the interior of the apartment.

"Did he bother you?" Jose Luis asked, glancing at Mr. Lords as if he were something familiar and objectionable.

"No, he just helped me up with the boxes."

"A world class valet service, no?"

I nodded my head, yes.

"We've had much trouble with—"

"Black man needs work and some soul healin'. Ain't nothin' wrong wi' dat. Black man doin' whatever he—"

Jose Luis stepped forward threateningly, but he stopped when Roe appeared in the doorway.

"There he is!" she exclaimed, stepping by Jose Luis and kissing me on the cheek. "Did you have any trouble finding the place?"

"No problem, once I used my compass."

"Come in," Roe said. She glanced at Mr. Lords. "Who's this?"

"He helped me with your boxes from Mrs. Spitz's house. I thought you would want them."

"You doll. Thanks. I'd forgotten all about them. Jose Luis, can you give Merle a hand?"

"Yes, but that man must leave—now, pronto," Jose Luis kept staring at Mr. Lords. To settle matters, I accompanied Mr. Lords down to the elevator, paid him another ten dollars, then returned. The door to the apartment was left open, so I stepped inside.

Roe was on the phone and Jose Luis had disappeared. She smiled at me, pointing to some leather chairs in the corner. I watched her pace back and forth, absorbed in her conversation. With regular clothes on, she looked too skinny, an appearance that was magnified by her short hair. I hadn't noticed before, but she had a row of small gold rings along the edge of her ear. Minutes passed; I felt like I was invisible.

Bored, I picked up a magazine—*ZZZMYZ: A Feminist Film Criticism Quarterly*—and glanced inside at the complicated chapter titles. Greek to me, I said to myself, setting the magazine back on the coffee table.

I looked around the apartment, which was basically a high-ceilinged warehouse with tall windows along one wall giving a view of the nearby rooftops. Near the door was a makeshift kitchen, with a bar and stools and hanging lights; the far side of the room was sectioned off by low partitions (light flickered up onto the walls and windows in this area); a bunch of guitars and conga drums were crowded in the corner, by a bed with a red comforter. Putting my hands behind my head, I looked up at the ceiling: hung from the metal beams, giant papier-mâché masks stared down at me.

When Roe finally completed her call, she skipped over to me and, in a split second, without my having a chance to object, curled up in my lap.

"Hi," she said coyly, staring into my face, "do you remember me?"

Her closeness, the weight of her body, embarrassed me and I didn't know what to say.

"Come on—out with it."

"Out with what?" I asked.

"Admit it. You missed me, didn't you?"

"No."

"Yes, you did!"

"Didn't."

"Did."

"You lose again," I said, sticking my tongue out at her.

She poked me in the ribs with her finger and tickled under my arm. I let out a loud laugh and tickled her back. We tussled back and forth, like two animals confirming the identity of the other. When the giggling stopped, we became lost in a quiet meditation of things.

"How are the old folks?"

"Worried about you."

"Somehow I doubt it. Worried about something, but not me."

"They didn't know where you lived or what you were doing. I guess you know Papa's seeing a psychiatrist."

"Still?"

"He's screwy. I guess it's depression. He just mopes around all day, watching television."

"It's good for him to relax a little. All he's done his whole life is work. Work, work, work, I always hated that."

I listened to Roe's words and wondered how long had it been since she had seen Mother and Papa.

"Mother's working pretty hard," I continued. "All the political stuff." I was going to mention the affair with Bill Peterson, but I stopped myself.

"Mother . . ." Roe whispered, shaking her head. "When I first came here, I'd never felt so alone in all my life. I was scared to death of doing anything—just to be out on the streets with new people was frightening. There was just so much going on everywhere and here I was . . . from the outback.

I phoned Mother every week, complaining about the company, venting. But she was a stick in the mud."

"She said she didn't know anything about your situation," I remarked, remembering the letter.

"What a joke! Mother's selective listening. But I just had to adjust. I found a lot of people to support me and give me guidance and it's led to so many changes. You can see the changes all around you."

I wondered what changes she was referring to.

"Roe, did you visit Winona in Nixon?"

"Yes," she answered, showing little curiosity about why I hadn't been there. "Mother sent me, I didn't really want to go."

Then I noticed Jose Luis standing across the room, staring at us. I couldn't tell how long he'd been there.

"Roe, I need your assistance," he said, turning away. She glanced up and her body seemed to tighten. "Wait, Merle, I'll be right back." She climbed off my lap and walked quickly across the room, disappearing behind the partitions. Jose Luis began speaking to her in a rapid-fire voice. Roe responded defensively for a moment, then Jose Luis started up again, harsher than before. Their images were cast up on the wall like a shadow play; Jose Luis waving his arms, Roe shaking her head.

I forced my eyes to the ground, trying to concentrate on something else. I was tempted to just walk out the door.

After a minute, Roe returned.

"Merle, come here for a second."

I got up and followed Roe into the little maze of partitions. In the center were some chairs surrounding a video camera and small screen.

"I wanted you to see this," Roe said, breathing deeply. She looked worried and distracted now. Jose Luis sat with his back to me, fiddling with the camera, and Roe stood behind him, her hands on his shoulders. He turned and glanced at me. "Sit down, sit down, please," he said, starting the video. The dancers magically came to life on the screen. It was the same Raging Feet troupe I had seen that afternoon, except each performer was in full costume. Dancers held instruments, dressed like members of a mariachi band; others stood at attention, soldiers in green fatigues and helmets; there was a tall man on stilts, dressed in black, holding a sickle, and wearing a crown covered with dollar signs; the majority of the dancers wore elaborate sunflower masks. But each costume and prop was handmade, giving the scene a dream-like quality. And, in the center of it all, Roe in her bloodstained leotards. To my amazement, her hair was as long as I had remembered it.

"Look at your hair, Roe."

"Yea," she said without regret. "I got it done a few days ago. We were thinking of cutting it in the middle of the performance on opening night, just for dramatic effect, but it seemed too complicated."

Jose Luis suddenly took interest in what we were saying.

"The theme of the ballet," he said, keeping his hands together as if in prayer, "is the punishment of a village girl after she steals from a government store to feed her family. It is a very simple story line, with simple symbolism. There is little need to hit the audience over the head with the standard oppressor vs. oppressed thing. We want more the sense of a folk tale, with magical characters. The hair had to go. It did not look right with the costume. Too traditional. The costume—a symbol of punishment, grief, innocence lost—has to float across the stage like a banner, and the hair got in the way."

"I saved the braid as a keepsake—for sentimental reasons," Roe added, and I wondered if it was meant for me.

Jose Luis pointed to the screen. "Here, this is the problem," he said critically, pointing out how the village and mountain scene painted on the stage backdrop was obscured by the dancers. "I see what you mean," Roe said sympathetically, leaning forward for a better view. I couldn't see what they were talking about or why it was so important. While they debated back and forth, I stared at the back of Roe's head, the hair tapering off into the white skin of her slender neck.

Jose Luis suddenly burst up from his seat, throwing Roe's hands off his shoulders. He began pacing the cubicle.

"Please leave me alone," Jose Luis said, "I have to think about how to solve this before rehearsal tonight." He stretched out his hands, as if pleading for our immediate response: "Please go."

We stepped out of the screening area.

"I'm going to Miyoko's then, alright?" Roe said politely. "Think about it and we can talk later."

We left the apartment and walked to the opposite end of the poorly lit corridor.

"What's that guy's problem anyway?" I asked Roe.

"He hasn't got a problem, Merle. We have a performance at the Palace of Fine Arts tomorrow night, and he's just trying to get everything completed."

"But can't he ever smile?"

"He hasn't got time to smile. He's a very creative guy—a genius in his own way. He's the choreographer and artistic director of the company. He's super busy."

"Is he your boyfriend?"

"What a question. Yes, of course he is."

We stopped at a door at the end of the corridor and Roe pressed a buzzer, which made a harsh noise inside. An Asian woman opened the door, greeted Roe with a smile and a kiss on the cheek, and asked us in.

"Miyoko, this is my brother, Merle. He just got into town."

She offered her hand, smiling. "It's very nice to meet you, Merle. Are you here for opening night?"

"Well, not really. I just found out about it."

We walked inside the apartment, which was smaller and cozier than Roe and Jose Luis's spot. The ceiling gave the impression of being low because it was covered with folds of flower-printed material; the walls, the furniture, were pale lavender.

"My, my, look at you," Miyoko said to me. "The male counterpart of our beautiful Roe—but with a tan."

"Don't believe the flattery, Merle," my sister remarked. "She's Japanese—they act nice with everyone."

"I can't believe my ears," Miyoko said.

"No, I'm only kidding. Miyoko is Raging Feet's costume designer. She did all the work for *The Sunflower*." Roe sat down on a couch and began paging through the newspaper. "Did that critic, Barnsby, ever mention the Collective?"

"No, I don't think so," Miyoko answered, folding a piece of green fabric and placing it in a box.

"It figures, the jerk," Roe said, putting the newspaper down.

"Merle, please sit down," Miyoko said. "Would you like something to drink: some tea, a beer?"

"No thanks," I said, taking a seat beside Roe on the couch.

"Do you still want to go to Roberts?" Roe asked.

Miyoko stepped up on a stool and pushed the box into the top of a cabinet. She was a full-bodied woman compared to Roe, with very narrow eyes and a generous, big-toothed smile.

"Oh! I think we should, don't you?" she said, "I mean, I know it's going to be hard." She struggled to put another box in place, so I quickly got up and helped her.

"You're a true gentleman, Merle," she said. "Thank you." I sat back down. With nothing to say, I felt like an out-of-place piece of furniture.

"Jose Luis has been obsessing terribly about tomorrow night," Roe said sympathetically. "Maybe we should just skip it. It's bad timing."

"You can, but I'm going—at least for a while," Miyoko said. She ran her hand through her wild black hair, which was cut short, with a gold streak, above her left ear, but full and shoulder length on the right side.

Her ears perked up suddenly at a sound in the back of the apartment, and she walked out of the room. You could hear her speaking another language, her voice innocent and high-pitched.

Roe turned to me. "Merle, we have a get-together we have to go to later. I'm sorry for all these things that have to be done; this was a bad week for you to visit. One of our former ballet teachers, Robert Cousineau, is dying and there is a dinner honoring him. What do you want to do? You can stay here, or you can go check out the city and meet us later."

The possibility of separation from Roe, after the turmoil of finding her, seemed out of the question. She seemed so absorbed in things that I was suspicious that I would never meet her again if she were to leave me.

"Would it be cool if I just tagged along with you?"

Roe thought for a moment. "O.K. You're in for a big surprise, but it's about time you got oriented to modern life anyway."

Just then Miyoko appeared, with a young boy at her side. He was sleepy, shuffling along, fresh from a nap. He peered sideways at us, shy but curious, clinging to his mother's side.

"This is Chester. Do you want to say hello to Roe?" He didn't. The boy just stared, motionless, then was slowly escorted across the room by his mother. He was wearing a cute pair of overalls, covered with images of cowboys twirling lassos.

"Chester, this is Merle. He's Roe's little brother." Miyoko tousled and re-arranged his hair, which was one big cowlick stuck up in the air. "He's a cowboy, too. He lives on a ranch in Nevada?" Miyoko looked at me, whispering, "Pardon me if I change your identity momentarily."

"No problem. I always wanted to be a cowboy."

I glanced at Roe sitting beside me. What was wrong with her, I wondered, taking in her cold, aloof expression. I felt sorry for her: already the usual performance anxiety.

"You were the last person to know me as a cowboy," I said to Roe. She hinted at a smile then bit her fingernail.

But then, like a firecracker going off, Chester burst to life. He left Miyoko's side, ran over to a box of toys, and began rifling through them. He pulled out a plastic horse and came over to me. He made the horse jump up and down on the couch next to my leg, fascinated with his own hand movements.

Roe got up and asked Miyoko to come into the kitchen to talk.

"Good luck," Miyoko said, smiling at the two of us, then disappearing out of the room.

I reached out for the horse, but Chester hesitated, looking towards the kitchen. He held the toy to his chest for a moment then slowly handed it to me; he suddenly ran back to his toy box and dragged out a bent cardboard castle.

"You ride the horse to the castle," he said excitedly, "and see if I'm inside. Pretend like you can't see me, then I'll jump out and scare you.

Then we can play cowboys."

An hour later, all of us drove to Robert Cousineau's event.

"This is a great 4x4, Merle," Miyoko said. "I can't imagine having something like this to drive around in."

I looked in the rearview mirror: Miyoko had her arm around Chester, who seemed on the verge of another nap; Roe was hidden from view.

"I just might have to give up my dear little Volkswagen and buy something like this," Miyoko said.

"Better start looking for another job then," Roe said.

"You have a Volkswagen?" I asked Miyoko. "What year?"

"A 1984 Rabbit."

I laughed to myself—then Cracker Joe's image disturbed me for a split second. "Do you remember Beetles, those old Volkswagens with the weird front ends? In Nevada, we used to buy them from a wrecking yard and drive them off a cliff near our high school."

"Impressive extra-curricular activities," Miyoko joked. "I'm surprised: Roe told me you were a conservative type, raising livestock for Future Farmer's of America."

"Yea, right," I responded, chuckling. "Maybe dogs."

Jose Luis sat next to me in the front, scrutinizing the dashboard. "In Honduras—my native country—the only people with a truck like this are the military police. It is a bad sign when you see a new truck." His hand moved along the upholstery, the bracelets on his arm making a tinkling sound.

"When did you come to the United States?"

"Too long ago," he said, staring out the window.

"Merle, turn here on Sacramento," Miyoko said.

I turned left onto the broad one-way street and accelerated up the hill. Somehow, behind the wheel of the truck, I could forget about my nervousness, about who I was. There was a double-parked taxi ahead of me, so I stepped on the gas, changed lanes abruptly, and flew over the top of the hill. The truck bounced clumsily as we came down the other side.

"Be careful, Merle," Roe said, behind me.

Those words! Just hearing those words sent a shiver up and down my spine.

Did she know the meaning of what she said?

Did she remember anything about it? Not much, I concluded in a flash of anger.

I pressed on the gas pedal.

"Merle!" she said again. It felt so good to have her attention on me, focused right in the back of my head, helplessly suspended there, that I hurtled along for a few more blocks, the stores and cars and people flying by. Then I thought of Chester and slowed down, embarrassed.

"Sorry about that," I announced to everyone.

"We survived, Merle," Miyoko said. "My folks place is on Buchanan, the next left. It's the fourth house on the left."

I parked in Miyoko's parents driveway. She aroused Chester with a cooing voice, then, after good-byes, led him up the steps of the two-story home and disappeared inside.

I stared straight ahead, afraid to turn to either Roe or Jose Luis. We all sat in an awkward silence for a minute or two. Down the street the brilliant orange sunlight washed over the houses.

"Why is Miyoko coming along? She isn't necessary for rehearsal tonight," Jose Luis asked impatiently.

"She wants to see Robert," Roe answered sharply.

"We cannot stay long, Roe. We have to be at the Palace at eight o'clock."

"We're not going to stay long."

Jose Luis turned and looked back at Roe. "Why are we doing this now. Why, on the last night of rehearsal?"

"I don't know, Jose. To honor Robert, I suppose."

"What a stupid, crazy plan!"

"Robert's dying."

"I don't care if he's dying. If it's so, it's so. Will he be gone tomorrow or the next day? No. You're being stupid. Shit, you always do this."

Jose Luis's jewelry rattled again as he scratched his neck. He smoothed down his hair with both hands.

Listening to the guy's words, I found myself burning up inside. I just had to speak my mind.

"What's your fuckin' problem, man?"

"Please, don't bother me," Jose Luis said, shaking his head back and forth.

"I mean, let's turn the tables—"

Roe touched me on the shoulder from behind. "Don't worry about it, Merle."

"No, now wait a second. What if I was in Tijuana or South America or wherever you call home, and I called your sister stupid. What do you think would happen, huh?"

"I don't have time for this."

I lunged at him, catching him by the throat with my left

hand, then pushed his head up against the window. I pushed as hard as I could to keep him there, gagged, his arms reaching helplessly into the air. Roe screamed: "Stop it, Merle." She threw herself into the front seat and tugged at my arm to separate us.

I guess I expected Jose Luis to be strong and fight me, but he just gave in and went limp, waiting for me to loosen my grip, which I did—after gripping his neck tight one last time, then shaking it, just to get my point across.

Jose Luis opened the door and stumbled out, taking off down the street.

"God damn you," Roe said, getting out and following him.

I was breathing so hard I felt faint. I could smell the man's cologne on my hand. I didn't know why, but, as blood rushed through my veins, I felt warm and satisfied, more complete than I had in a long time.

I looked down the block. They were talking under a street sign. I put my head in my trembling hands: maybe I shouldn't have left Nevada after all; I was making a mess of things. But then again, what just happened made it all strangely worthwhile.

Out of the corner of my eye, I saw Miyoko come down the steps of her parent's house. She climbed in the back seat.

"Where is everybody?"

"They're talking."

Roe walked back up the street to the truck. She opened the front passenger door. "Just go with Miyoko to Robert's," she said angrily, "I'll meet you there."

"What's wrong Roe?" Miyoko asked.

"Nothing. Ask Merle."

Roe turned and walked away. She met Jose Luis and disappeared around the corner.

"What happened?" Miyoko asked.

"I got in a fight with Jose Luis."

"Really?" she asked, pausing. "You mean a real fight?"

"A real fight."

"What happened?"

"I don't know. He's just got an attitude that I can't stand."

"I'm envious—I wish I'd had the pleasure myself."

"Really?"

"Really."

"Do you want to sit upfront."

"Sure."

I followed Miyoko's directions past the Japan Center then south on Fillmore Street. At her suggestion, I opened the sunroof and the cool evening air flooded in, the sky glowing red like embers. I felt lucky having her as a companion, her presence helping me control the growing guilt I felt about attacking Jose Luis. Am I crazy, I kept repeating to myself, sure that I was destroying Roe on the eve of her most important performance.

I was totally lost as we crossed a whole new part of San Francisco, past half-built condominiums, open fields, and old Victorian homes with elaborate paint jobs and stained glass windows.

Miyoko put her hand up through the sunroof, as if touching the sky, her white teeth flashing in appreciation of the passing wind.

"This may be a somber affair," she said, bringing her hand back inside. Robert, whose house we're visiting, is dying of AIDS. Roe and I took class from him. He's a wonderful man. We're sort of paying our respects."

"You a dancer, too?" I asked.

"Well, not much anymore. I never quite had the skills, or the long legs, that someone like Roe had, so I've moved on to doing costume design and production kinds of things. Your sister is the dancer. My God, she's good. It took Jose Luis about a second to choose her for the lead in *The Sunflower*."

"Jose Luis, what an asshole—excuse my French."

"Yes, well, maybe I shouldn't say this, but Roe seems to have a penchant for getting connected with talented assholes. I've seen it before."

"What do you do, Merle?"

My mind spun like a slot machine, trying to formulate a good story. Why do people always ask that question? I wondered. There was no sense in lying.

"I'm just bumming around now. Just trying to decide where to live."

"Are you thinking of coming to San Francisco?"

"Anything's possible, I guess, but I can't decide about this city."

As we came up to a four-way stop, she asked: "Would these guys have anything to do with your indecisiveness?"

Crossing the street in front of the truck were four young men, who, I guessed right away, were a bunch of scumbags. They weren't much younger than me really, but with their shaved heads, black army boots and fatigues, and chains hanging from their belts, they looked like strange mutations of Cracker Joe's attackers in Fallon.

They wandered out into the street, two of the four breaking into a rowdy scuffle, slapping each other. They seemed oblivious to the waiting cars.

I honked the horn, again and again, but they didn't move, so I moved forward anyway, and when they saw that I was intent on passing through, they hovered around the side of the truck. One of the freaks looked straight at me through the window, making faces and opening his mouth wide and smashing his lips against the glass; then he reared back and spit on the window. I recoiled, putting my hand up to block the grotesque sight. Then they started yelling and banging on the truck with their hands.

I thought the truck was being damaged in some way, and started to get out, but Miyoko grabbed my arm. "Wait," she commanded.

In a split second, a police car sped into the intersection, lights flashing, siren blaring, and the four men fled down the street behind us. The chaos was over as quickly as it began, and in a moment everything was back to normal.

I drove the truck through the intersection and pulled over to the curb, shaking my head in disgust, embarrassed at having such a thing happen in the company of a woman. I got out and checked the side of the truck, concerned that the hoodlums might have dented or scratched it. I didn't see any damage and got back inside.

"Is everything O.K.?" Miyoko asked.

"Yea, that was just weird, wasn't it?"

"Do you want to get a newspaper and start looking for available apartments?"

I grinned. "Right, this is the neighborhood, no doubt about it."

"Merle, look at me for a second."

I looked her way. She seemed tender and close to me in that moment. She pressed a button between the seats and I heard the window to my left open.

"All right, I think we can go now." She started laughing, and when I looked back at the open window, I knew what she meant and started laughing, too—a warm, wonderful belly laugh.

Robert Cousineau's house was only a short distance away, up a winding road that passed by a park filled with oak trees.

We entered the house along with a group of men who arrived at the same time. We all walked down a long hallway into the back of the flat. Since word had it that Mr. Cousineau was dying, I had no idea what to expect from the proceedings. I loathed the idea of this being some sort of depressing event that I would have to patiently sit through, hanging out, not knowing a soul.

I followed Miyoko past a kitchen packed with people talking and eating, arriving at a large living room with a spectacular view of San Francisco.

The room was crowded mostly with men (fags, as far as I could see) and a few women. It was obvious from the get-go, what with the champagne bottles being passed around, the bursts of laughter, the thumping dance music, this event was meant to be a real party.

Miyoko began talking to an acquaintance, so I made my way over to the edge of the room and looked out at the jaw-dropping view. The house was built on the side of a hill, which dropped off precipitously into a bramble of brush and trees, giving me the same sense of falling into clear space that I experienced from my perch near the house in Red Pepper Canyon. Lights twinkled from the neighborhoods below, the downtown skyscrapers, and the arched physique of the distant Bay Bridge. The view was so large, it seemed small, like an exquisite Christmas decoration.

"Would you like a libation?"

I turned around and was startled to see Terry, the black guy I met downtown the day before.

"How are you? What a surprise," he said, pouring me a glass of champagne. "When did you get here?"

"Coupla' minutes ago."

"Do you know Robert?"

"No, my sister does."

"Wait a minute. Honeycutt, right? No, it can't be. Is Roe your sister?"

"You got it."

He rolled his eyes, laughing. His face seemed different—he was wearing a touch of make-up and looked spectacular in some sort of red crushed-velvet jumpsuit.

"We've danced together. She's tooo maaarvelous for words. I should have known from your exotic golden eyes that you were related somehow."

How could he have looked at me so closely? I thought suspiciously. I politely took a sip of the champagne, which was so sweet I wanted to spit it out. Then Miyoko appeared out of the crowd.

"Merle, I want you to meet someone," she said. I put the drink on the windowsill.

"Talk to you later, " I said to Terry.

"I hope so," he answered, his eyes latching onto me.

Miyoko took my hand and led me through the crowd, which seemed to be growing by the minute. She took me back down the hallway to a room adjacent to the kitchen. Upon entering, my eyes adjusted to the low, amber lamplight. The party now seemed to exist in a faraway, parallel world. The walls were lined with ornately framed posters from ballet openings, and I noticed Mr. Cousineau's name highlighted in each one.

The man I assumed to be Mr. Cousineau was in the corner of the room, sitting in an antique chair with a blanket across his lap. There were four other men sitting around him. Behind the chair was a freestanding metal stand holding plastic bags of what looked like medicine.

"Hello, Miyoko, how are you?" Mr. Cousineau said in a soft, genuine voice.

She stepped over to him and they held hands. He was obviously in bad health, his face tired and haggard, with three red sores on his forehead.

"Oh! I'm fine." she said. "How are you feeling?"

She continued to hold his hand, her emotions changing her ready smile.

"About as good as can be expected. My spirits are considerably better with a party going on in my house and being with old friends, like yourself, who I haven't seen in much too long a time."

Miyoko introduced me: "Robert, this is Roe's brother, Merle."

"Roe's brother?" he said, raising his eyebrows and stirring in his seat. "Well, well, this is very special."

"Good to meet you, sir."

"Listen to him: only a man with the name Merle would call me sir! It's wonderful to meet you. You look like your sister." Mr. Cousineau began to cough, and couldn't stop for a minute or so. One of the men patted his back and handed him a tissue.

"When did you arrive in Baghdad, Merle?"

"I got in town yesterday, Mr. Cousineau."

"How do you find it?"

"A little different than Nevada."

"Not too many unusual creatures for you?"

"No, we've got some creatures in Nevada, too."

"Yes, but I imagine the cowboys in our quarter may be a little—how should I put it?—different in the saddle." He smiled, folding limp hands in his lap. "Is your sister coming tonight?"

"Yes, she should be here in a few minutes."

"Good, I have some bones to pick with that woman. What is this ethnic dance extravaganza—this barbarian rite—she is involved in?"

"Robert, don't be bad," Miyoko said.

"I'm not commenting on the costumes—which are wonderful. However, at this late stage in my life, Miyoko, I take great liberty with my badness. I guess I'm just mourning the demise of a promising career.

I'm sorry to say these things, Merle. You'll have to excuse me. I just hate it when psychology gets in the way of artistic creativity. It drives me batty. We all have mothers, for heaven's sake."

"Isn't that the awful truth!" a man, sitting next to Mr. Cousineau, said. The other men laughed.

Then there was a flurry of activity at the doorway. Two men and two women walked in; the men were dressed in tuxedoes, the women in ballet outfits, walking on point; they carried bouquets of roses.

"Well, what have we here?" Mr. Cousineau exclaimed, spreading his hands out, like the teacher he was. As the women pirouetted across the room and the men broke into a song, Miyoko and I slipped over to the door.

"Miyoko and the stranger from Nevada, thank you," Mr. Cousineau said. Waving good-bye, we left the room.

Back in the living room, the party was going full throttle. The scent of marijuana wafted in the air. The crowd was dancing to music that was much too loud, with arms raised, hips thrusting, voices yelping in excitement. Miyoko began moving to the music, then she tapped me on the chest and pointed to the dance floor. Her delicate eyes twinkled, but I waved her off, frowning, pointing to my clumsy feet. She tapped me on the chest again, tipping her head towards the dance floor, faking an angry expression. All right, all right, I said to myself, remembering Mrs. Spitz's warning, here goes nothing.

We started dancing on the edge of the crowd, but Miyoko grabbed my hand and pulled me into the center of the frenzy. The music wasn't like anything I'd ever heard before: totally instrumental, pounding away without a beginning, middle, or end. I looked at Miyoko. She wagged her arms back and forth, twisting like rubber, hair falling freely all around her face; if only, at that moment, we could have been alone. I stumbled along as best I could, grateful I wasn't wearing my sandals. From across the room, I saw Terry gyrating, his forehead covered with sweat. He pointed at me with his finger: maybe it was my imagination, but it seemed that he was licking his lips as he gazed at me. I looked away, pretending I didn't see, keeping my eyes on Miyoko.

The dancing went on and on. No sooner did one song end than the synthesized back beat of a new song would kick into gear, keeping the crowd rocking. Soon my shirt was soaked with sweat and Miyoko's face looked steamy and red in the cheeks. I made a sign to stop, so we bumped and weaved our way over to the bay window.

"It feels so good. I haven't danced in ages," Miyoko said, patting her neck with a napkin.

"Did you check your toes?" I asked.

"You did great—no medical emergencies," Miyoko said affectionately, pinching me in the ribs.

Then, from across the room, I saw Roe. She was sipping on a drink and seemed serious and distracted amidst all the gaiety in the room. I knew that she saw me as well, but didn't acknowledge the fact in any obvious way. I pointed her out to Miyoko then went over to where she was standing.

"What's going on?" I asked, warm and loose in my limbs.

"Nothing," she said in an impersonal voice. "Can we talk?"

"Sure. Did you see Mr. Cousineau?"

"Yes, the past few minutes. Why don't we go up on the roof. Come with me." Down the hallway, back towards the front door, was a staircase, and we took it up to the second floor, then up to the third, where the party was nothing but a dull thud in the floor. Through a sliding door in a bedroom, we walked out onto a small rooftop patio. The cool air made my warm skin tingle. No sooner did I start taking in the diamond-like lights below, the intimate sounds of the buses and cars, than Roe started in on me.

"Merle, what were you thinking?"

"When?"

"Don't act like an idiot. At Miyoko's parents house."

An idiot? I said to myself, ruminating on that simple, cruel word. To me it seemed obvious what I was doing in attacking Jose Luis; was she ignorant of that fact?

A few moments passed. My eyes continued to wander over the city, but I could feel Roe's hostile stare pressing on my face. Finally, I turned and looked at her.

"Did you get to the rehearsal all right?" I asked innocently.

"We got there. Everything was delayed. Jose Luis couldn't even speak, he was so pissed. Why did you do it, Merle?"

"The guy's a jerk, Roe."

"That doesn't have anything to do with you. You're not in a relationship with him, I am."

"That's just it—why are you?"

"Why what?"

"Why are you involved with him? He calls you stupid, Roe. He thinks your stupid. Pretty—a ballerina—but stupid."

Roe slapped my face. The sting surged down through my body, to my feet. Two times in a week, I thought, forcing myself not to strike back.

"Roe, don't ever do that again—I'm family."

"I don't care who you are."

"Why do you always end up with these jerks, Roe? Always helpless."

"You're not listening. I don't care who you are. You don't have the right to just come here and wreck everything I've been building for myself, so just leave me alone."

I'd heard this demand before.

"Well, in the past you always cared."

"Oh! Right!"

"You always talk a good game, but in the end you need your little brother by your side for protection, to support your little dreams."

"What a pack of lies. When?"

"When? You know when," I spit out, nearly dizzy with anger. "Jesus Christ, don't ever ask me that."

Roe's eyes widened in a horrible moment of recognition. Throwing her wine glass over the side of the porch, she turned and disappeared inside the house.

Wine dripped down my hand. I wiped it off on my new jeans then rubbed my eyes, cursing myself for bringing up the past. I looked back to the galaxy of lights twinkling across the city . . .

"Merle, you think Tonopah is gonna win?"

From our hiding place behind a row of oleanders, I looked down the street and across the parking lot to the blazing rows of light over the football field. The crowd roared, then chanting started up.

"The sky could fall in. Doesn't make much difference to me."

"We're gonna destroy 'em. Slaughter 'em. Dwayne will run circles around 'em. I give us a three touchdown edge."

"Fuckin' right, Parnelli, that's the royal spirit," I yelled out, words slipping easily off my oily tongue. "We're going to crown you King of Spirit, if you keep that up."

I belched, then Parnelli belched, and we laughed at each other.

"Give me another beer," I said.

Parnelli walked to the back of his Oldsmobile and opened the trunk.

"Hey, while you're at it, get me two sixers," I added, as if talking to myself, thinking ahead to the team party after the game; rumor had it that the tribes were going to gather up the canyon at Ben Winter's parents summer house. Parnelli came back with the tall malt liquor. I gave him four bucks (dog food money that Papa had given me) then put it in the ice chest in the back of the station wagon.

"Hey, when did you get your license back? You dumb shit."

"Don't bring that up," I said, slapping Parnelli on the back. "We're havin' too gooda time."

"I was just wondering, dumb shit, how hard they nailed you for an open container."

"Six months, ass bite."

"Not bad. Good thing it was Number One."

"It wasn't, dip stick. I drove anyway."

I thought of asking Parnelli to play his tape deck, to drown out the sounds of the game. I missed drinking up in the hills, where you could be alone and closer to the stars.0

"Feels strange to be back here," Parnelli said.

"Yea, we're just ghosts coming back to haunt the place."

Just then there was a screech of tires out of the parking lot.

"Watch out," Parnelli said, turning his head to see who was passing. A Buick rumbled by, jacked up, hoodless, a strobe in the back.

"It's Billy Parton," Parnelli sneered. "The game must be over."

I gazed dreamily down to the parking lot and, sure enough, head-lights were coming on and cars were beginning to leave. Horns were honking, so we must have won the game. I tipped the cold can and guzzled as much of the beer as I could take in one breathe; then I guzzled it again and finished it, tossing the can in the dirt outside. My alcohol-fueled skin glowed warm against the crisp autumn night.

"You going up to Brian's?" I asked Parnelli.

"I'll be there."

"I have to pick up Roe first, then I'll see you."

"Drive straight."

"No pwawbwemm," I snorted.

I got in the station wagon and turned on the radio. A song I always loved—the Allman Brother's, Sweet Melissa—was playing and I turned it up. I pulled out from behind the cover of oleander and pulled into the flow of cars leaving Silver State Field. Roe was going to meet me on the far side of the field, near a storage facility where the cheerleaders always congregated after the games (waiting for admittance into the University of Utah dance program, she had taken a part-time job instructing the cheer-leader squad). I purposely drove slow and steady, nodding to the music, keeping my eyes on the rearview mirror, my every move translated by the beers I just drank. There was the blast of a horn and I saw Billy Parton speeding by again, his head sticking out his car window, screaming at me. He'll be hauled in next, I figured.

I left the traffic behind when I turned off Chaparral Street, onto a utility road that cut across the high school campus. I knew the narrow road well because it was from here that my friends and I made our raids to the school water fountain every spring, carrying large boxes of laundry detergent. At the time, it seemed like clever, important fun, but now, three years after graduation, it was disturbing to be back on the same road, with nothing better to do than to be giving my sister a ride.

Cheerleaders were everywhere when I pulled up and parked next to the storage building. They didn't walk so much as bounce as they threw blue and gold pompons in a pile at the entrance, breaking into spontaneous cheers. I looked around for Roe, but didn't see her anywhere. I slipped down in my seat to avoid being seen by any cheerleaders who might want to talk. I closed my eyes and listened to the disc jockey talk rock n'roll, impatiently waiting for the next song. I was tempted to sneak one of the beers out of the trunk.

Then there was a tap at the window. It was Roe, smiling, motioning for me to roll the window down, which I did.

"Great game."

"I didn't see it."

"Dwayne Smith got injured in the second quarter, and his substitute scored two times. Everyone loved the new cheerleader's routines. They even introduced me, which was nice."

"Sounds like you ought to give up your scholarship and come back."

"Oh! Shut up."

"Let's go," I said, sitting up.

"O.K., but there are a few things I need to do before the party. Merle, do me a favor and load those pompons in the back."

I scowled, then turned off the engine. I'd learned that it was always best to just do as my sister asked, no matter how big or small the request, because otherwise you paid the price with her pouting and bad temper. So I loaded the stuff in the station wagon (slipping a beer into my pocket in the process) as Roe said good-bye to the team, then we drove away.

"Merle, can you stop at the corner by the school auditorium? I need to meet someone."

"Come on, let's head up the canyon, Roe. I been waiting hours already."

"It'll just take a second. It's a friend of mine. We have the station wagon, let's make use of it."

Roe turned on the radio, changing the stations impatiently.

She nodded her head in time with the music, still vibrating with energy from the game.

I popped the beer top.

"What are you drinking?" she asked, leaning forward and brushing her hair.

"Beer. You want one?"

"No, I don't want one. Why would I want one? You shouldn't be driving and drinking, Merle."

"You want to drive instead?" I asked. Roe lacked confidence as a driver and I knew what her answer would be.

"No, but you're being foolish."

"That's my middle name, sister."

"Oh! Please, give me a break."

Roe turned away and looked out the window, avoiding the biting little arguments we engaged in so frequently. She put her brush back in her purse and put on some lipstick. When we came to the end of the utility road, the worst of the traffic had cleared out, so I drove around to the other side of the high school where the auditorium was located. It was dark and quiet on that side of the campus.

"Pull up here," Roe said emphatically, pointing to the curb. "There he is."

She opened the door and got out. I stared straight ahead, listening to

Roe and her friend talk in muffled tones, finishing my beer. At moments like this, I felt gloomy and disgusted; what was I, a chauffeur?

Then Roe got back inside. When the back door opened, Mr. Coolio, a student teacher from the high school, climbed in the back seat. I couldn't believe my eyes.

"Merle, you know Damion Coolio, don't you?"

"Sure, some friends of mine take your classes."

"Good evening, Merle. How are you?"

"Fine and dandy," I said. He leaned forward and shook my hand, his aftershave filling the air. I didn't have any more to say and pulled away from the curb.

Roe turned to the back seat. "Tonight, you're going to find out what the real Cherry Creek is like," she said, teasing.

He laughed, saying: "I can't wait. I've been hiding too long in the ivory towers of Lincoln High School."

I watched in the rearview mirror as they went on chitchatting. He was a self-confident guy, with wavy blonde hair and a ready smile; friends said he was fresh from graduate school in Southern California. What he was doing hanging around with us, I had no idea.

"Merle, can we go by Damion's house before we go to the party. He has a new puppy he wants to show me. It's right on the way, just off 5th Street West."

Mr. Coolio kept quiet.

What else could I do but, as always, go along with the plan. "Sure, I don't care," I said listlessly.

"How has life been since you graduated, Merle?" Mr. Coolio asked from behind my head.

"Just working out at the test sites."

"Yes, lots of jobs out there. The Feds are good to us."

"You gotta work."

"Yes, unfortunately, it's one of life's little exigencies."

When I turned onto 5th Street West, he pointed out his house half-

way up the block. It was a small place, with a thick windbreak of trees on the west side of the yard.

After they disappeared inside, I went to the back of the station wagon and got another beer. I'd like to have seen the puppy myself, but I guess I wasn't invited. I put down the back gate and sat on it, listening to the crickets conversing.

What was an "exigency" anyway, I asked myself, probably the first time I'd thought about the definition of a word since leaving high school.

I couldn't help admiring Mr. Coolio, his maturity, his job, and my resentment towards him made my blood boil. He was probably out for a little excitement with the locals, I guessed. Polishing off the beer, I threw the can into his yard as an insult then urinated in the weeds.

A few minutes passed. At one point, I thought I heard a noise—a faint voice, an exclamation—coming from the house, but it disappeared into the nothingness of the quiet neighborhood.

I turned on the radio, opened the doors, and returned to my seat. What was keeping them anyway? I was tempted to knock on the door and let them know I was ready to go, but I was suddenly repulsed by the notion of seeing the inside of Mr. Coolio's house.

I got another beer, lukewarm this time. The suds were starting to go to my head, which was always the case when I got past a six-pack. I lay back on the car hood and stared at the sky, so vast, so smeared with stars. If Cracker Joe hadn't gone north for the weekend, we'd already be at the party by now and I wouldn't be involved in this waiting game.

Then there was barking in the house. The porch light came on. When Roe and Mr. Coolio stepped out, I got up and closed the gate then got back behind the wheel, deciding to keep my mouth shut about the long wait.

To my surprise, Roe got into the back seat with Mr. Coolio. "Sorry Merle. Let's hit the party," Roe said, her voice faraway and distracted.

As we pulled out of the driveway, I rolled down the window because of Mr. Coolio's smell, which seemed stronger than before. I high-tailed it back towards the freeway and caught Wade Territory Road south. It was five miles to the turnoff to Ben Winter's folks place, so I nailed the accelerator, letting the heavyweight station wagon gain some momentum. "Be careful, Merle," Roe said from the darkness.

I kept slyly glancing at Roe and Mr. Coolio in the rearview mirror. They were quiet, each staring out opposite windows. Then I sensed something I couldn't see: maybe hands moving behind the seat.

In a split second, a thousand versions of "What is this all about?" went crashing through my mind. I checked the mirror again: Roe's face was hidden by the back of Mr. Coolio's head. He had moved over to her side. He was kissing her neck!

But glancing in the mirror was like looking through a keyhole, so I turned and looked over my shoulder.

Roe's dress was pulled up!

I looked back at the road. It was a black tunnel, except for the sparkling lane markers. What I had just seen made me drive even faster.

Roe cried out, then his voice. I turned again: Roe's hands were around his head and shoulders, one leg up against the window. Was she pushing him away? No, maybe not. Shut up and drive, I told myself, forcing my eyes to the road. Then banging started. I could see, in the mirror, Roe struggling with the teacher, who was like a vulture spread across his prey.

"Stop," Roe yelled out, as the back of my seat got kicked.

I reached back, trying to grab Mr. Coolio. His belt was undone.

"Hey, knock it off," I demanded.

"Just drive."

Just drive, just drive, I repeated, watching the road with the corner of my eye. Well, fuck that shit, I thought, checking the shoulder of the road, braking. In a quarter mile there was a wide turn-off that led out into a field. I stopped the car. Loaded with adrenaline, I jumped out and opened the back door. By now Mr. Coolio was separated from Roe—he looked out at me like a deer caught in some headlights. Roe was spread out behind him.

I had never done such a thing before, but I went in after the man and dragged him outside. He didn't put up much resistance, pleading: "O.K. Hold it. Let me explain." Then he put his hand up: "Wait, wait, just hold it." But I didn't have any ears for his explanations, so I hit him in the face. He tried to run off, but I grabbed him from behind and hit him again, this time in the stomach. He just crumbled like he was tissue paper; he didn't know how to fight. So I hit him again, and after a few seconds I realized he was just a punching bag, so I wailed on him with my fists, kicking him over and over as he collapsed on the ground.

When I was done, I heard Roe's voice echoing behind me, telling me to stop. I looked at her. She was still in the back seat, looking out, horror-stricken, but protected by the station wagon. My fists felt damaged.

Mr. Coolio let out a groan. "You son of a bitch," he said, turning over on his back. He was in no shape to stand up.

Roe got out of the car and went to him. She knelt down and put his head in her lap. "My eye, Rowena, look at my eye," he whimpered. "That son of a bitch."

Roe looked at me. "Merle," she wailed at the top of her lungs, "what did you do?"

Without a word, I rushed back to the station wagon and got inside. The engine was still running. I tried to calm down, but it was impossible. In the rearview mirror, Roe was sitting on the ground, consoling the asshole. I put it into drive and took off.

I'd never felt so lonely as driving down that stretch of highway, my heart pounding, eyes unfocused, with Roe and that man somewhere in the dark behind me. I flew, clickety-clack, over a cattle guard, then the lights of a small market appeared and disappeared like the explosion of a flash bulb.

And soon I was moving too fast. There were yellow signs, a curve in the road, and in a split second the wagon went into a long, uncontrolled slide—

—Sometime later, my mind emerged out of an oily black pool.

There were white and blue lights everywhere, flashing, beating, around and around, and voices—unrecognizable voices. Hands were pulling at me like I was a puppet . . .

"Merle?"

I looked up and saw Miyoko. I glanced away, startled and embarrassed.

"Hey, what's wrong?" she asked.

A thousand sad questions, and some answers, seemed to well up inside of me and I couldn't respond. I just stood there, shaking my head, self-conscious as never before.

Miyoko stepped closer, as if she sensed my struggle, and touched my back, then kept her hand there, rubbing in small circles.

"Roe and I got in a fight," I said in a subdued voice.

"I saw her inside. She left to go back to rehearsal."

"Good . . . No, I didn't mean it that way." I slammed my fist down on the porch rail. "I'm sorry, Miyoko. I've only known you a couple hours and here you have to deal with this soap opera. All I'm doing is fighting shit, I can't help it."

Miyoko kept silent, listening.

"But it's true, I—don't—want—to—see—Roe!" I announced, keeping time on the rail with my clenched fist. "It's funny, but it feels so good just to say that."

I loosened my hand and turned back to Miyoko, smiling and trying to lighten up a little bit.

Miyoko stepped in front of me. "What do you want?"

I looked at her; her hand stopped moving on my back, holding firm.

"You, that's for sure. I'd like to have you."

"Well, go for it," she said softly.

Go for it? I asked myself. No problem!

So I grabbed her around the waist and pulled her close. I

dug my hands into her hair, right down to the scalp, which caused her to murmur, then I kissed, again and again, her tasty champagne-flavored mouth.

The next morning birds chattered away outside the window above the bed in the cottage. Although the room was still dark, the sun was beginning to illuminate the tops of the curtains. I figured it was late morning.

I turned over on my back. Miyoko stirred and draped her arm across my chest, moving close to me. "My ears are still pounding," she said, her breathe warm on my face.

After leaving Mr. Cousineau's, we'd driven down to the Mission District and gone dancing in two nightclubs, happily lost in a tangle of feelings for each other. Afterwards, to my surprise, she suggested spending the night together, so, despite being guilt-ridden because of Mrs. Spitz, I snuck her into my temporary digs.

I kept staring at the ceiling, afraid to look at Miyoko for fear of breaking the wonderful spell I was under. I could hardly believe what had happened between us; I felt like the luckiest guy on earth.

"This is a wonderful place," she said, desiring conversation. "I never visited Roe here."

I didn't say anything.

"Do you do carpentry work, Merle? You seem like a guy who would build houses."

"Naw, I really haven't got any skills."

"Oh! Hardly," she said, kissing my arm.

Full of myself, but embarrassed too, I turned towards Miyoko. Taking her sleepy face in my hands, I kissed her passionately, nibbling her ear. She quietly accepted my affections, but wasn't moved the way she'd been during the nighttime. She kept talking.

"You'll find what it is you want to do," she said encouragingly. "I found costume design, then, of course, Chester changed my life more than anything."

My penis awakened. It was like a hungry trout between my legs, and I positioned myself to put it between hers. I brushed her bangs away and rubbed her neck, admiring her skin, which was so unblemished it was almost gray. I just wanted her to stop talking so I could enjoy this rare piece of heaven I'd found.

Then we heard a banging door and low voices. I guessed that Mrs. Spitz and Gustavo were talking. Miyoko seemed to hear the voices, too, because she fell silent. We lay still for a minute, the world outside invading the room.

"Merle?"

"Yea."

"Thank you so much."

"There is nothing to thank me for, darlin'. I'm the one—"

"No, you've been very generous and very nice, but I have to tell you something."

"Sure, go ahead. We've talked about pretty much everything, so give it a go."

She paused for a long moment. "I don't know what you have in mind about us, but this is about it. I'm not going to be able to see you any more after this."

I kept my mouth shut, numb, waiting.

Miyoko propped her head on her arm and looked at me.

"I've been seeing someone for a couple years, ever since I got divorced from Chester's father. He's been away. He's getting back from Europe at the end of the month."

I scratched the new stubble of my beard. "That's all right, don't worry about it."

Miyoko's expression turned serious.

"I've been selfish. I'm sorry. You seem like you really want something new in your life and I've just set up this, this disappointment. You just shouldn't have looked at me with those eyes of yours."

Son of a bitch, I thought, turning onto my back.

"But San Francisco has so much to offer," she continued. "You can find whatever—"

"Let's forget about it, Miyoko. I don't have any right to expect anything from you. It's water under the bridge."

A lawnmower started up outside, drowning out what peace remained between us, so we got up and showered and dressed, with the plan that I would drop her off at her parent's house.

When we came out of the door of the cottage, Mrs. Spitz was sitting on the back porch, sipping tea, talking to Gustavo. She called out to me and I told her I'd be right back; I walked Miyoko out to the truck then returned to the backyard.

"You act very quickly, young man, and without due consideration."

"I'm sorry, Mrs. Spitz, I had no right to do that. It was a total surprise."

"Don't you know, you have to be careful with surprises these days."

"Right."

"I don't want you to be a resident here without paying rent."

"Yes, ma'am."

"Did you talk with Roe?"

"Yea, I did."

"How is she?"

"She's real busy dancing."

"I'm glad to hear it."

"Listen," I said, dipping into my pant pocket, "I have the back rent money you asked about." I pealed off eight hundred dollars and handed it to Mrs. Spitz. She was surprised and seemed hesitant to take the money.

"Thank you. Roe must have received a considerable raise at her new dance troupe. Do you want to pay rent for yourself? You're welcome to have the cottage."

"Let me think about it, Mrs. Spitz. I'm kind of living one day at a time. I'm in a bit of a rush right now, but I appreciate the offer."

"I understand. Away with you."

I dropped Miyoko off at her parent's house. I offered to give her and Chester a ride back to Albion Place, but she said she had business to take care of. I had the feeling she didn't want her son to get any funny ideas by seeing the two of us together in the morning hours.

There was nothing to do but go and talk to Roe and try to clear up what had happened the previous day, so I drove back to Albion Place. When I knocked at the apartment door, Roe answered.

"Hi," she said, leaving the door open and walking away.

The apartment was deadly quiet. In daylight, the real features of the place—the rough brick walls, concrete floors, industrial windows—were visible, making the space less hospitable than it had been the previous night.

"Is Jose Luis here?"

"No, he's not here. He'd probably wring your neck."

No, I'd wring his neck, I said to myself with certainty.

We sat down on stools at the kitchen counter.

"I'm sorry about all that," I said.

"Don't worry about it," she said nervously. "He's already gone to the Palace of Fine Arts."

She was wearing a bathrobe, her hair wet and freshly combed. She poured a cup of coffee and handed it to me, then, about to pour her own, she started to cry. She put her hands on the counter and hung her head for a moment, then suddenly looked up and stared at me.

"You won't believe who I just talked to."

I told her to fill me in.

"Mother and Papa."

I laughed. "What are you talking about? When—just now?"

"About an hour ago," she said. "They're here—there in San Francisco."

I took a sip of coffee and cleared my throat, trying not to show my astonishment.

"Well, what did they say?"

"They want to see us. They're at the Marquis Hotel on Union Square. Shit, I don't need this right now." She walked over to a sound system against the wall and turned off the background music.

"But that works out all right," I said, encouragingly, "They can see you dance tonight."

"No, no! That's exactly what I don't want," Roe asserted, pacing around the center of the apartment, working herself into a rage. "Don't you understand? This piece I'm in, Mother would go crazy if she saw me doing it."

"So what—this is what you're committed to right now. Isn't that why you left the Academy?"

"Do they know I left?"

"I think."

"But I don't want them to know everything, Merle. It would be such a disappointment for them, such a complication. They'll just be here for a short visit, then they'll go back home and everything will return to normal, so let's just do what's easiest for everyone. We'll make up some story about what I'm doing."

She sat down on the stool again, wiping her eyes. "I need your help with this one. Are you with me?" She reached out and touched my knee. "I don't want to let Mother and Papa down any more than I already have."

"Whatever. It's your life," I said.

Just then I heard the elevator doors in the hallway outside, then Chester's voice.

"Miyoko's back from her parents."

"Yea. No doubt about it."

Roe dressed, then we drove over to the hotel. The whole way, Roe described and rehearsed exactly what we would say to our parents about her circumstances.

"This traffic is a mess," she commented when we reached Union Square. "Merle, park in that lot just past Neiman Marcus. We can walk over to the Marquis."

I pulled into the entrance and we plunged underground, circling three levels down before finding a parking space.

Waiting in the bleak shadows for an elevator to ground level, Roe commented sullenly, "City living."

"You ever miss Cherry Creek?"

"Not much. Sometimes I miss the fields of sage, the smell of it, especially after a spring rain. But nothing else."

"Are you going to come back and visit?"

"Not until I've accomplished what I need to accomplish."

But you can't even talk honestly about what that is, I noted silently, looking at her face, which seemed bizarre and distorted in the dim light.

We finally got in the elevator and lurched upward.

"I've been thinking about last night," Roe said, keeping her eyes on the changing numbers above the elevator door.

"What about it?"

"How I always get blamed for things."

I had to bite my lip to keep from insulting her.

The elevator doors opened and we stepped out into the sunlight. Roe led me up some steps into a small park in the center of the square. As if hypnotized by some need to talk, we sat down on a stone bench.

"Why do you and Mother and Papa always do that?" she asked.

"Do what? Blame you? Nobody's blaming you. I'm the one with the record around my neck. You're cruising."

"Just stop it," she said, as if giving me an order. She reached in her purse. I expected her to pull out a brush for her hair, but instead she brought out a pair of sunglasses. I looked away, scowling at a noisy group of young Asian children walking by, all dressed in identical dark blue outfits. I had to take the high dive, I thought, determined to know.

"Roe, I've been remembering—thinking about—a lot of things. Why didn't you help me that night?"

"Don't cling to the past, Merle; believe me, it won't do you any good," she said, putting on the sunglasses. Sitting back and crossing her legs, she had the haughty look of a model about to be photographed.

"I'm not clinging to anything, just remembering."

Silence. Roe tipped her head back and took in the weak sun.

"Why didn't you come back that night?" I repeated.

"I phoned the police."

"Shit, don't you think I know that? But why didn't you find me and help me."

"I couldn't."

"I was cracked up in the middle of nowhere. I could—"

"Damion didn't want me to."

Hearing that name lit a fuse inside of me. I sat up and held out my hands. "So what? Who cares if he didn't want you to?"

"What are you talking about? You had just beaten him to a pulp."

"But I was helping you."

"How can you say that?"

"He was attacking you."

"You're crazy, Merle."

"What did you want—a driver, so you could fuck him in the back seat? Was that it?" I stood up in front of her.

"It's all a blur."

"I'm your brother, Roe, and you were thinking of him, not me. Don't you see? That's what hurts."

"He was controlling me, Merle."

"And you were helpless?"

"Sexually."

"I knew that."

"He raped me, Merle."

"That's why I stopped."

"No, not there. Inside the house." She drew her legs up and encircled them with her arms, resting her face on her knees.

I stared at her, licking my dry lips.

"I was under his control. I did what I was told."

"And you were under his control when he brought charges?"

"I guess so."

I stood looking down at Roe, considering her words. She was damaged goods. I saw that now. But we were just comparing losses—what was the use of it? I knelt down in front of her.

"Listen, Roe. I'm sorry, I know the whole thing is a can of worms, but . . . don't you understand? *He* should have gone to prison, not me."

She raised her head up and took off her sunglasses, wiping tears off her face.

"I've never said anything about that to anyone," she said, as if she hadn't understood a thing about me, only the implications of her own words. Forget it, I thought bitterly.

On the far side of the park, an ensemble of black-clad musicians struck up a song, the sweetness of the jumping flutes and guitars ruined by a small, crude PA system. Both of us stared at the group, relieved at being distracted from each other.

"They need some new speakers," I said.

"You're right. They're from Peru."

I sat back down on the bench. We both looked at each other, then Roe put her hand on my leg affectionately.

"Don't you wish we'd been raised in San Francisco. Maybe in Pacific Heights, with a view of the water?"

I skeptically mulled over the idea.

"Then maybe Mother and Papa, all of us, would have been different." She continued: "The Honeycutt's together, not these separate . . . pieces of honey that we are now."

I hated Roe when she talked like that, dreaming out loud. "We should go," I said.

"Yea, we're late. God, I'm nervous as a cat about this."

The Marquis Hotel was just a couple blocks away. As Roe checked at the front desk for our parent's room number, I gawked at the fancy decor of white antique furniture, elaborate mirrors, and crystal chandeliers. When we arrived at their room on the 11th floor, Mother answered the door.

"Well, you've finally made it. Come in."

Roe tried to push me through the door first, but I held back, so she reluctantly stepped inside.

"What have you done to yourself?" Mother asked Roe, kissing her on the check, touching her hair. "You look so much older, so mature."

"Do you like it?" Roe asked.

"Yes, of course, dear," she smiled. "Just give me a moment to adjust."

We moved into the elegantly furnished room. Mother immediately opened the gold drapes framing a tall window. Streams of light entered the room, revealing an intimate view of the windows and fire escapes of neighboring buildings. On a table in the corner was an open briefcase with papers and pamphlets strewn about.

"Papa will be out in a minute. He's shaving. Hello, Merle. You I've seen recently."

"Hi, Mother."

We exchanged a hug in the center of the room.

"And look at you. What's going on here? Did your sister have anything to do with this transformation."

"What are you talking about?" Roe asked, sitting down and crossing her legs.

"A week ago Merle looked like a prospector, just off a bender. And now he's clean-cut and handsome."

"I like his tattoo," Roe said.

"That is entirely a matter of opinion. Obviously, it's a ridiculous looking thing."

"Mother, you haven't seen Roe's ear," I countered, settling down on the bed.

"What about it?" Mother asked curiously.

Roe proudly turned her head to the side, so that Mother could see the row of small gold rings.

"Good Lord. Don't do this to me so soon. You don't look like a dancer any longer." She moved over to the bathroom door. "Bob? The kids are here. Are you almost done?' There was the sound of water and a garbled voice from inside. Mother rolled her eyes, saying, "Everything takes so long now." She seemed self-conscious standing in front of us, and sat down in a chair across from Roe.

"Darling, tell me everything. What have you been doing? We've been worried to death."

Roe moved in her seat. "Well, I stopped dancing with the ballet—"

"Wait, don't mention that. We need to talk about your plans. I have some ideas and I want to talk to you about them, but later—alone. Anyway, what are you doing now?"

"Not much really."

"Are you working?"

"I'm teaching ballet classes."

"Are you really? Where?"

"At a small private school."

"And where are you living?"

"In the Mission."

"The Mission. Where is that? I don't know this city. I was just looking at some brochures to learn more about the different neighborhoods, events, things we could do during the visit."

The bathroom door opened and Papa stepped out. He didn't pay us any mind and went about putting away his accessories bag in his suitcase. Almost mechanically, without looking at one another, Roe and I stood up, waiting until he emerged out of the shadows of the closet.

"Hello kids," he said.

We echoed his greeting. Roe threw her arms around Papa, burying her head in his neck, and they stayed embraced for a few long moments. Then he shook my hand. He smelled of aftershave and the scent reminded me of innumerable mornings in years past—at the breakfast table, traveling to work.

"Look at us," Mother said, as we stood at attention like bowling pins, "all here together."

"Yea, who would have thought?" Roe remarked. "How long are you staying?"

"We aren't sure. Probably a few days," Mother said, putting a red scarf around her neck, which complemented her gray pant suit. She looked smart and fashionable. "We can only keep the plane at the airport until next Wednesday, so I doubt if it will be longer than that."

"You flew in the Cessna?" I said, trying not to let out that I was absolutely confounded as to how the two of them had come together and made the trip, taking into consideration Papas condition and their separate lives.

"It was a good flight," Papa reported in a low steady voice. He stood perfectly still, as if his feet had no function. "Some high turbulence down by Bakersfield, that was about it." He kept a steady eye on Roe, who kept smiling back at him. I sat down on the bed again. "But don't get the idea this is a vacation," he added.

"Oh! But there's lots of things to do in San Francisco," Roe said, "especially this time of year."

Papa kept his eyes on Roe. "Do you think we wanted to leave Cherry Creek? No, we came here to find you."

Mother turned and looked at herself in the mirror, checking the scarf. "Let's go downstairs everybody, maybe have some lunch."

"Where have you been, Rowena?" Papa continued.

Roe appeared frightened for a moment, then resentful. Papa faced her, hard as a statue, and it seemed that time stood still.

"Papa, you know where I've been. I haven't been hiding anything."

"We guessed. We guessed you were still in San Francisco. We heard nothing from you. Our daughter joins the ballet in California and we never hear from her again. Why? Tell me why?"

"I wrote letters. I talked with Mother."

"Letters? What letters? I didn't see anything. What good are letters you never see?"

"Papa, for God sake, stop this," Mother insisted. She picked up a blue windbreaker from the top of the chest of drawers and put it in Papa's unsuspecting hand. "We've been together five minutes and you're interrogating your own daughter. No matter what's being said, I'm here for a vacation, so let's enjoy ourselves."

Papa grunted, shaking his head in aggravation.

"I'm going to the bathroom," Roe said, fleeing the situation.

I sat on the bed, situated between Mother shuffling papers on the desk and Papa slowly putting on his jacket.

"Honey, try to control yourself," Mother complained to Papa, "you're upsetting Roe."

"But she's upset me. For months and months."

"You should have let me know."

"What could you have done?"

"I don't know, something. Do you have to go to a pharmacy?"

"No. No, I don't."

"Good."

Mother clapped her hands together.

"Merle, how are you?"

"I'm doing fine."

"San Francisco looks like it has done you good. I, myself, feel like a child in a candy shop being here. Do you have any suggestions about where to have lunch?"

"I wouldn't know, Mother. I've been all over the place, some good areas, some not so good."

The bathroom door opened and Roe stepped out.

"Roe, we were just talking about where to have lunch. I was reading about North Beach. Is that a good spot? Its history sounded so interesting, with the Italians, the Chinese, the Beat Poets."

"Sure, North Beach is filled with places to eat," Roe said, "What do you feel like having?"

"Well, your father isn't accustomed to anything too spicy.

But what about if you and I go do some shopping in Union Square first—let the boys here do what they want—and we'll have lunch in an hour or two."

"Whatever you want, Mother. But I have to be back at my place by four o' clock."

"Maybe we could go someplace nice for dinner tonight. Something fancy, for a celebration."

"I can't. I have classes to teach and a meeting to attend. I'm sorry, but your visit was a surprise and I already had these previous commitments. I can't change them."

"Well, I'm sorry to hear that. We'll do the best we can. Everybody ready to go?"

We left the hotel. As Mother and Roe took off down the street, Papa and I ambled along slowly. After a short distance, a city bus screeched up to the curb next to us. A crowd quickly formed to board. I stepped to the center of the sidewalk to avoid all the people, but Papa got surrounded.

"Pardon me," he said to no one in particular, clumsily, single-mindedly, trying to move straight ahead.

The bus door opened and people surged forward. I stepped over to help Papa, grabbing his arm, but he jerked it away.

"Move, I need to get through!" he pleaded in a louder voice.

"Excuse me. Excuse me. I'm standing here," a young man complained. He was dressed in a blue, three-piece suit with horn-rim glasses. He picked up a briefcase, which was the size of a suitcase, blocking Papa even more.

"Is this a line?" Papa asked.

"You're very observant, old man."

"Who are you calling old man? Get out of my way."

The man raised his hands up in mock fear, "Whoa, don't get mean on me now."

The driver yelled out: "Doors closing." The man quickly

stepped aboard the bus with the others, leaving us alone on the sidewalk.

Papa charged off in a huff and I skipped along to keep up.

We found Mother and Roe standing in front of a store, Gaylord's Antique Sellers.

"Anything wrong?" Mother asked.

"I don't think I've stood in a line in twenty years. I'm not starting now," Papa vented.

"Whatever are you talking about?" Mother asked, looking at me for an explanation. I shrugged my shoulders, unable to explain the ridiculous confrontation.

Mother took Papa's arm and they moved down the street.

"Merle, come over here," Roe said. "Look at this." On the wall, above a clutter of vases and gaudy costume jewelry, Roe pointed out a framed photograph, titled: "San Francisco City Dog Show Championships—Golden Gate Park, 1938."

"Look who took third place," Roe said. There was a Russian wolfhound standing with its handler on a low podium, alongside the other winners.

"Do you think Papa would like it?"

"That photograph?"

"Yea."

"He doesn't raise dogs anymore."

"He doesn't?" she said, laughing away her exasperation. "What's happening with this family? Is anything the same?"

"No, not really, not even the dogs."

We played catch up with our parents, who we could see down the sidewalk, close to the square.

"Can you believe Papa—verbally attacking me like that?"

"He's not quiet and strong anymore. He just spits the truth out now."

"The truth?"

"Well, it is the truth, isn't it," I said, glancing at my sister, who had a vulnerable look on her face. "I left without a word. You disappeared. What are they supposed to think?"

"But that's bullshit. That's not considering all the reasons why we left in the first place."

As we approached Mother and Papa were gazing up at a hotel. "I've seen this place in an old Clark Gable movie," Mother said. "It's the St. Francis. It's just gorgeous. And look at Union Square." She pointed admiringly at the statue of a bugler on top of the tower in the center of the square.

"Mother, you're sounding like a tourist—boring," Roe said.

"Stop it. I am a tourist. I don't have the opportunity to live here, like you."

"Well, sell the house," Roe said sarcastically. "Anyway, what's the plan?"

It was decided we would all meet in North Beach in two hours, at a restaurant that Roe recommended, Fior di' Italia. Mother and Roe would tour the stores in Union Square, then take a taxi to met us; Papa and I would drive the truck to North Beach and bide our time until lunch.

While everyone waited, I went to the parking garage and returned with the truck. Papa slowly climbed inside, looking in the rearview mirror at a driver who was repeatedly honking his horn at us. "Just take your time, Merle, don't mind that pest," he said. Mother and Roe said good-bye and walked off into the crowd of shoppers, while Papa and I pulled out into the congested traffic.

I didn't know where I was going and asked Papa to look at the city map. At a stop light, a cable car trundled by, bell clanging, loaded with people, so, for no good reason, I made a right turn and followed behind it for a block or two. Like rats lost in a maze, we eventually, accidentally, found ourselves in the middle of Chinatown, crawling along behind laundry trucks and taxis.

"Watch it," Papa blurted out, and I braked for the pedestrians surging off the sidewalk. "God damn, it's crowded."

"Missin' Cherry Creek already?"

"Don't you? Look what we're doing: sitting in traffic, surrounded by a bunch of strangers from all around the world. You call this fun? I'll take the open spaces, thank you."

To get off the crowded street, I turned into an alleyway that plummeted steeply downhill. We passed what seemed like the back doors of restaurants and markets, and everywhere there were rows of crates filled with vegetables and chickens. We finally came down to a stoplight. "This is Kearny Street, Papa, can you check the map again?" I asked.

Old Asian men dressed in dark suits were playing checkers at tables in a doorway.

"I was surprised you and Mother came here."

"Didn't think I could fly that far, did you?"

"Naw, it wasn't that. It's just that you two didn't seem like you were on the same wave length."

"I went to the front house to break the ice. We were concerned about Roe, that was pretty much it."

"Roe's changed, Papa."

"We've all changed."

"She's not a ballerina anymore."

"Well, your mother is going to see to that."

"What do you care if she dances ballet or not? I mean, what difference does it really make?"

"Hell, I don't know. It's your mother's idea, always has been. I suppose it's always been Roe's ticket out of Cherry Creek."

"What's my ticket then?"

"I don't know what your ticket is, Merle." He looked up from the map. "You sure are filled with a lot of questions today. The light's green. We should turn left."

I was expecting North Beach to be near the water, the wharves, with seagulls flying around, but it was just another business area filled with restaurants, bookstores and strip joints. We drove around for a good ten minutes looking for parking, finally finding a spot on a hill above the shopping district.

We climbed out of the truck and looked around, like two scouts on a mountain peak gazing into uncharted territory. The street was so steep, it was difficult to walk normally. I started laughing.

"What's wrong?" Papa asked.

"We're lost. I've been a mile up in the sky with you, and a hundred miles into the test sites, but I've never seen you lost before."

A twinkle of recognition came into his eyes, and he grumbled, "That's why they make cities: to get lost in. We should expect this."

We looked down the hill, at the mass of buildings and rush of activity along the streets. A car horn blared annoyingly, answered by another. "Well, we know that down there is where we're meeting the girls. Why don't we avoid that mess as long as we can."

After Papa took a minute to pull out, prepare, and light a cigar, we carefully crossed the street, which dropped off just as precipitously on the eastern side of the hill.

A woman, walking a dog, strolled by. "Just like a postcard, isn't it?" she said. I waited for Papa to respond, but he didn't say anything, so I told the woman that, yes, it was a beautiful view.

"Let's stick to the high road here," I said, pointing north along a narrow lane. "We can stay on level ground that way."

Papa shuffled along, lost in thought, the cigar jutting out of his mouth. I was tempted to take his arm, out of affection, but I knew he would throw a fit if I did.

"Where did you say you were working these days?"

"I didn't say."

"But I'm asking you."

"Papa, why don't we enjoy San Francisco a little bit? This is the first time we've been here."

"I am enjoying it, every last step."

"I'm working at a rock shop in Fallon. Just a temporary gig."

"Doesn't sound like that's going to make you much money. I can talk to Bill Phelps at Shelby and see if he can put you on."

"I don't think so."

"Now, don't give me that. Just because I'm not working—disabled—crazy as a road lizard—doesn't mean I can't pull a couple strings for my own son."

"But I don't want to work on the test sites."

"You can get in the union, get some stability."

"But I don't want to work in Cherry Creek."

"You want to be a grunt in Fallon? Is that right?"

"I don't know right now."

"Well, decide. It's time you decided what you want to do with your life. When I go back to work, I'll bring you aboard."

"Thanks, but no thanks."

"I didn't kill anybody, Merle," Papa said strangely. "Don't worry."

"Jesus Christ, Papa, take it easy. I wasn't talking about that. Come on, enjoy your vacation."

"Son, you can't take a vacation when you're not working."

We came to a bend in the street, where we passed a little restaurant, Julia's Castle, which was huddled by itself in the otherwise residential area. We looked inside, hoping to have a quiet place to stop and relax, but the establishment was closed for renovation.

"It's all for the best, I can't have a drink because of the medication anyway."

I agreed; I didn't want a drink either. Like an unexpected

falling star, the Rambling Rose dropped into my mind, and I was hit by a momentary feeling of physical revulsion.

We kept walking. Passing a hillside covered with a large public garden, the lane opened up into a wider street, with a bridge-to-bridge view of the bay. Sailboats were scattered like confetti across the water; the sky was a vivid blue, the only clouds to be seen, clustered far away on the southern horizon.

Just then the air cracked with a high-pitched sound, and I practically jumped out of my skin.

"What was that?" I asked.

"Fighters—look."

Down below, four jets shot across the surface of the bay, not a hundred feet above the water. The jets were an identical dark blue, with gold stripes on the short wings. The two inside jets were spinning repeatedly.

"The Blue Angels! How about that," Papa said with admiration, squinting his eyes to see more clearly. Twirling the cigar in his mouth, Papa stood on his tiptoes, watching the jets speed under the Golden Gate Bridge and disappear out into the Pacific Ocean. "Did you know about this?" he asked.

I wished I had, but I told him, no, it was a total surprise.

We kept our eyes on the Golden Gate Bridge: within a minute, a distant whining could be heard and the jets shot under the bridge, weaving as they skimmed the water. In a matter of moments, they crossed to the eastern side of the bay, then, in unison, made a looping turn and, single-file, disappeared south under the Bay Bridge.

"They're the best, those F-16 Eagles, and the pilots flying them. Cream of the crop.

Freddie Betts, a guy who lived down the street in Mercury, used to be an Angel; he could do anything—anything—with a stick. I didn't know the squad was still around; thought it might have been eliminated in a budget cut or some nonsense.

Remember them at the spring air shows on the base?"

"I remember," I said.

Our eyes were caught again, like children at a circus, as two jets met in the middle of the bay, shooting straight up in the air, defying gravity like rockets. Then each made back dives down towards the water, pulling out and averting disaster at the last second.

A crowd of people on the hill above us, standing at the base of a tower, burst into cheers, and we found ourselves applauding, too. The flying continued on for another fifteen minutes, then, as a finale, all four jets said good-bye with one last sonic blast, disappearing into the northern sky.

Everything was suddenly still and quiet. The air was filled with intersecting white lines of engine exhaust, now growing in size, diffusing. I looked over at Papa. He was staring at the ground, his hands, the cigar, shaking slightly.

"Papa, are you O.K.?"

He nodded his head slowly, methodically, as if trying to control the meaning of his own thoughts.

"You know, I tried every which way to get in a jet cockpit: the Air Force, the air lines, private companies. Those jets—I don't know how to explain it—flying one of those always seemed like gravy to me, like freedom. Everything else was just the same old stuff: running crews, you kids, the bills.

I spent fifteen years chasing that dream, but I never could pass the spatial perception exam. Too stupid, I guess."

I patted him on the shoulder.

"Hell, Papa, you flew here, didn't you? A lot of people are afraid to ride a roller coaster."

"Yea, but it's hard when you look back and don't like what you see." He looked over at me, flicking the ash from his cigar. "You—you have your freedom in the palm of your hand. Damn it, Merle, do something with it."

I looked out to the Golden Gate Bridge; ant-like cars swarmed along the span. In that moment, I wished I'd had a grand design for myself, an ambitious plan that I could express to Papa—something he would be proud of—but I couldn't conjure up what it would be. I was on the run, and running wasn't freedom, no matter what anybody said.

"Sorry, Papa. I do want you to be proud of me."

"Don't be a baby, Merle. Forget about Breckenridge."

"I'm not thinking about Breckenridge," I said, shocked by his words.

"Yes, you are. Everybody sees it."

I felt stunned; my face felt like a puzzle that didn't fit together right. I was so pissed I could have taken Papa's cigar and shoved it in his eye. I turned away for a long, uncomfortable minute.

"I'm sorry, son. I'm shooting off at the mouth," Papa finally said. "You're the one who did time, so you're the one who knows about all that, not me, not the family, not anybody."

I faced him again. "Yea, Papa, it was no fun. And you never came to see me."

"I was trying to teach you a lesson," he said, pausing. "I was wrong."

"You ever been in jail?" I asked.

"Sure."

"When?"

"Starting in 1957, when I moved to Cherry Creek." He smiled with his sad wrinkled eyes, and it made me smile, too. For a moment we just stood there, eye to eye, understanding each other.

"That sounds like something Mother would complain about," I said.

"You got a point there. She's a walking contradiction, that woman, always negative about the very place she's chosen to spend her whole life. I could barely drag her here to San Francisco."

"Why's that?"

"It's hard to explain. She has her reasons—old reasons—most of which I'm tired of."

The woman with the dog strolled by again. She reminded me of a middle-aged Mrs. Spitz in her confident, dignified manner.

"Is that racket over with?" she asked. The dog, a Pekinese, tiptoed up, then yipped shrilly.

"The skies are clear," Papa answered.

"Good. This is the last year they're having that show. There have been complaints about how loud the whole thing is."

"That's too bad. I enjoyed it. That sure is a handsome dog you have there," Papa said. He knelt down and put out his hand.

The Pekinese moved its hind legs in nervous excitement, then yipped again.

"Desmond, quiet. He is not on his best behavior today, I'm afraid."

"That's all right," Papa stood up, smiling, "We all have our moods."

After saying good-bye to the woman and her annoying companion, we walked back to the truck and drove down to Fior di' Italia.

Two hours later, Mother and Roe walked into the restaurant.

Mother rushed up to the table. She was carrying a Macy's shopping bag. "I'm sorry we're late," she said, sitting down at our table near the window, placing the package in her lap.

"Mother had to go shopping," Roe said, collapsing in a chair. "There were crowds everywhere. It was a major pain."

Papa tore off a piece of sourdough bread and began chewing it.

"What have you two been doing?" Mother asked.

"Sitting here, waiting for you," Papa said.

"The whole time?"

"No. We saw an air show from up on the hill," Papa said, pointing with his finger, his mouth filled with bread.

"An air show—what do you mean?" Roe asked.

"The Blue Angels flew over the bay," I said.

Mother responded: "With this lovely view outside, I can't say I really care. Just look at it." We all glanced out the large sunny window, across a small square surrounded by trees, to a church. Mother continued: "Did you know that Marilyn Monroe and Joe DiMaggio were married in that church. That's straight from the expert here."

Roe looked over at the bar, raising her hand for the waiter. "That's me—San Francisco tour guide. Herb Caen is dead, so anything you need to know about the Barbary Coast, just ask me."

Mother turned and looked around the room, admiring the mural of the Italian countryside over the bar.

"Have you eaten anything yet?" she asked, turning back.

"No," Papa answered.

"Let's order quickly. Roe has a dance lesson to teach."

"When is that?" Papa asked.

"At five o' clock," Roe said. "Can you give me a ride, Merle?"

"Sure. We parked close by."

After we examined the menu, a waiter came up to the table and introduced himself as Rafael, talking in a cigarette-worn Italian accent. He took our food and drink orders, collected the menus, then stepped away.

"Isn't this nice that we're all here together?" Mother said.

"Just like the old days," Roe said, "except that Merle isn't such a little brat any more. Don't you think he looks dashing in his new haircut?"

"I wouldn't talk about haircuts, Roe," I said, looking at my sister and laughing. "And try to make it through the meal without crying."

She leaned back to let the waiter serve the drinks, glancing at me with sweet maliciousness. "A dagger to my heart. I'm collapsing."

"Don't slip a disc," I said, sipping my soda, "you won't be able to dance."

"Children, children, some things never change," Mother said sarcastically. "Roe, where are you staying now? When are Papa and I going to see your place?"

Roe shrugged before she spoke. "I'm actually in between apartments and staying with some friends. It might be better for me just to drop by the hotel."

Mother turned to Papa.

"Roe said that she is going to be returning to the Academy in the fall. She just needed a break—she was physically worn out with the practice routine. It was six days a week, six hours a day."

Papa nodded his head, brushing some bread crumbs into his hand. "When are you going to come home and visit?" he asked, dumping the crumbs in an ashtray.

"I don't know, Papa. It's been pretty crazy. I haven't had any money."

"You can ask us for plane fare. Or I can fly you."

"I know, I've just been too busy."

He stared at Roe.

She kept her eyes down, sipping her juice, and asked, "What's going on at work, Papa?"

"You're changing the subject."

"I was just curious, that's all."

"I'm just retired for a while."

"You're not retired. Don't say that," Mother insisted.

"Still on the couch with Dr. Pfund?"

"Sure, he's a good man."

"I just can't imagine you seeing a psychiatrist, Papa," Roe said, raising her eyebrows and smirking. "Does he have a little goatee?"

"I don't know what you're talking about, Rowena," Papa answered.

"Good," Mother said quickly. "Roe, let's change subjects."

Mother tasted her wine, announcing to the open air, "I've got a headache from rushing around." She picked up the package she'd set on the chair and opened it.

"This is for you, Merle," she said, handing me the open box. It was a blue, pinstriped shirt with a matching tie.

"Pretty fancy," I said, holding the apparel to my chest and turning to everyone.

"Isn't it nice?" Mother said. "Roe thought I should get a shirt with some God-awful design on it: some rock n" roll group—"

"I didn't think he would want to wear institutional blue again," Roe said.

I tipped my head towards Roe, annoyed by her comment, but she kept her eyes on the sidewalk outside, ignoring me.

"Do you like it?" Mother asked.

I looked back at the shirt. "Thanks. I'm just not sure where I'm going to wear it." I put the garment back in the box and set it on the chair.

"That's a good question," Papa agreed. "I have a closet full of them."

"If he went to school he could wear it; for interviews he could wear it; if he worked for a business he could wear it. It's very practical."

"I told him he should come back and work on the crew."

"He's done that, Bob," Mother said.

The waiter came up and set up his serving tray, then quickly returned with the plates of food. Papa and I were served our spaghetti with meatballs; Mother, her breaded calamari appetizer; and Roe, a salad—no doubt avoiding eating too much because of the evening's performance.

"What's little brother going to do with himself?" Roe asked provocatively, picking up her fork and looking at me before examining her salad.

"I don't know. I haven't given it much thought. Been too busy tracking you down."

"Leaving home and traveling would do you good," she insisted.

"O.K., God," I said, stirring my spaghetti, cooling it off.

"Are you thinking about coming to San Francisco?"

"I haven't thought about it one way or the other."

"Sure you haven't—" she said, poking at an anchovy.

"I've been away from home, Roe," I pointed out. In a flash, I thought of Biggs, the spring site on King Lear peak, his mysteriously, criminally, knowing about the artifacts, his staking out the string line and digging. "For two years I've been away."

"No, I mean getting out of Nevada, getting some culture."

"I just got here. Leave me alone."

"Speaking of culture, isn't the architecture great in San Francisco—the Victorians, the Art Deco buildings," Mother said, silencing all of us. She squeezed some lemon on her calamari, then continued. "Bob, doesn't this park outside remind you a little bit of Bethlehem, where Stanton's used to be?"

Papa made no effort to look outside, but kept to his meal. "Stanton's was a little hole in the wall, Evelyn."

"No—outside. The park, the trees. You don't even remember, do you?"

"It's possible I don't. That was a lifetime ago."

Mother turned to Roe and me, smiling. "Your father and I used to sneak away and meet at this place, Stanton's Inn. This was after our first few dates." She looked over at Papa. "It was a little place that served beer and bread and clams in big bowls, with garlic—lots of garlic."

Papa nodded his head, adding: "It was a dump where we didn't think your parents would find us."

"Oh! That's not true."

"The hell it isn't," Papa pulled his chair up to the table, pulling on his belt. "You two wouldn't know," he went on, "but Mother was from a fancy family in Pennsylvania, and all she wanted to do was get away from them. She could escape with me, so every Thursday we would go over to Stanton's. We would dance to this stand-up piano.

It was a big deal because I was from the Madison Avenue neighborhood near the steel factory, which was the wrong side of town, and Mother was from up on the knoll, near the Moravian church and the high school."

"Bethlehem. What a great town," Mother said nostalgically.

"You didn't think so at the time," Papa said, wiping spaghetti sauce from his face with a napkin. "You couldn't wait to get out of Pennsylvania—to get away from your parents. Carl and Beth Blanda, I'll never forget them."

"Oh, I loved that town. We should go back."

Papa looked at Mother, shaking his head in frustration. He furiously shook some cheese on his spaghetti, taking a large bite.

"What?" Mother said, staring at him, asking for an answer.

Papa waited a few moments, chewing, thinking.

"Why do you even talk like that?" Papa said.

"We could go, Bob."

"Then you would have to do what you've never been able

to do," he said, sticking his fork in the spaghetti again. "And I don't think you have the guts, Evelyn."

"What's that mean?" Roe asked.

"Let's talk about something else," Mother said, pushing her calamari around on the plate. "This is too complicated. Outside is the most beautiful city in the world."

"No," Roe insisted. "I'm serious. Papa, what does that mean, what you just said?"

"Skip it. It's nothing," Mother said, sipping her wine. "It's between Papa and me."

We continued eating, in silence, but then Papa started reminiscing again. "We left without getting married and were barely able to get across country in this old jalopy we were driving. I wanted to find work in Los Angeles, but once—"

"No, wait a second," Mother objected.

Papa wiped his mouth. "You didn't want to go to California, honey."

"That's not true. I was in love with you, that's all. I didn't know the difference between California and New York and Timbuktu."

"I wish you had known the difference," Roe said, sitting back in her chair.

"Why is that?" Papa asked Roe. "What difference would it have made to you?"

"Oh nothing, it's too complicated. It's between me and myself."

Papa kept eating his pasta, staring at Roe, and with each bite his mind seemed to spin faster and faster.

Roe sat up and pushed her salad plate towards the middle of the cable. "I'm going to the bathroom," Roe said. She got up and walked away from the table, catching the eye of a man leaning against the bar.

"Carl Blanda. That bastard hated my poor, working class guts," Papa continued, pressing his point.

"Would you please be quiet!" Mother hissed under her breath.

"Why? Because he's still alive? Is that what you're afraid of?" he answered, smiling cynically. "Because you've never returned in thirty years?"

"You do need a psychiatrist."

"No, I'm just tired of the status quo. Tired of secrets. That was your choice, Evelyn. He's old now, it's over."

"Waiter," Mother said, her voice trembling, "could we have our check please?" She turned back and stared blankly out the window.

After a minute, Mother asked, "Merle, how do think Roe is doing?"

I didn't hear her at first, still trying to understand what Mother and Papa had just said to each other. I knew Papa's parents were dead—he was an orphan—but my mother's father, still alive?

"Seems fine to me, Mother," I said absentmindedly.

"Where was she dancing?"

Mother confronted me with a lie, which I decided to tell.

"A little studio near Union Street."

"Is she dancing or teaching? What's the arrangement?"

"I don't know really, I just picked her up at the place. She seems to like it."

The conversation stopped as Roe returned and took her seat.

"Is Bethlehem near New York?" she asked, quickly devouring her salad.

Both Mother and Papa looked at each other, remembering, calculating distances.

"What—3 hours?" she asked.

"No, more like 7 hours," Papa said. He paused and thought

to himself. "I went to New York one time: Brooklyn Heights, Times Square."

"When was that?" Mother asked, as if jealous of his memory.

"Before I met you. With an old buddy of mine—Andy Waghazen. He drove a truck to New York twice a week, and one weekend I rode shotgun."

"I might be able to go to New York in December," Roe said with her mouth full.

"How?" Mother asked.

"That's a long story. And it's not confirmed yet. It's through a dance grant." Roe put her fork down. She pulled out a brush from her purse and aggressively stroked her hair.

"Would you please wait until I'm through eating to brush your hair," Mother complained, dipping her calamari in a red sauce and taking a bite.

"Sorry, I just need to get going. Are you ready, Merle?"

I took one last taste of my unfinished pasta then placed my napkin on the table. "At your command," I said.

"What are you doing later, Rowena?" Mother inquired.

"There's a meeting I can't get out of. I'm sorry."

"Too bad. We'll just see you tomorrow then, darling. I'll give a call in the morning. Merle, come by the room after you drop your sister off. The three of us can go sightseeing tonight, all right? I've read there's a gorgeous view from the top of the Bank of America building."

"O.K. Sounds like a plan," I said.

"Papa and I are going to finish our lovely meal, then take a taxi back to the hotel. That's if we can be civil with each other."

"And not talk about the past," Roe added.

We all stood up from the table. I shook Papa's hand and Roe kissed Mother on the cheek. I purposely left the shirt hidden on the chair. Without looking at Papa, Roe checked her watch, mentioned again that she was late, and rushed me out the door.

We walked across the park, past an art exhibit set in the middle of the grass.

"Did you see how he was staring me down?" Roe said. "He's always been like that—the whole fascist thing, when he just reads you the riot act and tells you who you are and who you aren't. I can't stand that."

"He's just proud," I said, looking up at the beautiful bell tower above the church. We crossed the street bordering the park and walked up the church steps. "He just wants you to be part of the family."

"Fuck that," she said, staying on the step below me. "That's pieces of honey, again."

The doors of the church were open and I was about to suggest that we walk inside, when Roe said: "Jose Luis abhors the Church. The destroyer of Civilization, he says. He rants about it all the time."

We were distracted for a moment by loud music blaring from a truck going by. I noticed Mother and Papa's window at Fior di' Italia was blocked by a row of trees.

"God, I have to perform tonight. I feel exhausted already. Just take me straight to the Palace of Fine Arts. I'll dress there."

"Are we late?"

"No, we have a little time. I just had to get away from the folks."

I stepped down to Roe and put my arms around her shoulders. She felt strong and firm, but unnaturally so, a spring tightened one turn beyond capacity.

"You know I went through your things at the house. They're all in a big pile of boxes in an empty room upstairs. And Mother showed me a letter you sent."

"Yea, well, do me a favor and make a bonfire of that stuff, O.K.? And then burn the house down, too." Her shoulders shook with laughter, then her tears burst.

"You should tell Mother and Papa about the show tonight."

She paused for a moment, wiping her wet cheeks. "No," she said, "I couldn't think straight if they were there."

"Come on, I'll go over and tell them right now. It's no big deal, you've danced in front of them a thousand times before."

"Before Mother maybe, not Papa. And besides, this is different; it's not ballet, it's political. They'll get blown away." Quickly, escaping my affection, she turned and walked off down the steps. "Let's get going—come on."

We walked to the truck and I followed her directions west to the Palace of Fine Arts.

"What shall we do with the parents tomorrow?" I asked, turning the radio on.

"I don't think I'm going to see them."

"Really?"

"Jose Luis has something lined up. He expects me to go—and don't say anything to me about it, I'm too stressed out already."

"There only here a couple days."

Roe ignored me.

"You shouldn't lie so much Roe," I said. The moment I made the comment, I was tempted to tell her that I'd paid Mrs. Spitz her back rent, but decided against it.

"Who are you anyway, George Washington?" she said, stroking her few braids of long hair. "You sound so corny."

"Since I've been here, you've told about five lies to the parents. Don't you feel strange doing that?"

"Would you mind your own fucking business. We're brother and sister, but, Merle, I'm very different from you. Get it through your thick skull. I don't need you to be hovering around me, questioning me."

"You know, you're full of shit when you say stuff like that," I said, stepping on the gas.

"You know it's the truth."

"No, I don't."

"You make me feel guilty and I don't like that. Why don't you just stop it, or leave me alone."

No problem, I said to myself, you bitch. We passed through a mile of busy intersections in silence, the street curving north. She told me to turn right into a neighborhood of white, Spanish-style homes with tile roofs. The street dead-ended at a small lake, with a large, ornate complex of buildings on the opposite side.

"Just park over here," she said, so I found a spot along the lake. It was still awkward between us, so I bided my time, looking at the swans drifting on the water, the lily pads, the impressive ring of tall columns in front of the buildings.

"So that's the Palace of Fine Arts, huh?" I asked.

"Yea."

"What a great looking place."

"Wasn't that weird when Mother and Papa started talking about Pennsylvania. What did they say when I left the table?"

I found myself hesitant to tell Roe. "What did they say?" she repeated.

"Papa said something like, "Because he's alive."

"What!" Roe exclaimed. "What was it exactly?"

"Papa said, Mother would be doing something she had never been able to do—"

"I heard that," Roe said impatiently, "what else?"

"He mentioned her parents. I'd forgotten their names were Carl and Beth, hadn't you? Anyway, Mother told him to shut up and that's when Papa asked: "Why, because he's still alive?"

"Alive—do you know what that means? Papa was from St. Peters Orphanage, we knew that, but Mother has always said her parents were deceased. She always used that word: deceased. She said there was nothing to return home to. But evidently that's bullshit. She has family that she's never revealed!"

"We have a grandparent," I said naively.

"I can't think about all this stuff right now," Roe said, shaking her head. "Let's go."

We got out of the truck and started walking around the lake.

Roe was quiet and serious. I imagined she was thinking about Jose Luis, Raging Feet, her performance. We passed a small lawn with statuary and a gazebo covered with purple blooms. Out beyond the Palace, angling north, loomed the Golden Gate Bridge.

"This is the most beautiful place I've ever seen."

"Yea, it is, but let's just stop here," Roe said. "Once I get inside, I'm going to be distracted."

We faced each other. Roe kissed me on the cheek and squeezed my hand.

"Good luck. I'll see you at curtain time. Hope you like it."

"When can I see you tomorrow?" I asked.

"I told you. I can't see you."

"I thought that was the parents, not me?" I complained. I looked down, embarrassed at being so vulnerable in wanting her attentions.

"Sorry, no can do."

I thought to myself: she's always apologizing for something, without any feeling behind it.

"Do you ever have memories of when we were growing up?" I asked, knowing I was wasting her time.

"I avoid that stuff at all costs," Roe said.

"That parade, when I let Buster out into the street."

"I'm feeling sicker by the minute. I gotta run. So long, Merle."

She turned and walked away. I just stood there, dumbfounded, and watched her take long strides around the lake. Her figure shrunk as she passed below the immense colonnade; without her long hair, I could hardly recognize her. She disappeared around the corner of the building. I felt lonely and awkward standing there by myself, so I walked back to the truck.

I found myself simmering with anger. I couldn't understand her walking away like that—like I was just a distant friend or something; but maybe I was someone different to her now.

I sat behind the wheel for a long time, staring across the lake. The air was thick and moist, putting a chill in my bones, so I rolled up the window, started the engine, and put the heater on. I was unable to decide what to do or where to go. Although a series of plans entered my mind—going back to see the parents, visiting Mrs. Spitz, or even calling up Miyoko—none of them seemed like the right thing to do. I looked at the clock: three hours before curtain time. I thought about being inside, watching Roe perform, maybe hanging out with the company afterwards, Jose Luis; it all put a bad taste in my mouth.

I drove the truck back out to the busy street and pulled into a gas station. In a phone booth, I looked up the number for the Marquis Hotel.

When I called, the receptionist told me my parents weren't in. Did I want to leave a message? Yes, I said, then the voice mail beeped: "This is Merle. I don't know whether this thing is recording or not. Listen, Roe is dancing tonight at eight o'clock at the Palace of Fine Arts. You'll have to ask somebody where that's at exactly, I couldn't tell you. I know this is all last minute, but I thought you might want to know. That's it. So long."

I gassed up then took the long drive through the city to the freeway. Coming up the on-ramp, I noticed the sun fading out west, disappearing into a quilt-like bank of fog. I passed the wall of downtown skyscrapers and the billboards for John Ascuaga's Nugget, then, stepping on the gas, drove onto the Bay Bridge, leaving San Francisco behind. Passing over the island in the middle of the span, contrary thoughts entered my mind—go back and watch Roe, see the folks, be reasonable—but they vanished in one blast of warm air from the eastern hills, which were purple as plums.

I caught Interstate 80 north, heading for the Sierra Mountains, some one hundred miles away. That night I took a room in Truckee, and in the morning, I headed into Reno, arriving just before noon.

I pulled off on Virginia Street and stopped at a gas station near the Circus Circus casino. When I got out of the truck, my lips were already dry and chapped.

I phoned the Waterstone's in Nixon. The phone rang repeatedly and I almost hung up, when a voice answered that I didn't recognize.

"Is Winona or Joe there?" I asked.

"Just a second," said the male voice.

"Hello?" It was Winona.

"It's Merle, Winona."

"Hi, where are you?"

"In Reno."

"What are you doing?"

"I just got back from San Francisco. I saw Roe."

"That's funny. How's she doin'?"

I didn't know what to say. "Same old, same old," I said, trying to laugh.

Silence.

"Winona, where's Cracker Joe? I need to talk with him."

Another silence.

"That may be hard to do."

"Why?"

"He's near you, actually. He's at the Washoe Medical Center. He's been there for a few days. He's recovering from being beaten up in Fallon."

"What's wrong with him."

"He has a broken arm and a brain injury. He's not thinking right."

"Jesus Christ," I said, dying inside. This was the last thing I wanted to hear.

"We've been in Reno most of the week. I just came home last night. He's going to be in there for awhile longer."

"I was with him," I said, regretting my honesty the moment I opened my mouth.

"When was that?" Winona asked.

"That night! It's hard to explain. I just lost track of him; I was fucked up big time. Why'd this have to happen?"

"You tell me, you stupid fool," Winona said, cold and impersonal. I thought she might hang up. "He mentioned you a few times," she went on.

"Can I see him?"

"Sure. There's visiting hours today. You know where Washoe Medical Center is, right? Just off the freeway."

"Yea. No problem."

Silence.

"What a drag, huh?" I said.

"Lots of things are a drag these days. See for yourself. Let me know what you think," she said.

"I will. So long," I said, putting down the receiver. I couldn't move; tears filled my eyes and I just stood there looking out across the street at the silly families entering the pink sliding doors at Circus Circus. The sun, hot and oppressive, streamed into the booth, so I busted out and returned to the truck. Then I drove down 4th Street to a large medical complex, where I parked.

At the front desk, I identified myself and was referred back to Ward B. I was told to follow the green stripe on the floor, which I did, making my way, left and right, through a series of hallways, passing nurses and patients and family members along the way. After identifying myself, again, through a speaker at a set of wide doors, I was finally buzzed into the Head Trauma Unit.

I walked up to a glass-walled office.

"Can I help you?" a nurse asked.

"I'm trying to find Joseph Waterstone."

"I think he's outside, in recreation. You have about thirty minutes before visiting hours are over. Sign in here, please." She handed me a clipboard; I put down my name, the time.

She walked me through a large treatment room, where hospital staff worked with patients in a mock kitchen, along a low gymnastic bar, and on an exercise pad on the floor.

The nurse opened a sliding glass door and pointed outside. "He's over there. Let me know if you need anything."

I saw Cracker Joe across the courtyard, sitting on a bench. I walked over to him and he looked up, recognizing me. He was wearing a Walkman, and took the headset off.

"Hey, there he is, again," he said, smiling broadly. He stuck his hand in the air, so I slapped it. I sat down beside him, more ashamed than I'd ever been.

"What's happening?" I said.

"Aerosmith, man. *"Dream on, dream on, dream on—dream on until your dreams come true*, dow, dow, dow, da, daaaa" He chopped at the air, his arm in a cast. He put the headset up to his ear again.

"Winona told me you were here."

Cracker seemed to ignore me, looking around the courtyard. "They got me, Merle."

"Who got you?"

"The Air Force dicks. They got me."

"I'm sorry, Cracker, I just—"

"I did the best I could, but—did you see that nurse?"

"Cracker, I blew it, man, I have to apologize for— "

"Fine, baby," Cracker Joe exclaimed, slapping his knee. "Fine. I'll do it right now—you know what I mean? And I see her every day."

"Yea, I agree, she's cute. How are you, man?"

"I'm here. Nothin's wrong with me," Cracker Joe said. His face was puffy, a row of stitches on the side of his nose. When he looked me in the eye, it didn't seem to mean anything. He pulled the headset plug out of the Walkman and the music blared, scratchy and raw; he slapped his leg to the beat.

"Turn it down a little, Cracker, so we can talk."

He did as I asked.

"But I'm going to get 'em, you watch," he continued. "You wait, maybe tonight, maybe ten years from now, I'm going to sneak up and I'm going to get those jugheads."

"You broke your arm, huh?"

"Something's wrong in there, yea. You want to sign?"

"Sure. You have a pencil or something?"

"No, I don't. God damn this place. You can't get nothin' when you need it." Cracker said, his smile turning to an agitated grimace. He reached over and repeatedly pressed a red button on a post next to the bench. A buzzer went off inside the building.

The nurse appeared at the sliding door and stepped outside.

"Can I be of any help?" she asked.

"Yea, get a pencil. My friend wants to sign my cast."

"Just a moment." The woman disappeared and returned shortly, walking out and giving us the pencil. She stood by us, waiting.

"I'm sorry," the nurse said, "I have to return it to the ward. It's our policy."

"I'll take care of it," I said. "I'll bring it right back to you."

"No problem. I'm right inside. It's almost lunch time, Joseph, do you want to have the turkey sandwich, like yesterday?"

"No, I don't eat turkey. Not even when it's Thanksgiving, or any holiday."

"What can I get you then? We have tuna salad, roast beef, or cheese. What sounds good?"

"Roast beef, I guess."

She offered me lunch, but I told her I wasn't hungry. As she returned to the building, a man and woman came out into the courtyard. The man was obviously a visitor, the way he helped the woman along. She wore a powder blue robe and moved slowly, dragging her left leg. They sat down on a bench under some maple trees.

"I just went to San Francisco, to see Roe," I said.

"Who is that?" Cracker Joe asked.

"Roe—my sister. You know, the ballet dancer," I said, shocked by his confusion.

"Don't know nothin' about her. When did I meet her? When?"

I didn't press the matter any further.

"I need to get out of here, Merle. I been in here a long, long time. It's not fair. I got things to do. Sherrie . . . Oh! Sherrie. Boy, that's a trip, isn't it. And the Air Force boys. Are you going to be talking with them? If you do, tell them it's going to be big time pay back."

"Are you filing any charges against those guys? Were the police involved?"

"I don't need the police. Why would we want that? I'd stay away from the police if I were you, they're evil." He started laughing, but smiling hurt his face. He stopped and touched his nose. Tears suddenly came to his eyes and he just seemed to stew in his own mixed-up emotions.

"Here, give me the cast, I'll put my John Hancock on it."

"Put something good, Merle. Look where the nurse drawed those flowers. Nice, huh? Do something like that."

I thought for moment . . . then I wrote "*For Cracker Joe, the man with the rock n' roll heart*" and drew a heart, and a guitar, in the background.

"Hey, I like that. I like that," he said, excited, spit on his lip.

The nurse stuck her head out the sliding door: "Joseph, your lunch is ready in the cafeteria."

"Good. Star Trek is on, too." He looked at his wristwatch. "I'm late for Star Trek."

Cracker Joe stood up slowly, balancing himself. We walked towards the building, and from his painful gait I could see how damaged he really was.

"Cracker, maybe I can bring you some music when I come next time."

"Yea, but make it oldies," he said, stopping for a moment to rest. "Shit, I might use that wheelchair again. My legs don't work." We finally got inside, crossed the activity room, and made our way to the open doorway of the cafeteria.

Cracker Joe noticed that the television, which was positioned in the middle of the wall, was already turned on.

"So long Merle. I gotta go—Star Trek is on." I was going to ask him if he wanted to have lunch together the next day, but he just shuffled away without looking at me, without shaking my hand. He sat down among the other patients; although I stood there for a couple minutes, he never turned to look back at me, but just kept his excited eyes on the screen, leaving his sandwich untouched.

I left and once again followed the green line back towards the entrance of the building. The walls of the corridor were covered with children's drawings from a local school. Then Cracker Joe's nurse stepped out of an office and practically bumped into me.

"Excuse me. I have to watch where I'm going," she said. She was a cute, athletic-looking blonde.

"How did your visit go?"

"It's hard to say. He sure is banged up."

"He was unconscious for a good while."

"How long do you think he'll be in here?"

"Not too much longer here, maybe a week, then he'll prob-ably go to a transitional cognitive rehab facility. There's one on Keystone, up by the university." She took off her rubber gloves.

"To get his thinking straight?"

"Yes, his orthopedic problems will heal fine, but the mental part of it will take some time. You just never know how he'll end up down the road. But the more support from friends and family, the better." I thanked her, gave her the pencil, then went out to the parking lot.

I sat in the truck, exhausted and depressed. I looked down-town, at the dome of the Silver Legacy, the El Dorado, Harrah's three towers. Without the gaudy extravaganza of night-time lights, the casinos seemed dull, meaningless. I drove back down to Virginia Street and gassed up again. Inside the Stop n' Go, I bought Cracker Joe four tapes: Ozzy Ozborne, AC/DC, Thin Lizzy, and Cheap Trick—then continued east on Interstate 80. After passing through Sparks, I drove into the sun-drenched des-olation of the desert.

The brownish Truckee River—so shallow it appeared mo-tionless—winded through the canyon, past a basalt plant, a trailer park, a dump, and the turnoff to the Mustang Ranch whore-house. I rubbed skin from my dry lips and stretched my back; the warm air through the open window felt so good, I passed on the air conditioning.

I reached over into the box between the seats and pulled out the gun. It felt like the misplaced part of some evil machine that I didn't know how to use. With a quick jerk of my arm, I tossed it out the window. Looking in the side mirror, I saw it skid on the road, bouncing into the sage.

It took me an hour to get to King Neptune's in Fallon. I parked the 4x4 in its proper place by the flat bed truck and got out. Everything was quiet, as if time had stood still since I was last there.

A station wagon was parked in front door of the shop. The early afternoon sun had a familiar August sting, making my clean-shaven face feel pale and vulnerable, like I'd been living underground. Looking towards the back house, I saw Crystal curled up on the steps, sleeping. I scratched my scalp and bite my lip apprehensively. Here goes nothing, I murmured, then walked over to the shop and stepped inside.

Mr. Farnsworth was behind the cash register, leaning back with his arms folded, talking to a young, red-haired man. He glanced at me, but betrayed no sense of surprise.

"Well, if you want to bring the load next week, that sounds O.K.," he said. "Afternoon would be better for me. 7 cents a pound, is that correct?"

"Yea, that's what I was told."

"Great, but ask your old man about the serpentine. I'm still interested in a quarter ton of that." They shook hands then the man stepped by me and left.

Mr. Farnsworth didn't pay me any mind. He read a piece of paper by the cash register, then signed it. I walked over and set down the keys on the glass case. I regretted not having the stolen necklet to return, but I'd tossed it with my overalls.

"The truck's outside—in the same shape as before. I'm sorry for doing what I did, I didn't mean any harm."

"I thought you might have been a criminal, but I didn't take you for a thief, so I'm glad to see you brought it back."

"I was honored to drive it."

"One more week and I would have reported you to the police. Then it wouldn't have been so much fun."

"Thanks for being patient. The Blue and Silver I don't need."

"Where did you go?"

"Down south to see my folks in Cherry Creek, then to San Francisco to see my sister."

Mr. Farnsworth took a long sip of coffee, smirking. "Damn, maybe I should have you hauled in—putting a thousand miles on my vehicle.

San Francicsco. Your first time?"

"Yea, probably my last, too."

"Oh, don't say that. It's a great town. I used to have an old buddy from my college days who taught at UCSF. I'd go see him every five years or so. Not as much night life in San Francisco as Fallon, but it's interesting just the same."

I smiled. He stood up and suggested going outside. We walked out the backdoor and crossed the yard into the workshop.

"When you first stepped through the door, I didn't recognize you. Who took you to the car wash?"

"Yea, well, I used to be even shinier. I haven't got around to cleaning myself up for a couple days," I said. "It's a hard habit to develop."

"You got a point there."

Mr. Farnsworth checked one of the cutting machines, opening the hooded top. I petted the cat, who, hearing us move about, had settled into a box under a sunny window.

"What are your plans?"

"I'm going up to Nixon, see a friend."

"No buses going that way."

"Naw, I'll just hitchhike. I'll get a ride now 'cause I look so respectable." Since Mr. Farnsworth was being gentlemanly about my stealing the truck, I thought for a moment that he might offer it to me, to go see Winona. But he didn't make the offer, and I felt guilty for even thinking that he might.

"Don't be too spic n' span or you'll get robbed," he said. "Help me with this, will you?" I leaned over and grabbed one end of a wooden box filled with obsidian and lifted it up on a shelf.

"Mr. Farnsworth, I know this is kind of crazy to say, after I stole from you and everything, but is that job offer still good?"

Mr. Farnsworth took off his glasses and cleaned them with a handkerchief, pinching his eyebrows together. He put them back on and stared right through me.

"You think I'm an old fool, don't you?" he said.

"No," I responded nervously.

He paused again, then said: "I can pay $400 a month, plus a room at the back of the shop, near the shower. But you have to work in the yard and in the shop dealing with the customers. I'm tired of being tied to that cash register. It's six days a week, ten to five."

"I'll do it. I'm ready. When do you want me to start?"

"I have work in a week. You heard me making the deal."

"I really appreciate it. I really do. I'll work hard for you, you'll see."

"I'll determine that, thank you," Mr. Farnsworth said.

"Mr. Farnsworth, I have something to tell you."

"What, more?"

"Yea, more. Before I met you, I was involved in, in a sort of ring of people who found and sold artifacts."

"What?" Mr. Farnsworth uttered.

"It was just a stupid thing I fell into. We worked up in the mountains: the Jackson range, up above the Black Rock."

"Could you find the place again?"

"Sure."

Mr. Farnsworth took a step back and leaned against the workbench, crossing his arms, his eyes burning with anger.

"Who was it you worked for?"

"A guy named Biggs."

"What did he deal in?"

"It was like the stuff you have in the shop. Some old pottery. I dropped the things off in Nixon, to some guy named Ed Morgan."

"Morgan? I know him. I've had my suspicions about that two-faced bastard for years. I used to be in a professional association with him."

I reached into my pocket and pulled out the remaining one thousand dollars in cash, then set it on the workbench. "I made money from what I did. I don't want it anymore—it's dirty money."

"What do you want me to do with it?"

"Keep it, give it to a museum, burnt it, whatever. I don't want it."

"Merle, I got a Ph.D. in Geology, not Social Work. God Almighty, what am I supposed to do with you." He shook his head. "We'll see what we can do. There's been a lot of black market activity the last few years. It's hard to stop it."

"Another thing."

"What?"

"I need a fifty dollar advance on my salary. I'm broke."

He slapped his leg and laughed, his face a mass of wrinkles.

"You're a crafty devil, aren't you? You remind me of my old students, always something up their sleeve?" He picked up a one hundred dollar bill off the workbench and gave it to me.

"How's that?"

"Great."

"Now you're making three hundred dollars the first month," he said.

We went to the house and he gave me a glass of soda. Confirming our agreement once again, I said good-bye and walked out to the highway and starting hitchhiking, just like I'd done earlier in the week.

By evening, in two rides, I made it to the road leading into Nixon. I half-expected to witness something caused by the political unrest in town, but the highway was desolate, except for a rancher who rumbled by on a tractor.

When I arrived at the Waterstone's house, Winona's truck was parked in front, next to Cracker Joe's station wagon. I glanced skeptically at my new clothes—bright blue and almost spotless—then knocked on the door. Budweiser barked, then Marcos answered the door.

I raised my arms, surrendering, saying, "What, no rifle this time?"

He gave me a cold stare, turning away, leaving the door open.

I stepped into the living room. Nanna was in her rocking chair, darning a sock. I walked up to her, and we nodded at each other, smiling, then she continued her handiwork.

I followed Marcos into the kitchen. The refrigerator door closed and Winona turned around to face me.

"Boy, you're getting around these days," she said. She walked over to the table and set down a platter of chicken.

"Are you hungry?"

"No, thanks anyway," I said. She picked up two bowls and put them in the refrigerator, then took a sponge and began wiping down the sink.

Marcos sat down at the table, watching me.

"How did things turn out with the hostages?" I asked.

"Lousy. Did you see Joe?" he inquired.

"Yea," I answered, shaking my head. "He's fucked up. I got some tapes I'm going to give him tomorrow."

"He'll like that," Winona said.

"Are you pressing charges?" I asked.

"We don't know what to do," she said, rinsing the sponge. "The witnesses said that Joe started assaulting them. No one really saw what happened. He was found out in a field. He'd been bingeing."

"What if we were pressing charges, so what?" Marcos asked, biting into a piece of chicken.

"I could be a witness, if you needed me. I saw all those guys."

"It's a little late for that, isn't it?" he complained.

"I don't know. Is it?" I shot back.

Winona looked over at her brother, trying to quiet him with a look.

"We can't get any straight answers out of Joe about exactly what happened," she said.

"I know what happened," I said, leaning against the door, trying to conceptualize just what had gone down that night. Shit, I don't want to describe this, I said to myself, but I have to.

"We were partying pretty hard. Real hard, actually. It was my fault. The whole mood of the thing was my fault.

I convinced Cracker to drive me to Fallon. But he wanted to go to the Rambling Rose, this whorehouse. These military guys showed up—just a bunch of punks really—but the whole time we're there, Cracker is getting on their wrong side. When all the fighting started up, I was outside in the car. I was in a bad way— all fucked up—and couldn't really function well enough to help him. They drove him away. Maybe I was a coward or a bad friend, but I just couldn't get it together."

"But what happened to you?" Marcos asked.

"I was out of it. I went unconscious or something. I didn't come to until the next day."

"Did you try to find out what happened?" he questioned, more loud and critical, popping the top of a beer.

"I went back the next day. The car was there, but there was no trace of Cracker."

"Well, of course there wasn't. They drove off with him and

beat him to smithereens. Why didn't you report it to the police?"

"I don't know, Marcos. I just ran from it."

"Yea, you did—asshole."

I straightened up. "Well, fuck you, too," I said.

Keeping his eyes on me, he slowly set his beer down and pushed back his chair and stood up. He was going to rush me, except Winona put out her hand.

"Stop it, both of you," she said in a stern voice.

"He's a traitor, Winona. I don't trust him."

"Just calm down, brother. He's here, dealing with it, isn't he?"

"But it's too late," Marcos said miserably. He sat down and quietly started eating his food again. "Shit!" he said, to the wall.

Winona went to the sink and shut off the water.

"We're going to talk with an attorney this week," she said, wiping her hands. "We'll see what can be done and what our options are, O.K.? We should be glad he's alive."

"Yea. I'm sorry, Merle," Marcos said. "I just feel bad for Joe."

"I know. I haven't been able to stop thinking about it either," I said.

Finished with her chores, Winona looked at me, tipping her head slightly, telling me to go outside. I said good-bye to Marcos then stepped out the sliding glass door. She followed right behind.

"Come on, let's take a walk," she said. We left the house behind and took the narrow path through the sage to Pyramid Lake.

"I'm sorry about all that," she said, putting her hands in the pockets of her khaki shorts, her sandals crunching the ground.

"He's right. Come on, I can see my own guilt. But I love Cracker as much as—"

"Just shut up and leave it alone," she said. She stopped and broke off a piece of sagebrush, crushing it in her hand. She put it under my nose and I took in the rich pungent odor, then she smelled it herself.

"Isn't that nice? No matter how many times you smell it, it's always nice."

"Yea, that's Nevada, right there," I said.

At trail's end, we stopped and looked out across the lake.

"Did you see Roe?"

"Yea."

"How was it?"

I thought about the question for a long time, turning back and staring at Nixon, then facing the lake again.

"To be honest, I found out I don't like her."

Winona gave a short laugh. She walked over to the water's edge, the wind blowing her hair. "We don't like the things we worship, do we?"

"I also found out I have a grandfather."

"What? Say it again."

"Mother always said her parents were dead. But it turns out she has a father, who's alive and living back East somewhere."

"Your mother said that?"

"Well, somehow it just got uncovered with everything that was going on."

"That's so strange," Winona said. "Now you have your own grandpa, just like I have Nanna."

I bit my lip. I hadn't really thought about it one way or the other. *My very own grandpa . . .*

We looked at each other. Alone, and surrounded by nothing but the desert, sky and water, it seemed like we both felt the same thing at once. I walked over and kissed her, then kissed her some more. Her strong shoulders, her back, felt so good to squeeze and lean against, followed by the joy of touching her long hair. We just held each other for a couple minutes, then Winona asked: "Do you want to go out?"

"Swimming?"

"No, beyond the rock there, we have a canoe we can use."

"Yea, sure, let's go." I said.

Winona took my hand and we strolled along the shore towards a flat-topped boulder a short distance away.

Then I heard a voice: "Hey, Merle! Stop! Merle!"

We both turned and looked back towards the path through the field. It was Marcos.

"Merle, you have a call," he yelled out, waving. "It's your sister calling long distance."

I looked at him, for a moment not understanding his words. "My sister?" I asked out loud. "What the hell is going on?"

Winona pressed my hand, saying, "I don't know, but you better check it out."

I looked at her. I didn't want to leave her—not even for a moment—and wanted her permission first, which her brown eyes immediately gave me. I kissed her. "I'll be right back," I said.

I returned to the house and got on the phone.

"Hello?"

"Merle?"

"Yea."

"It's Roe." There was a ripe pause.

"How did you know I was here?"

"Just a guess," she said. "Listen, I wanted to tell you that I felt like a bad host. I was in a shitty mood. I'm sorry."

Roe apologizing; I couldn't believe my ears.

"Did Mother and Papa see you dance?"

"Yes, you little shit, but it turned out all right. They didn't freak out or anything, and they were able to met Jose Luis."

The phone line faded in and out for a second.

"You still there?" she asked.

"Yea."

"Listen, I wanted to ask you something. It turns out I'll be going to New York in the fall. Do you want to go back there with me, maybe try to see our grandfather."

I scratched my young beard, not knowing what to think.

"Sure, I guess so," I said, filled with doubt. "I don't know how I would pay for it though. I haven't got any money."

"Well, I owe you eight hundred dollars, don't I?"

"You saw her?"

"Yea. I intended to pay."

I glanced into the living room, at Marcos lying on the couch, napping, and Nanna rocking nearby. A few moments passed and we didn't know what to say to each other.

"Well, I got a job in Fallon. You can phone me there if you want. It's the King Neptune rock shop, or you can call me here ..."

"Are you getting back together with Winona?"

"Yea, anything's possible."

"That's good, I liked her."

"Well, give me a call anytime. And I know your number at Albion Place."

"O.K. little Merlin, I just wanted to touch base with you."

"Thanks for phoning."

"Bye."

I put down the phone, my mind spinning. "Thanks, Marcos," I said, rushing out of the sliding door. For the third time that week, I started walking back down the path to the lake. I touched my shirt pocket, feeling Roe's letter there ...

Someone was coming. I turned and faced the curtain, looking like I was busy. Where was my sister?

The crowd outside hummed like bumblebees, waiting for The Nutcracker Suite.

When I looked over my shoulder, all I could see was costumes and more costumes. There were kids dressed like dolls and candy canes and The Mouse King and flowers. Everyone was preparing to take some position for the be-

ginning of the Christmas extravaganza. Waiting nervously for curtain call.

But where was Rowena?

I couldn't believe my position in this whole thing. How had this happened? I was a tin soldier, and part of the group that was going on stage first. There had been a call to the mobile home the day before. One of the participants had come down with food poisoning. Did my Mother have any recommendations for a replacement? Of course, she did—me! I was coming south to the Las Vegas Convention Center anyway, to see Rowena dance, so there was no problem. So here I was, after a few practice marches backstage that afternoon, expected to march out on stage, in step, in time, in front of thousands of people.

A group of five young girls tiptoed by: fairies with pink tutus and wands.

"Merle?" someone said. I looked up. It was Mrs. Jensen. "Merle, come on now. Don't be nervous.

See those speakers where the curtain opens up. Go over there and get in line. The horns are there already, leaning up against the curtain. I'm getting everyone together. We have to hurry." She patted me on the back then disappeared across the room.

I hurried over to the spot she was talking about, the first one there. I felt ridiculous, dressed in a blue suit, with gray knee socks, cobbler shoes, a bow tie, and a big hat—someone called it a "Napoleon" hat. Since I was at the far end of the line, stage right, I was the first one to step out on stage. Ten paces straight out, five to the right, then ten to the left; after a kick of the leg, a salute, then a blow of the horn. Then repeat it going back. But, I just hadn't tried it enough times!

Rowena, the princess ballerina in the production, was around some-where. Where was she? Who could I ask?

Across the room, I saw Kathy Mulvaney and bolted over and tapped her on the shoulder.

"Have you seen Rowena?" I asked.

She was putting rouge on the cheeks of another girl and didn't both-

er to look at me. "I saw her in the back getting dressed," she said. "I think she might be in the bathroom."

I walked across the hardwood floor, away from the main stage, past a group of adults and a set of tables covered with clothes and costumes and baggage. Behind all this, in the corner of the huge building, were the rest rooms.

I stopped at the Girls sign and looked around. Nobody was watching. I tried the door: it was open.

"Rowena, are you in there?"

I heard a weak voice say something I couldn't understand.

I stepped inside, locking the door.

There, next to the stalls, she had set out a blanket to stretch on. She sat on the ground, one leg extended out, forcing her head towards her knee. I walked up slowly.

"What are you doing?"

"Getting ready."

"I was waiting outside and—"

"I don't think I can do it, Merle," she said, resting her head on her knee, closing her eyes. "I'm scared."

"I'm, like, scared too," I said.

But she didn't pay me any mind. She got up, walked into one of the stalls, and threw up into a toilet. This is, like, a bad one, I thought, remembering the others times in Cherry Creek, when Rowena would get crazy before a performance.

I stepped over to the door of the stall, concerned, but she had already finished. She walked by me and went over to her bag and wiped her mouth with a towel "I hate this," she said, returning to her place on the floor. She started twisting at the waist, putting an arm behind her neck. "What are you doing here?"

"I'm trying to get ready."

"I'm almost done. I'll be out in a second."

The orchestra struck up a song in the main auditorium. I stood there, not knowing what to do, wondering if all the other guys were ready.

"Just think, last night at this time we were taking Romulus for a walk."

"Get out of here, Merle," Rowena said, ignoring me.

I walked back across the floor to the curtain, where the other tin soldiers were waiting in line. I took my place at the head of the group, then picked up my horn.

It was bent! Bent, bent, bent!

A boy standing next to me explained, "Jimmy stepped on it. It was an accident."

I picked up the thick cardboard version of an instrument; the end hung down, like it was on a hinge. I looked at the other soldiers in line; they were all handling their instruments, practicing their moves.

I tried to catch Jimmy Peterson's eye, but he was turned away, talking to another boy.

I looked around, panicked. Mrs. Jensen came up, her hands touching all of us, whispering instructions, but she was too busy to notice my predicament.

Then the orchestra went into full swing, not a hundred feet away, and the audience felt like a big magnet that was tugging at me from beyond the curtains.

Across the room, I saw Rowena. She had just come out of the rest room and was setting her bag down. She didn't dance until the beginning of the second act, so I knew she had some time to kill.

I motioned to her frantically. She peered at me from across the floor and zoomed over.

"Hi. Ready to go?" she asked. She was dressed in silver leotards, on point.

"Look at my trumpet!" I complained, grimacing.

She raised up the damaged end of the horn.

"Some guy stepped on it," I said, wanting to laugh and cry at the same time.

She tried to bend it into shape, but it didn't hold.

"You have the worst luck," she said. "Why do you always do this to me?" She turned and looked all around the room, examining every corner.

"Wait," she said, and ran over to a storage closet by some tables.

Mrs. Jensen walked by, barking orders: "Now, remember your steps. Don't think about the crowd, just what steps you're taking, and snap your heels at the end." She walked up to the opening in the curtains, looking out at the stage. "Now stand up proud and tall."

Rowena hurried back towards me. She had a short broom, and she was twisting the head. She spun it off, then quickly gave me the handle.

"Put that in the horn."

"What?" I asked.

"Put it inside the horn," she insisted.

I pushed it through, from the mouthpiece to the end. It fit! I put the trumpet up to my mouth. The broken end pointed upward, straight and secure.

I gave Rowena a quick victorious look, smiling nervously (she stepped back, waving good luck) then Mrs. Jensen motioned with her hand: now, now, now.

Ten steps straight out, then five to the right . . .

When I got back to the lake, Winona was knee keep in the water, getting the canoe ready.

"What'd she say?"

"She wants to go back East, to see our grandfather," I said, taking off my shoes and socks and rolling up my pant legs.

She smiled then carefully climbed into the front of the canoe. "Ready to go?" she asked.

I wadded into the water and hopped up into the back. She handed me an oar.

"I like your new preppie look, Merle," Winona said, glancing back at me. "Just your short whiskers, nothing else."

I laughed as I pushed off, pulling the oar through the water and trying to build up some steam.

"I got a job in Fallon, running this rock shop," I said in a loud voice.

"Oh! Yea, I've heard that before."

"I'm serious. The King Neptune: a free room and some cash. I start next week."

"That means you're not going to be living with me?" she asked, alternating the oar from side to side.

I looked longingly at her strong arms, her swaying hair.

"Depends on whether you want to loan me your truck six days a week. Anyway, your welcome to come and visit. Maybe we could break in the room together."

She glanced back, so that I could see the side of her face. "No problem with that, Merle."

The water, which had been choppy close to shore, became smooth as we got a half-mile out into the lake.

"I don't see any pelicans out today," I said, checking the sky above the island and the jutting Pyramid.

"It has to be closer to sunset."

We paddled hard for a few more minutes, working up a sweat.

"I don't know what's wrong with me," I said. "I'm not afraid of the Kui-Qui fish anymore."

Winona stopped rowing and put her oar down. With her hands, she grabbed both sides of the canoe and began rocking it back and forth.

"We'll see," she yelled out, laughing. "Wait until I tip you over!"

I could've kept my balance, no problem, but I gladly gave up trying and fell into the water, clothes and all.

The End

www.ingramcontent.com/pod-product-compliance
Lightning Source LLC
Chambersburg PA
CBHW050727180626
46814CB00002B/634